DEFENDING THE BRAND

"Tell your boys to round up your Bar O cattle and run them back over your line. If you don't, I'll make you run 'em back afoot!" Jed Asbury demanded.

"*What?*" Besovi was incredulous. "I'll see you in hell first!"

Jed knew this dispute could be settled in two ways. If he went for his gun there would be shooting and men would be killed. He chose the other way.

Acting so suddenly the move was unexpected, he grabbed Besovi by the beard and jerked the rancher sharply toward him, at the same time he kicked the rancher's foot loose from his stirrup, then shoved hard. Besovi, caught unawares by the attack fell off his horse and Jed hit the ground beside him.

Besovi came to his feet, clawing for his gun.

"Afraid to fight with your hands?" Jed taunted the big man. He stripped off his gun-belts and put them aside, then moved warily toward Besovi. . . .

Bantam Books by Louis L'Amour
Ask your bookseller for the books you have missed

BENDIGO SHAFTER
BORDEN CHANTRY
BOWDRIE
BOWDRIE'S LAW
BRIONNE
THE BROKEN GUN
BUCKSKIN RUN
THE BURNING HILLS
THE CALIFORNIOS
CALLAGHEN
CATLOW
CHANCY
THE CHEROKEE TRAIL
COMSTOCK LODE
CONAGHER
CROSSFIRE TRAIL
DARK CANYON
DOWN THE LONG HILLS
DUTCHMAN'S FLAT
THE EMPTY LAND
FAIR BLOWS THE WIND
FALLON
THE FERGUSON RIFLE
THE FIRST FAST DRAW
FLINT
FRONTIER
GUNS OF THE TIMBERLANDS
HANGING WOMAN CREEK
HELLER WITH A GUN
THE HIGH GRADERS
HIGH LONESOME
THE HILLS OF HOMICIDE
HONDO
HOW THE WEST WAS WON
THE IRON MARSHAL
JUBAL SACKETT
THE KEY-LOCK MAN
KID RODELO
KILKENNY
KILLOE
KILRONE
KIOWA TRAIL
LAW OF THE DESERT BORN
THE LONESOME GODS
THE MAN CALLED NOON
THE MAN FROM SKIBBEREEN
MATAGORDA
MILO TALON
THE MOUNTAIN VALLEY WAR
NORTH TO THE RAILS
OVER ON THE DRY SIDE
PASSIN' THROUGH
THE PROVING TRAIL
THE QUICK AND THE DEAD
RADIGAN
REILLY'S LUCK
THE RIDER OF LOST CREEK
RIDING FOR THE BRAND
RIVERS WEST
THE SHADOW RIDERS
SHALAKO
SHOWDOWN AT YELLOW BUTTE
SILVER CANYON
SITKA
SON OF A WANTED MAN
THE STRONG SHALL LIVE
TAGGART
TO TAME A LAND
TUCKER
UNDER THE SWEETWATER RIM
UTAH BLAINE
THE WALKING DRUM
WAR PARTY
WESTWARD THE TIDE
WHERE THE LONG GRASS BLOWS
YONDERING

Sackett Titles by
Louis L'Amour

---

1. SACKETT'S LAND
2. TO THE FAR BLUE MOUNTAINS
3. THE DAYBREAKERS
4. SACKETT
5. LANDO
6. MOJAVE CROSSING
7. THE SACKETT BRAND
8. THE LONELY MEN
9. TREASURE MOUNTAIN
10. MUSTANG MAN
11. GALLOWAY
12. THE SKY-LINERS
13. THE MAN FROM THE BROKEN HILLS
14. RIDE THE DARK TRAIL
15. THE WARRIOR'S PATH
16. LONELY ON THE MOUNTAIN
17. RIDE THE RIVER

RIDING FOR THE BRAND

Louis L'Amour

BANTAM BOOKS
TORONTO • NEW YORK • LONDON • SYDNEY • AUCKLAND

RIDING FOR THE BRAND

A Bantam Book / published by arrangement with the author

Bantam edition / March 1986

ISBN 0-553-26189-4

Published simultaneously in the United States and Canada

Bantam Books are published by Bantam Books, Inc. Its trademark, consisting of the words "Bantam Books" and the portrayal of a rooster, is Registered in U.S. Patent and Trademark Office and in other countries. Marca Registrada. Bantam Books, Inc., 666 Fifth Avenue, New York, New York 10103.

PRINTED IN THE UNITED STATES OF AMERICA

KR 0 9 8 7 6 5 4 3 2 1

To my loyal fans,
with gratitude for
riding for the brand.

Contents

Foreword

Beginning a writing career is never easy, and the stories in this collection were often written when the going was rough. Nobody wanted to buy a story from somebody named Louis L'Amour so, for a time, I used the name of one of my characters named Jim Mayo.

The material from the stories came from sitting on a bale of hay eating a lunch in a shady spot by an irrigation ditch or out on a mountainside with an old-timer with whom I'd become friends. They did not tell me these stories, which are my own creation, but they did talk of old-time fights, rustling cattle, round-ups, camp cooks, and drifting cowhands who might have come from anywhere.

Long ago I'd learned to listen more than talk and the stories came easily to those old men, not talking to me but to each other. I was just an innocent by-sitter storing memories.

They talked of whiskey and women, of mossy-horn steer and wild mustangs, of cutting horses and ropers, of nights in town and long rides home, of gold discoveries, lost mines, buried tresures, and outlaws.

They had lived in the west when it was wild and the memories did not fade. Some of them as boys had seen the last of the moutain men come down with their furs, and they had seen buffalo hunted and Indian war parties.

They had eaten the dust of the trail herds, smelled the branding fires and coffee boiling in cowboy camps. To listen to them was to hear the saga of the west at first-hand, and to remember many a night rolled up in my own blankets, still thinking of the stories, and seeing again how it must have been when those fine old men were young.

My title story, *Riding for the Brand*, begins with the main character taking the name of a man he never knew and laying claim to his property. It is fitting that his actions should have a passing similarity to the circumstances surrounding this book's publication.

My publisher, Bantam Books, and I have rushed into print with this volume, and a second frontier collection, *Dutchman's Flat*, because a publisher I'm in no way associated with is issuing early magazine versions of some of my stories in a book that bears both my name and the same title as this edition. They're doing this without my authorization or permission, and without even having the courtesy of telling me what they plan to publish.

In 1983, this same publisher issued unauthorized editions of some of my frontier and detective stories in two collections, *Law of the Desert Born* and *The Hills of Homicide*. To offer my readers the chance to have the proper presentation of these stories, Bantam Books quickly published them in expanded editions, and I am pleased to note the demand for the authorized Bantam titles was so great that the unauthorized paperbacks quickly faded from the marketplace.

Now, two and a half years later, this publisher is back, again trying to profit from my hard work.

Their publication of an unauthorized version of *Riding for the Brand* is outrageous and unfair. Unfortunately the old copyright law fails to protect the stories they've taken for their volumes. As I said once before, while this publisher may be legally cleared to bring out these totally unauthorized versions, each of us must make his or her decision about the ethics of that kind of publishing.

My anger toward them has quickly been channeled into a renewed sense of determination to publish my short stories the way I see fit to best serve my readers.

I put aside the new novel I'm writing and worked into the night to select and edit the stories in this volume and to prepare the introductory historical notes that precede them. Many of the Bantam staff as well worked around the clock to bring this book to you as quickly as possible.

The unauthorized editions shortchange the reader by offering fewer stories than I've selected for my edition, and they do not have any of my newly written commentary.

Bantam Books is my official publisher and has been so for more than thirty years. They are the only publisher authorized to issue my short stories in book form. Only accept short story collections with my name on them that are published by Bantam.

I know my loyal fans—who certainly know how to read a brand—will want to own only the enhanced, enlarged Bantam edition of this book. It will come as no surprise to them that I will never autograph one copy of the unauthorized edition of *Riding for the Brand*. As far as I'm concerned, it simply doesn't exist.

I hope you enjoy reading this new collection as much as I appreciate you "riding for the brand" with me.

Louis L'Amour
Los Angeles, California
February, 1986

AUTHOR'S NOTE

RIDING FOR THE BRAND

The term "riding for the brand" was an expression of loyalty to a man's employer or the particular outfit he rode for. It was considered a compliment of the highest order in an almost feudal society. If a man did not like a ranch or the way they conducted their affairs he was free to quit, and many did, but if he stayed on he gave loyalty and expected it.

A man was rarely judged by his past, only by his actions. Many a man who came west left things behind him he would rather forget, so it was not the custom to ask questions. Much was forgiven if a man had courage and integrity and if he did his job. If a man gave less than his best, somebody always had to take up the slack, and he was not admired.

Riding for the Brand

He had been watching the covered wagon for more than an hour. There had been no movement, no sound. The bodies of the two animals that had drawn the wagon lay in the grass, plainly visible. Farther away, almost a mile away, stood a lone buffalo bull, black against the gray distance.

Nothing moved near the wagon, but Jed Asbury had lived too long in Indian country to risk his scalp on appearances, and he knew an Indian could lie ghost-still for hours on end. He had no intention of taking such a chance, stark naked and without weapons.

Two days before he had been stripped to the hide by Indians and forced to run the gauntlet, but he had run better than they had expected and had escaped with only a few minor wounds.

Now, miles away, he had reached the limit of his endurance. Despite little water and less food he was still in traveling condition except for his feet. They were lacerated and swollen, caked with dried blood.

Warily, he started forward, taking advantage of every bit of cover and moving steadily toward the wagon. When he was within fifty feet he settled down in the grass to study the situation.

This was the scene of an attack. Evidently the wagon had been alone, and the bodies of two men and a woman lay stretched on the grass.

Clothing, papers, and cooking utensils were scattered, evidence of a hasty looting. Whatever had been the dreams of these people they were ended now, another sacrifice to the westward march of empire. And the dead would not begrudge him what he needed.

Rising from the grass he went cautiously to the wagon, a tall, powerfully muscled young man, unshaven and untrimmed.

He avoided the bodies. Oddly, they were not mutilated, which was unusual, and the men still wore their boots. As a last resort he would take a pair for himself. First, he must examine the wagon.

If Indians had looted the wagon they had done so hurriedly, for the interior of the wagon was in the wildest state of confusion. In the bottom of a trunk he found a fine black broadcloth suit as well as a new pair of hand-tooled leather boots, a woolen shirt, and several white shirts.

"Somebody's Sunday-go-to-meetin' outfit," he muttered. "Hadn't better try the boots on the way my feet are swollen."

He found clean underwear and dressed, putting on some rougher clothes that he found in the same chest. When he was dressed enough to protect him from the sun he took water from a half-empty barrel on the side of the wagon and bathed his feet; then he bandaged them with strips of white cloth torn from a dress.

His feet felt much better, and as the boots were a size larger than he usually wore, he tried them. There was some discomfort, but he could wear them.

With a shovel tied to the wagon's side he dug a grave and buried the three side by side, covered them with quilts from the wagon, filled in the earth, and piled stones over the grave. Then, hat in hand, he recited the Twenty-Third Psalm.

The savages or whoever had killed them had made only a hasty search, so now he went to the wagon to find whatever might be useful to him or might inform him as to the identity of the dead.

There were some legal papers, a will, and a handful of letters. Putting these to one side with a poncho he found, he spotted a sewing basket. Remembering his grandmother's habits he emptied out the needles and thread, and under the padded bottom of the basket he found a large sealed envelope.

Ripping it open he grunted with satisfaction. Wrapped in carefully folded tissue paper were twenty twenty-dollar gold pieces. Pocketing them, he delved deeper into the trunk. He found more carefully folded clothes. Several times he broke off his searching of the wagon to survey the country about, but saw nothing. The wagon was in a concealed situation where a rider might have passed within a few yards and not seen it. He seemed to have approached from the only angle from which it was visible.

In the very bottom of the trunk he struck paydirt. He found a steel box. With a pick he forced it open. Inside, on folded velvet, lay a magnificent set of pistols, silver plated and beautifully engraved, with pearl handles. Wrapped in a towel nearby he found a pair of black leather cartridge belts and twin holsters. With them was a sack of .44 cartridges. Promptly, he loaded the guns and then stuffed the loops of both cartridge belts. After that he tried the balance of the guns. The rest of the cartridges he dropped into his pockets.

In another fold of the cloth he found a pearl-handled knife of beautifully tempered steel, a Spanish fighting knife and a beautiful piece of work. He slung the scabbard around his neck with the haft just below his collar.

Getting his new possessions together he made a pack of the clothing inside the poncho and used string to make a backpack of it. In the inside pocket of the coat he stowed the legal papers and the letters. In his hip pocket he stuffed a small leather-bound book he found among the scattered contents of the wagon. He read little, but knew the value of a good book.

He had had three years of intermittent schooling, learning to read, write, and cipher a little.

There was a canteen and he filled it. Rummaging in the wagon he found the grub box almost empty, a little coffee, some moldy bread, and nothing else useful. He took the coffee, a small pot, and a tin cup. Then he glanced at the sun and started away.

Jed Asbury was accustomed to fending for himself. That there could be anything wrong in appropriating what he had found never entered his head, nor would it have entered the head of any other man at the time. Life was hard, and one lived as best one might. If the dead had any heirs, there would be a clue in the letters or the will. He would pay them when he could. No man would begrudge him taking what was needed to survive, but to repay the debt incurred was a foregone conclusion.

Jed had been born on an Ohio farm, his parents dying when he was ten years old. He had been sent to a crabbed uncle living in a Maine fishing village. For three years his uncle worked him like a slave, sending him out on the Banks with a fishing boat. Finally, Jed had abandoned the boat, deep-sea fishing, and his uncle.

He walked to Boston and by devious methods reached Philadelphia. He had run errands, worked in a mill, and then gotten a job as a printer's devil. He had grown to like a man who came often to the shop, a quiet man with dark hair and large gray eyes, his head curiously wide across the temples. The man wrote stories and literary criticism and occasionally loaned Jed books to read. His name was Edgar Poe and he was reported to be the foster son of John Allan, said to be the richest man in Virginia.

When Jed left the print shop it was to ship on a windjammer for a voyage around the Horn. From San Francisco he had gone to Australia for a year in the goldfields, and then to South Africa and back to New York. He was twenty then and a big, well-made young man hardened by the life he had lived. He had gone west on a riverboat and then down the Mississippi to Natchez and New Orleans.

In New Orleans Jem Mace had taught him to box. Until then all he had known about fighting had been acquired by applying it that way. From New Orleans he had gone to Havana, to Brazil, and then back to the States. In Natchez he had caught a cardsharp cheating. Jed Asbury had proved a bit quicker, and the gambler died, a victim of six-shooter justice. Jed left town just ahead of several of the gambler's irate companions.

On a Missouri River steamboat he had gone up to Fort Benton and then overland to Bannock. He had traveled with wagon freighters to Laramie and then to Dodge.

In Tascosa he had encountered a brother of the dead Natchez gambler accompanied by two of the irate companions. He had killed two of his enemies and wounded the other, coming out of the fracas with a bullet in his leg. He traveled on to Santa Fe.

At twenty-four he was footloose and looking for a destination. Working as a bullwhacker he made a round-trip to Council Bluffs and then joined a wagon train for Cheyenne. The Comanches, raiding north, had interfered, and he had been the sole survivor.

He knew about where he was now, somewhere south and west of Dodge, but probably closer to Santa Fe than to the trail town. He should not be far from the cattle trail leading past Tascosa, so he headed that way. Along the river bottoms there should be strays lost from previous herds, so he could eat until a trail herd came along.

Walking a dusty trail in the heat, he shifted his small pack constantly and kept turning to scan the country over which he had come. He was in the heart of Indian country.

On the morning of the third day he sighted a trail herd, headed for Kansas. As he walked toward the herd, two of the three horsemen riding point turned toward him.

One was a lean, red-faced man with a yellowed mustache and a gleam of quizzical humor around his eyes. The other was a stocky, friendly rider on a paint horse.

"Howdy!" The older man's voice was amused. "Out for a mornin' stroll?"

"By courtesy of a bunch of Comanches. I was bullwhackin' with a wagon train out of Santa Fe for Cheyenne an' we had a little Winchester arbitration. They held the high cards." Briefly, he explained.

"You'll want a hoss. Ever work cattle?"

"Here and there. D'you need a hand?"

"Forty a month and all you can eat."

"The coffee's a fright," the other rider said. "That dough wrangler never learned to make coffee that didn't taste like strong lye!"

That night in camp Jed Asbury got out the papers he had found in the wagon. He read the first letter he opened.

Dear Michael,

When you get this you will know George is dead. He was thrown from a horse near Willow

Springs, dying the following day. The home ranch comprises 60,000 acres and the other ranches twice that. This is to be yours or your heirs if you have married since we last heard from you, if you or the heirs reach the place within one year of George's death. If you do not claim your estate within that time the property will be inherited by next of kin. You may remember what Walt is like, from the letters.

Naturally, we hope you will come at once for we all know what it would be like if Walt took over. You should be around twenty-six now and able to handle Walt, but be careful. He is dangerous and has killed several men.

Things are in good shape now but trouble is impending with Besovi, a neighbor of ours. If Walt takes over that will certainly happen. Also, those of us who have worked and lived here so long will be thrown out.

Tony Costa

The letter had been addressed to Michael Latch, St. Louis, Missouri. Thoughtfully, Jed folded the letter and then glanced through the others. He learned much, yet not enough.

Michael Latch had been the nephew of George Baca, a half-American, half-Spanish rancher who owned a huge hacienda in California. Neither Baca nor Tony Costa had ever seen Michael. Nor had the man named Walt, who apparently was the son of George's half-brother.

The will was that of Michael's father, Thomas Latch, and conveyed to Michael the deed to a small California ranch.

From other papers and an unmailed letter, Jed discovered that the younger of the two men he had buried had been Michael Latch. The other dead man and the woman had been Randy and May Kenner. There was mention in a letter of a girl named Arden who had accompanied them.

"The Indians must have taken her with them," Jed muttered.

He considered trying to find her, but dismissed the idea as impractical. Looking for a needle in a haystack would at least be a local job, but trying to find one of many roving bands of Comanches would be well-nigh impossible. Nevertheless, he would inform the army and the trading posts. Often, negotiations could be started, and for an appropriate trade in goods she might be recovered, if still living.

Then he had another idea.

Michael Latch was dead. A vast estate awaited him, a fine, comfortable, constructive life, which young Latch would have loved. Now the estate would fall to Walt, whoever he was, unless he, Jed Asbury, took the name of Michael Latch and claimed the estate.

The man who was his new boss rode in from a ride around the herd. He glanced at Jed, who was putting the letters away. "What did you say your name was?"

Only for an instant did Jed hesitate. "Latch," he replied, "Michael Latch."

Warm sunlight lay upon the hacienda called Casa Grande. The hounds sprawling in drowsy peace under the smoke trees scarcely opened their eyes when the tall stranger turned his horse through the gate. Many strangers came to Casa Grande, and the uncertainty that hung over the vast ranch had not reached the dogs.

Tony Costa straightened his lean frame from the doorway and studied the stranger from under an eye-shielding hand.

"Señorita, someone comes!"

"Is it Walt?" Sharp, quick heels sounded on the flatstoned floor. "What will we do? Oh, if Michael were only here!"

"Today is the last day," Costa said gloomily.

"Look!" The girl touched his arm. "Right behind him! That's Walt Seever!"

"Two men with him. We will have trouble if we try to stop him, Señorita. He would not lose the ranch to a woman."

The stranger on the black horse swung down at the steps. He wore a flat-crowned black hat and a black broadcloth suit. His boots were almost new and hand tooled, but when her eyes dropped to the guns, she gasped.

"*Tony!* The guns!"

The young man came up the steps, swept off his hat, and bowed. "You are Tony Costa? The foreman of Casa Grande?"

The other riders clattered into the court, and their leader, a big man with bold, hard eyes, swung down. He brushed past the stranger and confronted the foreman.

"Well, Costa, today this ranch becomes mine, and you're fired!"

"I think not."

All eyes turned to the stranger. The girl's eyes were startled, suddenly cautious. This man was strong, she thought suddenly, and he was not afraid. He had a clean-cut face, pleasant gray eyes, and a certain assurance born of experience.

"If you are Walt," the stranger said, "you can ride back where you came from. This ranch is mine. I am Michael Latch."

Fury struggled with shocked disbelief in the expression on Walt Seever's face. "*You?* Michael Latch? You couldn't be!"

"Why not?" Jed was calm. Eyes on Seever, he could not see the effect of his words on Costa or the girl. "George sent for me. Here I am."

Mingled with the baffled rage, there was something else in Walt's face, some ugly suspicion or knowledge. Suddenly Jed suspected that Walt knew he was not Michael Latch. Or doubted it vehemently.

Tony Costa had moved up beside him. "Why not? We have expected him. His uncle wrote for him, and after Baca's death, I wrote to him. If you doubt it, look at the guns. Are there two such pairs of guns in the world? Are there two men in the world who could make such guns?"

Seever's eyes went to the guns, and Jed saw doubt and puzzlement replace the angry certainty.

"I'll have to have more proof than a pair of guns!"

Jed took the letter from his pocket and passed it over. "From Tony. I also have my father's will and other letters."

Walt Seever glanced at the letter and then hurled it

into the dust. "Let's get out of here!" He started for his horse.

Jed Asbury watched them go, puzzling over that odd reaction of Walt's. Until Seever saw that letter he had been positive Jed was not Michael Latch. Now he was no longer sure. But what could have made him so positive in the beginning? What could he know?

The girl was whispering something to Costa. Jed turned, smiling at her. "I don't believe Walt was too happy at my being here," he said.

"No," Costa's expression was unrevealing, "he isn't. He expected to have this ranch for himself." Costa turned toward the girl. "Sēnor Latch? I would introduce to you Señorita Carol James, a—a ward of Señor Baca's and his good friend."

Jed acknowledged the introduction.

"You must bring me up to date. I want to know all you can tell me about Walt Seever."

Costa exchanged a glance with Carol. "Of course, Señor. Walt Seever is a *malo hombre*, Señor. He has killed several men, is most violent. The men with him were Harry Strykes and Gin Feeley. They are gunmen and believed to be thieves."

Jed Asbury listened attentively, yet wondered about Carol's reaction. Did she suspect he was not Michael Latch? Did she *know* he was not Latch? If so, why didn't she say something?

He was surprised they had accepted him so readily, for even after he had decided to take the dead man's place he had not been sure he could go through with it. He had a feeling of guilt and some shame, yet the real Michael Latch was dead, and the only man he was depriving seemed to be a thoroughly bad one whose first action would have been to fire the ranch's foreman, a man whose home had always been this hacienda.

He had made a wild ride over rough country to get here in time, but over all that distance he had debated with himself about the rights and the wrongs of his action.

He was nobody, a drifter, worker at whatever came to hand, an adventurer, if you will, but not unlike hundreds of others who came and went across the West and more often than not left their bones in the wilderness, their flesh to feed the ancient soil.

He had not known Michael Latch, or what kind of man he had been, but he suspected he had been a good man and a trusted one. Why could he not save the ranch from Walt Seever, find a home for himself at last, and be the kind of man Michael Latch would have been?

All through that wild ride west he had struggled with his conscience, trying to convince himself that what he did was the right thing. He could do Latch no harm, and Costa and Carol seemed pleased to have him here, now that he had arrived. The expression on Seever's face had been worth the ride, if nothing more.

There was something else that disturbed him. That was Walt Seever's odd reaction when he had said he was Michael Latch.

"You say," Jed turned to Carol, "that Seever was sure he would inherit?"

She nodded. "Yes, though until about three months ago he was hating George Baca for leaving the ranch to you. Then suddenly he changed his mind and seemed sure he would inherit, that you would never come to claim your inheritance."

It had been about three months ago that Jed Asbury had come upon the lone wagon and the murdered people, a murder he had laid to Indians. But leaving the corpses with their clothing and the wagon unlooted did not seem like any raiding parties of which he had known.

Three people murdered—could Seever have known of that? Was that why he had suddenly been sure he would inherit?

The idea took root. Seever must have known of the killings. If that was so, then the three had not been killed by Indians, and a lot remained to be explained. How did the wagon happen to be alone, so far from anywhere? And what had become of the girl, Arden?

If Indians had not made the attack and carried Arden off, then somebody else had captured her, and wherever she was she would know he was not the real Michael Latch. She would know Jed Asbury, for an imposter, but she might also know who the killers were.

Walking out on the wide terrace overlooking the green valley beyond the ranch house, Jed stared down the valley, his mind filled with doubts and apprehensions.

It was a lovely land, well watered and rich. Here, with what he knew of land and cattle, he could carry on the work George Baca had begun. He would do what Michael Latch would have done, and he might even do it better.

There was danger, but when had he not known danger? And these people at the ranch were good people, honest people. If he did not do more than save the ranch from Seever and his lawless crowd he would have adequate reason for taking the place of the dead man. Yet he was merely finding excuses for his conduct.

The guns he wore meant something, too. Carol had recognized them, and so had Seever. What was their significance?

He was in deep water here. Every remark he made must be guarded. Even if they had not seen him before, there must be family stories and family tradition of which he knew nothing. There was a movement behind him, and Jed Asbury turned. In the gathering dusk he saw Carol.

"Do you like it?" She gestured toward the valley.

"It's splendid! I have never seen anything prettier. A man could do a lot with land like that. It could be a paradise."

"Somehow you are different than I expected."

"I am?" He was careful, waiting for her to say more.

"You're much more assured than I expected you to be. Mike was quiet, Uncle George used to say. Read a lot, but did not get around much. You startled me by the way you handled Walt Seever."

He shrugged. "A man changes. He grows older, and coming west to a new life makes a man more sure of himself."

She noticed the book in his pocket. "What book do you have?" she asked curiously.

It was a battered copy of Plutarch. He was on safe ground here, for on the flyleaf was written, *To Michael, from Uncle George*.

He showed it to her and she said, "It was a favorite of

Uncle George. He used to say that next to the Bible more great men had read Plutarch than any other book."

"I like it. I've been reading it nights." He turned to face her. "Carol, what do you think Walt Seever will do?"

"Try to kill you or have you killed," she replied. She gestured toward the guns. "You had better learn to use those."

"I can, a little."

He dared not admit how well he could use them, for a man does not come by such skill overnight, nor the cool nerve it takes to use them facing an armed enemy. "Seever has counted on this place, has he?"

"He has made a lot of talk." She glanced up at him. "You know, Walt was no blood relation to Uncle George. He was the son of a woman of the gold camps who married George Baca's half-brother."

"I see." Actually, Walt Seever's claim was scarcely better than his own. "I know from the letters that Uncle George wanted me to have the estate, but I feel like an outsider. I am afraid I may be doing wrong to take a ranch built by the work of other people. Walt may have more right to it than I. I may be doing wrong to assert my claim."

He was aware of her searching gaze. When she spoke it was deliberately and as if she had reached some decision.

"Michael, I don't know you, but you would have to be very bad, indeed, to be as dangerous and evil as Walt Seever. I would say that no matter what the circumstances, you should stay and see this through."

Was there a hint that she might know more than she admitted? Yet it was natural that he should be looking for suspicion behind every phrase. Yet he must do that or be trapped.

"However, it is only fair to warn you that you have let yourself in for more than you could expect. Uncle George knew very well what you would be facing. He knew the viciousness of Walt Seever. He doubted you would be clever or bold enough to defeat Seever. So I must warn you, Michael Latch, that if you do stay, and I believe you should, you will probably be killed."

He smiled into the darkness. Since boyhood he had

lived in proximity to death. He was not foolhardy or reckless, for a truly brave man was never reckless. He knew he could skirt the ragged edge of death if need be. He had been there before.

He was an interloper here, yet the man whose place he had taken was dead, and perhaps he could carry on in his place, making the ranch safe for those who loved it. Then he could move on and leave this ranch to Carol and to the care of Tony Costa.

He turned. "I am tired," he said. "I have ridden long and hard to get here. Now I'd like to rest." He paused. "But I shall stay, at least—"

Jed Asbury was already fast asleep when Carol went into the dining room where Tony Costa sat at the long table. Without him, what would she have done? What could she have done? He had worked with her father for thirty years and had lived on the hacienda all his life, and he was past sixty now. He still stood as erect and slender as he had when a young man. And he was shrewd.

Costa looked up. He was drinking coffee by the light of a candle. "For better or worse, Señorita, it has begun. What do you think now?"

"He told me, after I warned him, that he would stay."

Costa studied the coffee in his cup. "You are not afraid?"

"No. He faced Walt Seever and that was enough for me. Anything is to be preferred to Walt Seever."

"Sí." Costa's agreement was definite. "Señorita, did you notice his hands when he faced Seever. They were ready, Carolita, ready to draw. This man has used a gun before. He is a strong man, Carolita!"

"Yes, I think you are right. He is a strong man."

For two days nothing happened from the direction of town. Walt Seever and his hard-bitten companions might have vanished from the earth, but on the Rancho Casa Grande much was happening, and Tony Costa was whistling most of the time.

Jed Asbury's formal education was slight, but he knew men, how to lead them and how best to get results. Above all he had practical knowledge of handling cattle and of range conditions.

He was up at five the morning after his discussion with Carol, and when she awakened, old Maria, the cook, told her the señor was hard at work in his office. The door was open a crack, and as she passed by she glimpsed him deep in the accounts of the ranch. Pinned up before him was a map of the Casa Grande holdings, and as he checked the disposition of the cattle, he studied the map.

He ate a hurried breakfast and at eight o'clock was in the saddle. He ate his next meal at a line camp and rode in long after dark. In two days he spent twenty hours in the saddle.

On the third day he called Costa to the office and sent Maria to request the presence of Carol. Puzzled and curious, she joined them.

Jed wore a white shirt, black trousers, and the silver guns. His face seemed to have thinned down in just the two days, but when he glanced at her, he smiled.

"You have been here longer than I and are, in a sense, a partner." Before she could interrupt he turned to Costa. "I want you to remain as foreman. However, I have asked you both to be here as I plan some changes."

He indicated a point on the map. "That narrow passage leads into open country and then desert. I found cattle tracks there, going out. It might be rustlers. A little blasting up in the rocks will close that gap."

"It is a good move," Costa agreed.

"This field—" Jed indicated a large area in a field not far from the house, "must be fenced off. We will plant it to flax."

"Flax, Señor?"

"There will be a good market for it." He indicated a smaller area. "This piece we will plant to grapes, and all that hillside will support them. There will be times when we cannot depend on cattle or horses, so there must be other sources of income."

Carol watched in wonderment. He was moving fast, this new Michael Latch. He had grasped the situation at once and was moving to make changes that Uncle George had only thought about.

"Also, Costa, we must have a roundup. Gather the cattle and cut out all those over four years old, and we'll sell them. I saw a lot of cattle from five to eight years old back there in the brush."

After he had ridden away to study another quarter of the ranch, Carol walked to the blacksmith shop to talk to Pat Flood. He was an old seafaring man with a pegleg whom Uncle George had found broke and on the beach in San Francisco and who had proved to be a marvel with tools.

He looked up from under his bushy brows as she stopped at the shop. He was cobbling a pair of boots. Before she could speak he said, "This here new boss, Latch? Been to sea, ain't he?"

Surprised, she said, "What gave you that idea?"

"Seen him throw a bowline on a bight yesterday. Purtiest job I seen since comin' ashore. He made that rope fast like he'd been doin' it for years."

"I expect many men handle ropes well," she commented.

"Not sailor fashion. He called it a line, too. 'Hand me that line!' he says. Me, I been ashore so long I'm callin' them ropes m'self, but not him. I'd stake my supper that he's walked a deck."

Jed Asbury was riding to town. He wanted to assay the feeling of the townspeople toward the ranch, toward George Baca and Walt Seever. There was a chance he might talk to a few people before they discovered his connection. Also, he was irritated at the delay in the showdown with Seever. His appearance in town might force that showdown or allow Seever an opportunity if he felt he needed one. If there was to be a meeting he wanted it over with so he could get on with work at the ranch.

He had never avoided trouble. It was his nature to go right to the heart of it, and for this trip he was wearing worn gray trousers, boots, his silver guns, and a battered black hat. He hoped they would accept him as a drifting puncher.

Already, in riding around the ranch and in casual talk with the hands, he had learned a good deal. He knew the place to go in town was the Golden Strike. He tied his horse to the hitching rail and went inside.

Three men loafed at the bar. The big man with the scar on his lip was Harry Strykes, who had ridden with Seever. As Jed stepped to the bar and ordered his drink, a man seated at a table got up and went to Strykes. "Never saw him before," he said.

Strykes went around the man and faced Jed. "So? Cuttin' in for yourself, are you? Well, nobody gets in the way of my boss. Go for your gun or go back to Texas. You got a choice!"

"I'm not going to kill you," Jed said. "I don't like your manner, but if you touch that gun I'll have to blow your guts out. Instead, I'd rather teach you a lesson."

His left hand grabbed Strykes by the belt. He shoved back and then lifted, and his left toe kicked Strykes's foot from under him as Jed lifted on the belt and then let go.

The move caught Strykes unaware, and he hit the floor hard. For an instant he was shaken, but then he came off the floor with a curse.

Jed Asbury had taken up his drink with his left hand, leaning carelessly against the bar. Jed's left foot was on the brass rail, and as Strykes swung his right fist, Jed straightened his leg, moving himself out from the bar so that the punch missed, throwing Strykes against the bar. As his chest hit the bar Jed flipped the remainder of his drink into Strykes's eyes.

Moving away from the bar he made no attempt to hit Strykes, just letting the man paw at the stinging whiskey in his eyes. When he seemed about to get his vision cleared, Jed leaned forward and jerked open Strykes's belt. Strykes's pants slid toward his knees, and he grabbed at them. Jed pushed him with the tips of his fingers. With his pants around his knees Strykes could not stagger, so he fell.

Jed turned to the others in the room. "Sorry to have disturbed you, gentlemen! The name is Mike Latch. If you are ever out to the Casa Grande, please feel free to call."

He walked out of the saloon, leaving laughter behind him as Strykes struggled to get up and pull his pants into place.

Yet he was remembering the man who had stepped

up to Strykes saying he had never seen Jed before. Had that man known the real Mike Latch? If Walt Seever knew of the covered wagon with its three murdered people, he would know Jed Asbury was an impostor and would be searching for a way to prove it. The vast and beautiful acres of Rancho Casa Grande were reason enough.

Riding homeward he mulled over the problem. There was, of course, a chance of exposure, yet no one might ever come near who could actually identify him.

His brief altercation with Strykes had gotten him nowhere. He had undoubtedly been observed when riding into town, and the stranger must have known the real Latch. Nevertheless, the fight, if such it could be called, might have won a few friends. In the first place he could not imagine a man of Seever's stamp was well liked; in the second he had shown he was not anxious to get into a gun battle. Friends could be valuable in the months to come, and he was not catering to the rowdy element who would be Seever's friends.

Seever, however, would now be spoiling for a fight, and Jed might be killed. He must find a way to give Carol a strong claim on the ranch. Failing in that, he must kill Walt Seever.

Jed Asbury had never killed a man except to protect his own life or those close to him. Deliberately to hunt down and shoot a man was something he had never dreamed of doing, yet it might prove the only way he could protect Carol and Tony Costa. With a shock he realized he was thinking more of Carol than of himself, and he hardly knew her.

Apparently the stranger had known he was not Mike Latch. The next time it might be a direct accusation before witnesses. Jed considered the problem all the way home.

Unknown to Jed, Jim Pardo, one of the toughest hands on the ranch, had followed him into town. On his return, Pardo drew up before the blacksmith shop and looked down at Pat Flood. The gigantic old blacksmith would have weighed well over three hundred pounds with two good legs, and he stood five inches over six feet. He rarely left the shop, as his wooden leg was always giving him trouble.

"He'll do," Pardo said, swinging down.

Flood lit his corncob pipe and waited.

"Had a run-in with Harry Strykes."

Flood drew on the pipe, knowing the story would come.

"Made a fool of Harry."

"Whup him?"

"Not like he should of, but maybe this was worse. He got him laughed at."

"Strykes will kill him for that."

Pardo rolled a cigarette and explained. "If Strykes is smart he will leave him alone. This here Latch is no greenhorn. He's a man knows what he can do. No other would have handled it like he did. Never turned a hair when Strykes braced him. He's got sand in his gizzard, an' I'm placin' my bets that he'll prove a first-class hand with a shootin' iron. This one's had trouble before."

"He's deep," Flood said, chewing on his pipe stem.

"Old George always said Latch was a book reader, an' quiet-like."

"Well," Flood was thoughtful, "He's quiet enough, an' he reads books."

Tony Costa learned of the incident from Pardo, and Maria related the story to Carol. Jed made no reference to it at supper.

Costa hesitated after arising from the table. "Señor, since Señor Baca's death the señorita has permitted me to eat in the ranch house. There was often business to discuss. If you wish, I can—"

"Forget it, and unless you're in a hurry, sit down. Your years on the ranch have earned you your place at the table."

Jed took up the pot and filled their cups. "Yesterday I was over in Fall Valley and I saw a lot of cattle with a Bar O brand."

"Bar O? Ah, they try it again! This brand, Señor, belongs to a very big outfit! Frank Besovi's ranch. He is a big man, Señor, a very troublesome man. Always he tries to move in on that valley, but if he takes that he will want more. He has taken many ranches, so."

"Take some of the boys up there and throw those cattle off our range."

"There will be trouble, Señor."

"Are you afraid of trouble, Costa?"

The foreman's face tightened. "No, Señor!"

"Neither am I. Throw them off."

When the punchers moved out in the morning, Jed mounted a horse and rode along. And there would be trouble. Jed saw that when they entered the valley.

Several riders were grouped near a big man with a black beard. Their horses all carried the Bar O brand.

"I'll talk to him, Costa. I want to hear what Besovi has to say."

"Very bad man," Costa warned.

Jed Asbury knew trouble when he saw it. Besovi and his men had come prepared for a showdown. Jed did not speak, he simply pushed his black against Beosvi's gray. Anger flared in the big man's eyes. "What the hell are you tryin' to do?" he roared.

"Tell your boys to round up your Bar O cattle and run them back over your line. If you don't, I'll make you run 'em back, afoot!"

"*What?*" Besovi was incredulous. "You say that to *me*?"

"You heard me. Give the order!"

"I'll see you in hell first!" Besovi shouted.

Jed Asbury knew this could be settled in two ways. If he went for a gun there would be shooting and men would be killed. He chose the other way.

Acting so suddenly the move was unexpected, he grabbed Besovi by the beard and jerked the rancher sharply toward him, at the same time he kicked the rancher's foot loose from his stirrup and then shoved hard. Besovi, caught unawares by the sheer unexpectedness of the attack, fell off his horse, and Jed hit the ground beside him.

Besovi came to his feet, clawing for his gun. "Afraid to fight with your hands?" Jed taunted.

Besovi glared and then unbuckled his gun belts and

handed them to the nearest horseman. Jed stripped off his own gun belts and handed them to Costa.

Besovi started toward him with a crablike movement that made Jed's eyes sharpen. He circled warily, looking the big man over.

Jed was at least thirty pounds lighter than Besovi, and it was obvious the big man had power in those mighty shoulders. But it would take more than power to win this kind of a fight. Jed moved in, feinting to get Besovi to reveal his fighting style. Besovi grabbed at his left wrist, and Jed brushed the hand aside and stiffened a left into his face.

Blood showed, and the Casa Grande men yelled. Pardo, rolling his quid of tobacco in his jaws, watched. He had seen Besovi fight before. The big man kept moving in, and Jed circled, wary. Besovi had some plan of action. He was no wild-swinging, hit or miss fighter.

Jed feinted again and then stabbed two lefts to Besovi's face, so fast one punch had barely landed before the other smacked home. Pardo was surprised to see how Besovi's head jerked under the impact.

Besovi moved in, and when Jed led with another blow, the bigger man went under the punch and leaping close encircled Jed with his mighty arms. Jed's leap back had been too slow, and he sensed the power in that grasping clutch. If those huge arms closed around him he would be in serious trouble, so he kicked up his feet and fell.

The unexpected fall caught Besovi off balance and he lunged over him, losing his grip. Quickly, he spun, but Jed was already on his feet. Besovi swung and the blow caught Jed on the cheekbone. Jed took the punch standing and Pardo's mouth dropped open in surprise. Nobody had ever stood up under a Besovi punch before.

Jed struck then, a left and right that landed solidly. The left opened the gash over Besovi's eye a little wider, and the right caught him on the chin, staggering him. Jed moved in, landing both fists to the face. The big man's hands came up to protect his face and Jed slugged him in the stomach.

Besovi got an arm around Jed and hooked him twice

in the face with wicked, short punches. Jed butted him in the face with his head, breaking free.

Yet he did not step back but caught the rancher behind the head with his left hand and jerked his head down to meet a smashing right uppercut that broke Besovi's nose.

Jed pushed him away quickly and hit him seven fast punches before Besovi could get set. Like a huge, blind bear Besovi tried to swing, but Jed ducked the punch and slammed both fists to the body.

Besovi staggered, almost falling, and Jed stepped back. "You've had plenty, Besovi, and you're too good a fighter to kill. I could kill you with my fists, but I'd probably ruin my hands in doing it. Will you take those cattle and get out of here?"

Besovi, unsteady on his feet, wiped the blood from his eyes. "Well, I'll be damned! I never thought the man lived—! Will you shake hands?"

"I'd never shake with a tougher man or a better one!"

Their hands gripped, and suddenly Besovi began to laugh. "Come over to supper some night, will you? Ma's been tellin' me this would happen. She'll be pleased to meet you!"

He turned to his riders. "The fun's over, boys! Round up our stock an' let's go home."

The big rancher's lips were split; there was a cut over his right eye and another under it. The other eye was swelling shut. There was one bruise on Jed's cheekbone that would be bigger tomorrow, but it wasn't enough to show he had been in a fight.

"Can't figure him," Pardo told Flood, later. "Is he scared to use his guns? Or does he just like to fight with his hands?"

"He's smart," Flood suggested. "Look, he's made a friend of Besovi. If he'd beaten him to the ground, Besovi might never have forgiven him. He was savin' face for Besovi just like they do it over China way. And what if he'd gone for his guns?"

"Likely four or five of us might not have made it home tonight."

"That's it. He's usin' his head for something more

than a place to hang a hat. Look at it. He's made a friend of Besovi and nobody is shot up."

Jed, soaking his battered hands, was not so sure. Besovi might have gone for a gun, or one of his hands might have. He had taken a long gamble and won; next time he might not be so lucky.

At least, Rancho Casa Grande had one less enemy and one more friend.

If anything happened to him Carol would need friends. Walt Seever was ominously quiet, and Jed was sure the man was waiting for proof that he was not Michael Latch. And that gave Jed an idea. It was a game at which two could play.

Carol was saddling her horse when he walked out in the morning. She glanced at him, her eyes hesitating on the bruise. "You seem to have a faculty for getting into trouble!" she said, smiling.

He led the black gelding out. "I don't believe in ducking troubles. They just pile up on you. Sometimes they get too big to handle."

"You seem to have made a friend of Besovi."

"Why not? He's a good man, just used to taking in all he can put his hands on, but he'll prove a good neighbor." He hesitated and then glanced off, afraid his eyes would give him away. "If anything happens to me, you'll need friends. I think Besovi would help you."

Her eyes softened. "Thank you, Mike." She hesitated just a little over the name. "You have already done much of what Uncle George just talked of doing."

Costa was gathering the herd Jed wanted to sell, and Pardo was riding with him. Jed did not ask Carol where she was going, but watched her ride away toward the valley. He threw a saddle on his own horse and cinched up. At the sound of horses' hoofs he turned.

Walt Seever was riding into the yard. With him were Harry Strykes and Gin Feeley. The fourth man was the one he had seen in the saloon who had told Walt he was not Michael Latch. Realizing he wore no guns, Jed felt naked and helpless. There was no one around the ranch house of whom he knew.

Seever drew rein and rested his hands on the pommel of his saddle. "Howdy! Howdy, Jed!"

No muscle changed on Jed Asbury's face. If trouble came he was going right at Walt Seever.

"Smart play," Seever said, savoring his triumph. "If it hadn't been for me doubtin' you, you might have pulled it off."

Jed waited, watching.

"Now," Seever said, "your game is up. I suppose I should let you get on your horse an' ride, but we ain't about to."

"You mean to kill me like you did Latch and his friends?"

"Think you're smart, do you? Well, when you said that you dug your own grave."

"I suppose your sour-faced friend here was one of those you sent to kill Latch," Jed commented. "He looks to be the kind."

"Let me kill him, Walt!" The man with the sour face had his hand on his gun. "Just let me kill him!"

"What I want to know," Seever said, "is where you got them guns?" Walt said, holding up a hand to stop the other man.

"Out of the wagon, of course! The men you sent to stop Latch before he got here messed up. I'd just gotten away from a passel of Indians and was stark naked. I found clothes in the wagon. I also found the guns."

"About like I figured. Now we'll get rid of you, an' I'll have Casa Grande."

Jed was poised for a break, any kind of a break, and stalling for time. "Thieves like you always overlook important things. The men you sent messed up badly. They were in too much of a hurry and didn't burn the wagon. And what about Arden?"

"Arden? Who the devil is Arden?"

Jed had come a step nearer. They would get him, but he was going to kill Walt Seever.

He chuckled. "They missed her, Walt! Arden is a girl. She was with Latch when he was killed."

"A girl?" Seever turned on the other man. "Clark, you never said anything about a girl!"

"There wasn't any girl," Clark protested.

"He killed three of them, but she was out on the prairie to gather wild onions or something."

"That's a lie! There was only the three of them!" Clark shouted.

"What about those fancy clothes you threw around in the wagon? Think they were old woman's clothes?"

Walt was furious. "Damn you, Clark! You said you got all of them!"

"There wasn't no girl," Clark protested. "Anyway, I didn't see one!"

"There was a girl, Walt, and she's safe. If something goes wrong here you will have to answer for it, Walt. You haven't a chance!"

Seever's face was ugly with anger. "Anyway, we've got you! We've got you dead to rights!" His hand moved toward his gun, but before Jed Asbury could move a muscle, there was a shot.

From behind Jed came Pat Flood's voice. "Keep your hands away from those guns, Walt. I can shoot the buttons off your shirt with this here rifle, and in case that ain't enough I got me a scattergun right beside me. Now you gents just unbuckle your belts, real easy now! Your first, Seever!"

Jed dropped back swiftly and picked up the shotgun.

The men shed their guns. "Now get off your hosses!" Flood ordered.

They dismounted and Flood asked, "What you want done with 'em, Boss? Should we bury them here or give them a runnin' chance?"

"Let them walk back to town," Jed suggested. "All but Clark. I want to talk to Clark."

Seever started to speak, but the buffalo gun and the shotgun were persuasive. He led the way.

"Let me go!" Clark begged. "They'll kill me!"

Jed gathered the gun belts and walked to the blacksmith shop, behind Clark.

"How much did you hear?" he asked Flood.

"All of it," the big blacksmith replied bluntly, "but my memory can be mighty poor. I judge a man by the way he handles himself, and you've been ridin' for the brand. I ain't interested in anything else."

Jed turned on Clark. "Get this straight. You've one chance to live, and you shouldn't have that. Tell us what happened, who sent you and what you did." He glanced at Flood. "Take this down, every word."

"I got paper and pencil." Flood said. "I always keep a log."

"All right, Clark, a complete confession and you get your horse a and runing start."

"Seever will kill me."

"Make your choice. You sign a confession or you can die right here at the end of a rope behind a runaway horse. Seever's not going to kill anybody, ever again."

Clark hesitated, and then he said, "I was broke in Ogden when Seever found me. I'd knowed him before. He told me I was to find this here wagon that was startin' west from St. Louis. He said I was to make sure they never got here. I never knew there was a woman along."

"Who was with you?"

"Feller named Quinby and a friend of his'n named Buck Stanton. I met up with 'em in Laramie."

At Jed's exclamation, Flood glanced at him. "You know them?"

"I killed Buck's brother Cal. They were crooked gamblers."

"Then you were the man they were huntin'!" Clark exclaimed.

"Where are they now?"

"Comin' this way, I suppose. Seever sent for 'em for some reason. Guess he figured they could come in here and prove you was somebody different than you said."

"Seever ordered the killing?"

"Yes, sir. He surely did."

A few more questions and the confession was signed.

"Now get on that horse and get out of here before we change our minds and hang you."

"Do I get my guns?"

"You do not. Get going!"

Clark fairly threw himself into the saddle and left at a dead run.

Flood handed the confession to Jed. "Are you going to use it?"

"Not right now. I'll put it in the safe in the house. If Carol ever needs it, she can use it. If I brought it out now it would prove that I am not Michael Latch."

"I knew you weren't him," Flood said. "Old George told me a good bit about him, but just seein' you around told me you'd covered a lot more country than he ever did."

"Does Carol know?"

"Don't reckon she does, but then she's a right canny lass."

If Stanton and Quinby were headed west, then Seever must have telegraphed for them to come, and they would certainly ally themselves with Seever against him. As if he did not have trouble enough!

Costa and Jim Pardo rode into the yard, and Costa trotted his horse over to Jed, who was wearing the silver guns now.

"There were many cattle! More than expected! We came to see if the Willow Springs boys can help us."

"Later. Was Miss Carol out with you?"

"No, Señor. She went to town."

Jed swore. "Flood, you take care of things here. We're riding into town!"

Seever would stop at nothing now, and if Quinby and Stanton had arrived in town Jed's work would be cut out for him. No doubt Seever had known how to reach them, and it must have been from Stanton that Seever learned his name. A description from Seever would have been enough for Stanton to recognize who he was.

The town lay basking in a warm sun. In the distance the Sierras lifted snowcapped peaks against the blue sky. A man loitering in front of the Golden Strike stepped through the doors as Jed appeared in the street with his Casa Grande cowboys. Walt Seever stepped into the doorway, nonchalant, confident.

"Figured you'd be in. We sort of detained the lady, knowin' that would bring you. She can go loose now that you're where we want you."

Jed stepped down from the saddle. This was a trap, and they had ridden right into it.

"There's a gent in front of the express office, Boss," Pardo said.

"Thanks, and watch the windows," Jed suggested. "Upstairs windows."

Jed was watching Seever. Trouble would begin with him. He moved away from his horse. No sense in getting a good animal killed. He did not look to see what Costa and Pardo were doing. They would be doing what was best for them and for what was coming.

"Glad you saved me the trouble of hunting you, Seever," he said.

Seever was on the edge of the boardwalk, a big man looking granite hard and tough. "Save us both trouble. Folks here don't take to outsiders. They'd sooner have somebody like me runnin' the outfit than a stranger. Shuck your guns, get on your horses, and you can ride out of town."

"Don't do it, Boss!" Pardo warned. "He'll shoot you as soon as your back is turned."

"The ranch goes to Miss Carol, Seever. You might get me, but I promise you, you will die."

"Like hell!" Seever's hand swept for his gun. "I'll kill—!"

"Look out!" Pardo yelled.

Jed stepped aside as the rifle roared from the window over the livery barn, and his guns lifted. His first bullet took Walt Seever in the chest; his second went into the shadows behind a rifle muzzle in the barn loft.

Seever staggered into the street, his guns pounding lead into the street. Oblivious of the pounding guns around him, Jed centered his attention on Seever, and when the man fell, the pistol dribbling from his fingers, Jed looked around, keeping his eyes from this man he had killed, hating the sight of what he had done.

Costa was down on one knee, blood staining the left sleeve of his shirt, but his face was expressionless, his pistol ready.

A dead man sprawled over the windowsill above the barn. A soft wind stirred his sandy hair. That would be

Stanton. Pardo was holstering his gun. There was no sign of Stryker or Feeley.

"You all right, Boss?" Pardo asked.

"All right. How about you?"

Tony Costa was getting to his feet. "Caught one in the shoulder," he said. "It's not bad."

Heads were appearing in doors and windows, but nobody showed any desire to come outside. Then a door slammed down the street, and Carol was running to them.

"Are you hurt?" She caught his arm. "Were you shot?"

He slid an arm around her as she came up to him, and it was so natural that neither of them noticed. "Better get that shoulder fixed up, Costa." He glanced down at Carol. "Where did they have you?"

"Strykes and Feeley were holding me in a house across the street. When Feeley saw you were not alone he wanted Harry Strykes to leave. Feeley looked out the door and Pat Flood saw him."

"Flood?"

"He followed you in, knowing there'd be trouble. He came in behind them and had me take their guns. He was just going out to help you when the shooting started."

"Carol," he hesitated. "I've got a confession to make. I am not Michael Latch."

"Oh? Is that all? I've known that all the time. You see, I was Michael Latch's wife."

"His what?"

"Before I married him I was Carol Arden James. He was the only one who ever called me Arden. During the time we were coming west I was quite ill, so I stayed in the wagon and Clark never saw me at all.

"He convinced Michael there was a wagon train going by way of Santa Fe that would take us through sooner, and if we could catch them it would help. It was all a lie to get us away from the rest of the wagons, but Michael listened, as the train we were with was going only as far as Laramie.

"After we were on the trail, Clark left us to locate the wagon train, as he said. Randy Kenner and Mike decided to camp, and I went over the hill to a small pool to bathe. When I was dressing I heard shooting, and believing it was Indians, I crept to the top of a hill so I could see our wagon.

"It was all over. Clark had ridden up with two men and opened fire at once. They'd had no warning, no chance.

Randy was not dead when I saw them. One of the men kicked a gun out of his hand—he was already wounded—and shot him again. There was nothing I could do, so I simply hid."

"But how did you get here?"

"When they left I did not go back to the wagon. I simply *couldn't*, and I was afraid they might return. So I started walking back to the wagon train we had left. I hadn't gone far when I found Old Nellie, our saddle mare. She knew me and came right up to me, so I rode her back to the wagon train. I came from Laramie by stage."

"Then you knew all the time that I was faking?"

"Yes, but when you stopped Walt I whispered to Costa not to say anything."

"He knew as well?"

"Yes. I'd showed him my marriage license, which I always carried with me, along with a little money."

"Why didn't you say something? I was having a battle with my conscience, trying to decide what was right, always knowing I'd have to explain sooner or later."

"You were doing much better with the ranch than Michael could have. Michael and I grew up together and were much more like brother and sister than husband and wife. When he heard from his Uncle George, we were married, and we liked each other."

Suddenly it dawned on Jed that they were standing in the middle of the street and he had his arm around Carol. Hastily he withdrew it.

"Why didn't you just claim the estate as Michael's wife?"

"Costa was afraid Seever would kill me. We had not decided what to do when you appeared."

"What about these guns?"

"My father made them. He was a gunsmith and he had made guns for Uncle George. These were a present to Mike when he started west."

His eyes avoided hers. "Carol, I'll get my gear and move on. The ranch is yours, and with Seever gone you will be all right."

"I don't want you to go."

He thought his ears deceived him. "You—what?"

"Don't go, Jed. Stay with us. I can't manage the ranch alone, and Costa has been happy since you've been here. We need you, Jed. I—I need you."

"Well," he spoke hesitantly, "there are things to be done and cattle to be sold, and that quarter section near Willow Springs could be irrigated."

Pardo, watching, glanced at Flood. "I think he's going to stay, Pat."

"Sure," Flood said. "Ships an' women, they all need a handy man around the place!"

Carol caught Jed's sleeve. "Then you'll stay?"

He smiled. "What would Costa do without me?"

AUTHOR'S NOTE

FOUR-CARD DRAW

As I have written elsewhere it has never been necessary to guess at what happened in the West. We know.

There are newspaper accounts of most of the gun-fighting period. There are court records in many cases and military records; above all there are letters, diaries and journals, some of which have been published. Others are still in manuscript form but available in the archives of universities, libraries, and historical societies. Moreover, there are photographs, for in the period after the Civil War there were many photographers traveling throughout the West.

In many cases there are several sources so one may be balanced against the another. Dates can be checked and if they are of importance, should be checked for western men rarely had calendars available and just as rarely were not concerned about dates. The matter of accurate time is a comparatively new one, largely a result of the birth of the railroad timetable.

Mountain men, cowboys, or miners had no particular reason to note down a day or a time. If they got the month right they were lucky. To we of a time-conscious period this seems rather amazing, but with the exception of the need to get cattle to market at a time when the prices were right a cattleman needed to calendars or clocks.

The discovery of fresh material on the West is still occurring with the opening up of old trunks and the discovery of records that had been forgotten. Above all, here as elsewhere in the world, there are many archives that have never been examined or catalogued, papers gathered and stacked against some time when people and time might be available to study them. Discoveries are constantly being made, but who knows what remains untouched, unsuspected?

Four-Card Draw

When a man drew four cards he could expect something like this to happen. Ben Taylor had probably been right when he told him his luck had run out. Despite that, he had a place of his own, and come what may, he was going to keep it.

Nor was there any fault to find with the place. From the moment Allen Ring rode his claybank into the valley he knew he was coming home. This was it; this was the place. Here he would stop. He'd been tumbleweeding all over the West now for ten years, and it was time he stopped if he ever did, and this looked like his fence corner.

Even the cabin looked good, although Taylor told him the place had been empty for three years. It looked solid and fit, and while the grass was waist high all over the valley and up around the house, he could see trails through it, some of them made by unshod ponies, which mean wild horses, and some by deer. Then there were the tracks of a single shod horse, always the same one.

Those tracks always led right up to the door, and they stopped there, yet he could see that somebody with mighty small feet had been walking up to peer into the windows. Why would a person want to look into a window more than once? The window of an empty cabin? He had gone up and looked in himself, and all he saw was a dusty, dark interior with a ray of light from the opposite window, a table, a couple of chairs, and a fine old fireplace that had been built by skilled hands.

"You never built that fireplace, Ben Taylor," Ring had muttered, "you who never could handle anything but a running iron or a deck of cards. You never built anything in your life as fine and useful as that."

The cabin sat on a low ledge of grass backed up against the towering cliff of red rock, and the spring was not more than fifty feet away, a stream that came out of the rock and trickled pleasantly into a small basin before spilling out and winding thoughtfully down the valley to join a larger stream, a quarter of a mile away.

There were some tall spruces around the cabin, and a couple of sycamores and a cottonwood near the spring. Some gooseberry bushes, too, and a couple of apple trees. The trees had been pruned.

"And you never did that, either, Ben Taylor!" Allen Ring said soberly. "I wish I knew more about this place."

Time had fled like a scared antelope, and with the scythe he found in the pole barn he cut off the tall grass around the house, patched up the holes in the cabin where the packrats had got in, and even thinned out the bushes—it had been several years since they had been touched—and repaired the pole barn.

The day he picked to clean out the spring was the day Gail Truman rode up to the house. He had been putting the finishing touches on a chair bottom he was making when he heard a horse's hoof strike stone, and he straightened up to see the girl sitting on the red pony. She was staring openmouthed at the stacked hay from the grass he had cut and the washed windows of the house. He saw her swing down and run up to the window, and dropping his tools he strolled up.

"Huntin' somebody, ma'am?"

She wheeled and stared at him, her wide blue eyes accusing. "What are you doing here?" she demanded. "What do you mean by moving in like this?"

He smiled, but he was puzzled, too. Ben Taylor had said nothing about a girl, especially a girl like this. "Why, I own the place!" he said. "I'm fixin' it up so's I can live here."

"You own it?" Her voice was incredulous, agonized. "You couldn't own it! You couldn't. The man who owns this place is gone, and he would never sell it! Never!"

"He didn't exactly sell it, ma'am," Ring said gently.

"He lost it to me in a poker game. That was down Texas way."

She was horrified. "In a poker game? Whit Bayly in a poker game? I don't believe it!"

"The man I won it from was called Ben Taylor, ma'am." Ring took the deed from his pocket and opened it. "Come to think of it, Ben did say that if anybody asked about Whit Bayly to say that he died down in the Guadaloupes—of lead poisoning."

"Whit Bayly is dead?" The girl looked stunned. "You're sure? Oh!"

Her face went white and still and something in it seemed to die. She turned with a little gesture of despair and stared out across the valley, and his eyes followed hers. It was strange, Allen Ring told himself that it was the first time he had looked just that way, and he stood there, caught up by something nameless, some haunting sense of the familiar.

Before him lay the tall grass of the valley, turning slightly now with the brown of autumn, and to his right a dark stand of spruce, standing stiffly, like soldiers on parade, and beyond them the swell of the hill, and further to the right the hill rolled up and stopped, and beyond lay a wider valley fading away into the vast purple and mauve of distance and here and there spotted with the golden candles of cottonwoods, their leaves bright yellow with nearing cold.

There was no word for this; it was a picture, yet a picture of which a man could only dream and never reproduce.

"It—it's beautiful, isn't it?" he said.

She turned on him, and for the first time she seemed really to look at him, a tall young man with a shock of rust-brown hair and somber gray eyes, having about him the look of a rider and a look of a lonely man.

"Yes, it is beautiful. Oh, I've come here so many times to see it, the cabin, too. I think this is the most lovely place I have ever seen. I used to dream about—" She stopped, suddenly confused. "Oh, I'm sorry. I shouldn't talk so."

She looked at him soberly. "I'd better go. I guess this is yours now."

He hesitated. "Ma'am," he said sincerely, "the place is mine, and sure enough, I love it. I wouldn't swap this place for anything. But that view, that belongs to no man. It belongs to whoever looks at it with eyes to see it, so you come any time you like, and look all you please."

Ring grinned. "Fact is," he said, 'I'm aimin' to fix the place up inside, an' I'm sure no hand at such things. Maybe you could sort of help me. I'd like it kind of homey like." He flushed. "You see, I sort of lived in bunkhouses all my life an' never had no such place."

She smiled with a quick understanding and sympathy. "Of course! I'd love to, only"—her face sobered—"you won't be able to stay here. You haven't seen Ross Bilton yet, have you?"

"Who's he?" Ring asked curiously. He nodded toward the horsemen he saw approaching. "Is this the one?"

She turned quickly and nodded. "Be careful! He's the town marshal. The men with him are Ben Hagen and Stan Brule."

Brule he remembered—but would Brule remember him?

"By the way, my name is Allen Ring," he said, low voiced.

"I'm Gail Truman. My father owns the Tall T brand."

Bilton was a big man with a white hat. Ring decided he didn't like him and that the feeling was going to be mutual. Brule he knew, so the stocky man was Ben Hagen. Brule had changed but little, some thinner, maybe, but his hatchet face as lean and poisonous as always.

"How are you, Gail?" Bilton said briefly. "Is this a friend of yours?"

Allen Ring liked to get his cards on the table. "Yes, a friend of hers, but also the owner of the place."

"You own Red Rock?" Bilton was incredulous. "That will be very hard to prove, my friend. Also, this place is under the custody of the law."

"Whose law?" Ring wanted to know. He was aware that Brule was watching him, wary but uncertain as yet.

"Mine. I'm the town marshal. There was a murder committed here, and until that murder is solved and the killer brought to justice this place will not be touched. You have already seen fit to make changes, but perhaps the court will be lenient."

"You're the town marshal?" Allen Ring shoved his hat back on his head and reached for his tobacco. "That's mighty interestin'. Howsoever, let me remind you that you're out of town right now."

"That makes no difference!" Bilton's voice was sharp. Ring could see that he was not accustomed to being told off, that his orders were usually obeyed. "You will get off this place before nightfall!"

"It makes a sight of difference to me," Allen replied calmly. "I bought this place by stakin' everything I had against it in a poker game. I drew four cards to win, a nine to match one I had and three aces. It was a fool play that paid off. I registered the deed. She's mine legal. I know of no law that allows a place to be kept idle because there was a murder committed on it. If after three years it hasn't been solved, I suggest the town get a new marshal."

Ross Bilton was angry, but he kept himself under control. "I've warned you, and you've been told to leave. If you do not leave, I'll use my authority to move you."

Ring smiled. "Now listen, Bilton! You might pull that stuff on some folks that don't like trouble! You might bluff somebody into believin' you had the authority to do this. You don't bluff me, an' I simply don't scare—do I Brule?"

He turned on Brule so sharply that the man stiffened in his saddle, his hand poised as though to grab for a gun. The breed's face stiffened with irritation, and then recognition came to him. "Allen Ring!" he said. "You again!"

"That's right, Brule. Only this time I'm not takin' cattle through the Indian Nation. Not pushin' them by that ratty bunch of rustlers an' highbinders you rode with." Ring turned his eyes toward Bilton. "You're the law? An' you ride with *him*? Why, the man's wanted in ever' county in Texas for everythin' from murder to horse thievin'."

Ross Bilton stared at Ring for a long minute. "You've been warned," he said.

"An' I'm stayin'," Ring replied sharply. "And keep your coyotes away if you come again. I don't like 'em!"

Brule's fingers spread and his lips stiffened with cold fury. Ring watched him calmly. "You know better than that, Brule. Wait until my back is turned. If you reach for a gun I'll blow you out of your saddle."

Stan Brule slowly relaxed his hand, and then wordless, he turned to follow Bilton and Hagan, who had watched with hard eyes.

Gail Truman was looking at him curiously. "Why, Brule was afraid of you!" she exclaimed. "Who are you, anyway!"

"Nobody, ma'am," he said simply. "I'm no gunfighter, just an hombre who ain't got brains enough to scare proper. Brule knows it. He knows he might beat me, but he knows I'd kill him. He was there when I killed a friend of his, Blaze Garden."

"But—but then you must be a gunman. Blaze Garden was a killer! I've heard Dad and the boys talk about him!"

"No, I'm no gunman. Blaze beat me to the draw. In fact, he got off his first shot before my gun cleared the holster, only he shot too quick and missed. His second and third shots hit me while I was walkin' into him. The third shot wasn't so bad because I was holdin' my fire and gettin' close. He got scared an' stepped back, and the fourth shot was too high. Then I shot and I was close up to him then. One was enough. One is always enough if you place it right."

He gestured at the place. "What's this all about? Mind tellin' me?"

"It's very simple, really. Nothing out here is very involved when you come to that. It seems that there's something out here that brings men to using guns much faster than in other places, and one thing stems from another.

"Whit Bayly owned this place. He was a fixing man, always tinkering and fixing things up. He was a tall, handsome man whom all the girls loved—"

"You, too?" he asked quizzically.

She flushed. "Yes, I guess so, only I'm only eighteen

now, and that was three, almost four years ago. I wasn't very pretty or very noticeable and much too young.

"Sam Hazlitt was one of the richest men in the country around here, and Whit had a run-in with him over a horse. There had been a lot of stealing going on around, and Hazlitt traced some stock of his to this ranch, or so he claimed. Anyway, he accused Bayly of it, and Whit told him not to talk foolish. Furthermore, he told Hazlitt to stay off of his ranch. Well, folks were divided over who was in the right, but Whit had a lot of friends and Hazlitt had four brothers and clannish as all get out.

"Not long after, some riders from Buck Hazlitt's ranch came by that way and saw a body lying in the yard, right over near the spring. When they came down to have a look, thinking Whit was hurt, they found Sam Hazlitt, and he'd been shot dead—in the back.

"They headed right for town, hunting Whit, and they found him. He denied it, and they were goin' to hang him, had a rope around his neck, and then I—I—well, I swore he wasn't anywhere near his ranch all day."

"It wasn't true?" Ring asked keenly, his eyes searching the girl's face. She avoided his eyes, flushing even more.

"Not—not exactly. But I knew he wasn't guilty! I just knew he wouldn't shoot a man in the back! I told them he was over to our place, talking with me, and he hadn't time to get back there and kill Sam.

"Folks didn't like it much. Some of them still believed he killed Sam, and some didn't like it because despite the way I said it, they figured he was sparking a girl too young for him. I always said it wasn't that. As a matter of fact, I did see Whit over our way, but the rest of it was lies. Anyway, after a few weeks Whit up and left the country."

"I see—and nobody knows yet who killed Sam Hazlitt?"

"Nobody. One thing that was never understood was what became of Sam's account book—sort of a tally book, but more than that. It was a sort of record he kept of a lot of things, and it was gone out of his pocket. Nobody ever found it, but they did find the pencil Sam used on the sand nearby. Dad always figured Sam lived long enough to write something, but that the killer stole the book and destroyed it."

"How about the hands? Could they have picked it up? Did Bilton question them about that?"

"Oh, Bilton wasn't marshal then! In fact, he was riding for Buck Hazlitt then! He was one of the hands who found Sam's body!"

After the girl had gone Allen Ring walked back to the house and thought the matter over. He had no intention of leaving. This was just the ranch he wanted, and he intended to live right here, yet the problem fascinated him.

Living in the house and looking around the place had taught him a good deal about Whit Bayly. He was, as Gail had said, "a fixin' man," for there were many marks of his handiwork aside from the beautifully made fireplace and the pruned apple trees. He was, Ring was willing to gamble, no murderer.

Taylor had said he died of lead poisoning. Who had killed Bayly? Why? Was it a casual shooting over some rangeland argument, or had he been followed from here by someone on vengeance bent? Or someone who thought he might know too much?

"You'll like the place." Taylor had said—that was an angle he hadn't considered before. Ben Taylor had actually seen this place himself! The more sign he read, the more tricky the trail became, and Allen walked outside and sat down against the cabin wall when his supper was finished, and lighted a smoke.

Stock had been followed to the ranch by Sam Hazlitt. If Whit was not the thief, then who was? Where had the stock been driven? He turned his eyes almost automatically toward the Mogollons, the logical place. His eyes narrowed, and he recalled that one night while playing cards they had been talking of springs and waterholes, and Ben Taylor had talked about Fossil Springs, a huge spring that roared thousands of gallons of water out of the earth.

"Place a man could run plenty of stock," he had said and winked, "and nobody the wiser!"

Those words had been spoken far away and long ago,

and the Red Rock ranch had not yet been put on the table; that was months later. There was, he recalled, a Fossil Creek somewhere north of here. And Fossil Creek might flow from Fossil Springs—perhaps Ben Taylor had talked more to effect than he knew. That had been Texas, and this was Arizona, and a casual bunkhouse conversation probably seemed harmless enough.

"We'll see, Ben!" Ring muttered grimly. "We'll see!"

Ross Bilton had been one of the Hazlitt hands at the time of the killing, one of the first on the scene. Now he was town marshal but interested in keeping the ranch unoccupied—why?

None of it made sense, yet actually it was no business of his. Allen Ring thought that over and decided it was his business in a sense. He now owned the place and lived on it. If an old murder was to interfere with his living there, it behooved him to know the facts. It was a slight excuse for his curiosity.

Morning came and the day drew on toward noon, and there was no sign of Bilton or Brule. Ring had loaded his rifle and kept it close to hand, and he was wearing two guns, thinking he might need a loaded spare, although he rarely wore more than one. Also, inside the cabin door he had his double-barreled shotgun.

The spring drew his attention. At the moment he did not wish to leave the vicinity of the cabin, and that meant it was a good time to clean out the spring. Not that it needed it, but there were loose stones in the bottom of the basin and some moss. With this removed he would have more water and clearer water. With a wary eye toward the canyon mouth, he began his work.

The sound of an approaching horse drew him erect. His rifle stood against the rocks at hand, and his guns were ready, yet as the rider came into sight, he saw there was only one man, a stranger.

He rode a fine bay gelding and he was not a young man, but thick and heavy with drooping mustache and kind blue eyes. He drew up.

"Howdy!" he said affably, yet taking a quick glance

around before looking again at Ring. "I'm Rolly Truman, Gails' father."

"It's a pleasure," Ring said, wiping his wet hands on a red bandanna. "Nice to know the neighbors." He nodded at the spring. "I picked me a job. That hole's deeper than it looks!"

"Good flow of water," Truman agreed. He chewed his mustache thoughtfully. "I like to see a young man with get-up about him, startin' his own spread, willin' to work."

Allen Ring waited. The man was building up to something; what, he knew not. It came then, carefully at first, yet shaping a loop at it drew near.

"Not much range here, of course," Truman added. "You should have more graze. Ever been over in Cedar Basin? Or up along the East Verde bottom? Wonderful land up there, still some wild, but a country where a man could really do something with a few whiteface cattle."

"No, I haven't seen it," Ring replied, "but I'm satisfied. I'm not land hungry. All I want is a small piece, an' this suits me fine."

Truman shifted in his saddle and looked uncomfortable. "Fact is, son, you're upsettin' a lot of folks by bein' here. What you should do is to move."

"I'm sorry," Ring said flatly. "I don't want to make enemies, but I won this place on a four-card draw. Maybe I'm a fatalist, but somehow or other, I think I should stick here. No man's got a right to think he can draw four cards and win anythin', but I did, an' in a plenty rough game. I had everythin' I owned in that pot. Now I got the place."

The rancher sat his horse uneasily, and then he shook his head. "Son, you've sure got to move! There's no trouble here now, and if you stay she's liable to open old sores, start more trouble than any of us can stop. Besides, how did Ben Taylor get title to this place? Bayly had no love for him. I doubt if your title will stand up in court."

"As to that I don't know," Ring persisted stubbornly. "I have a deed that's legal enough, and I've registered that deed an' my brand along with it. I did find out that Bayly had no heirs. So I reckon I'll sit tight until somebody comes along with a better legal claim than mine."

Truman ran his hand over his brow. "Well, I guess I

don't blame you much, son. Maybe I shouldn't have come over, but I know Ross Bilton and his crowd, and I reckon I wanted to save myself some trouble as well as you. Gail, she thinks you're a fine young man. In fact, you're the first man she's ever showed interest in since Whit left, and she was a youngster then. It was a sort of hero worship she had for him. I don't want trouble."

Allen Ring leaned on the shovel and looked up at the older man. "Truman," he said, "are you sure you aren't buyin' trouble by tryin' to avoid it? Just what's your stake in this?"

The rancher sat very still, his face drawn and pale. Then he got down from his horse and sat on a rock. Removing his hat, he mopped his brow.

"Son," he said slowly, "I reckon I got to trust you. You've heard of the Hazlitts. They are a hard, clannish bunch, men who lived by the gun most of their lives. Sam was murdered. Folks all know that when they find out who murdered him and why, there's goin' to be plenty of trouble around here. Plenty."

"Did you kill him?"

Truman jerked his head up. "No! No, you mustn't get that idea, but—well, you know how small ranchers are. There was a sight of rustlin' them days, and the Hazlitts were the big outfit. They lost cows."

"And some of them got your brand?" Ring asked shrewdly.

Truman nodded. "I reckon. Not so many, though. And not only me. Don't get me wrong, I'm not beggin' off the blame. Part of it is mine, all right, but I didn't get many. Eight or ten of us hereabouts slapped brands on Hazlitt stock—and at least five of us have the biggest brands around here now, some as big almost as the Hazlitts."

Allen Ring studied the skyline thoughtfully. It was an old story and one often repeated in the West. When the war between the states ended, men came home to Texas and the southwest to find cattle running in thousands, unbranded and unowned. The first man to slap on a brand was the owner, with no way he could be contested.

Many men grew rich with nothing more than a wide

loop and a running iron. Then the unbranded cattle were gone, the ranches had settled into going concerns, and the great days of casual branding had ended, yet there was still free range, and a man with that same loop and running iron could still build a herd fast.

More than one of the biggest ranchers had begun that way, and many of them continued to brand loose stock wherever found. No doubt that had been true here, and these men like Rolly Truman, good, able men who had fought Indians and built their homes to last, had begun just that way. Now the range was mostly fenced, and ranches had narrowed somewhat, but Ring could see what it might mean to open an old sore now.

Sam Hazlitt had been trailing rustlers—he had found out who they were and where the herds were taken, and he had been shot down from behind. The catch was that the tally book, with his records, was still missing. That tally book might contain evidence as to the rustling done by men who were now pillars of the community and open them to the vengeance of the Hazlitt outfit.

Often Western men threw a blanket over a situation. If a rustler had killed Sam, then all the rustlers involved would be equally guilty. Anyone who lived on this ranch might stumble on that tally book and throw the range into a bloody gun war in which many men now beyond the errors of their youth, with homes, families, and different customs, would die.

It could serve no purpose to blow the lid off the trouble now, yet Allen Ring had a hunch. In their fear of trouble for themselves they might be concealing an even greater crime, aiding a murderer in his escape. There were lines of care in the face of Rolly Truman that a settled, established rancher should not have.

"Sorry," Ring said, "I'm stayin'. I like this place."

All through the noon hour the tension was building. The air was warm and sultry, and there was a thickening haze over the mountains. There was that hot thickness in the air that presaged a storm. When he left his coffee to return to work, Ring saw three horsemen coming into the canyon mouth at a running walk. He stopped in the door and touched his lips with his tongue.

They reined up at the door, three hard-bitten, hard-eyed men with rifles across their saddle bows. Men with guns in their holsters and men of a kind that would never turn from trouble. These were men with the bark on, lean fanatics with lips thinned with old bitterness.

The older man spoke first. "Ring, I've heard about you. I'm Buck Hazlitt. These are my brothers, Joe and Dolph. There's talk around that you aim to stay on this place. There's been talk for years that Sam hid his tally book here. We figure the killer got that book and burned it. Maybe he did, and again, maybe not. We want that book. If you want to stay on this place, you stay. But if you find that book, you bring it to us."

Ring looked from one to the other, and he could see the picture clearly. With men like these, hard and forgiving, it was no wonder Rolly Truman and the other ranchers were worried. The years and prosperity had eased Rolly and his like into comfort and softness, but not these. The Hazlitts were of feudal blood and background.

"Hazlitt," Ring said, "I know how you feel. You lost a brother, and that means somethin', but if that book is still around, which I doubt, and I find it, I'll decide what to do with it all by myself. I don't aim to start a range war. Maybe there's some things best forgotten. The man who murdered Sam Hazlitt ought to pay."

"We'll handle that," Dolph put in grimly. "You find that book, you bring it to us. If you don't—" His eyes hardened. "Well, we'd have to class you with the crooks."

Ring's eyes shifted to Dolph. "Class if you want," he flared. "I'll do what seems best to me with that book. But all of you folks are plumb proddy over that tally book. Chances are nine out of ten the killer found it and destroyed it."

"I don't reckon he did," Buck said coldly, "because we know he's been back here, a-huntin' it. Him an' his girl."

Ring stiffened. "You mean—?"

"What we mean is our figger, not yours." Buck Hazlitt reined his horse around. "You been told. You bring that book to us. You try to buck the Hazlitts and you won't stay in this country."

Ring had his back up. Despite himself he felt cold anger mounting within him. "Put this in your pipe, friend," he said harshly. "I came here to stay. No Hazlitt will change that. I ain't huntin' trouble, but if you bring trouble to me, I'll handle it. I can bury a Hazlitt as easy as any other man!"

Not one of them condescended to notice the remark. Turning their horses they walked them down the canyon and out of it into the sultry afternoon. Allen Ring mopped the sweat from his face and listened to the deep rumbling of far-off thunder, growling among the canyons like a grizzly with a toothache. It was going to rain. Sure as shootin', it was going to rain—a regular gully washer.

There was yet time to finish the job on the spring, so he picked up his shovel and started back for the job. The rock basin was nearly cleaned and he finished removing the few rocks and the moss that had gathered. Then he opened the escape channel a little more to insure a more rapid emptying and filling process in the basin into which the trickle of water fell.

The water emerged from a crack in the rocks and trickled into the basin, and finishing his job, Ring glanced thoughtfully to see if anything remained undone. There was still some moss on the rocks from which the water flowed, and kneeling down, he leaned over to scrape it away, and pulling away the last shreds, he noticed a space from which a rock had recently fallen. Pulling more moss away, he dislodged another rock, and there, pushed into a niche, was a small black book!

Sam Hazlitt, dying, had evidently managed to shove it back in this crack in the rocks, hoping it would be found by someone not the killer.

Sitting back on his haunches, Ring opened the faded, canvas-bound book. A flap crossed over the page ends, and the book had been closed by a small tongue that slid into a loop of the canvas cover. Opening the book, he saw the pages were stained, but still legible.

The next instant he was struck by lightning. At least, that was what seemed to happen. Thunder crashed, and something struck him on the skull and he tried to rise and something struck again. he felt a drop of rain on his face and his eyes opened wide and then another blow caught him and he faded out into darkness, his fingers clawing at the grass to keep from slipping down into that velvety, smothering blackness.

He was wet. He turned a little, lying there, thinking he must have left a window open and the rain was—his eyes opened and he felt rain pounding on his face and he stared, not at a boot with a California spur, but at dead brown grass, soaked with rain now, and the glistening smoothness of waterworn stones. He was soaked to the hide.

Struggling to his knees, he looked around, his head heavy, his lips and tongue thick. He blinked at a gray, rain-slanted world and at low gray clouds and a distant rumble of thunder following a streak of lightning along the mountaintops.

Lurching to his feet, he stumbled toward the cabin and pitched over the doorsill to the floor. Struggling, again to his feet he got the door closed, and in a vague, misty half world of consciousness he struggled out of his clothes and got his hands on a rough towel and fumblingly dried himself.

He did not think. He was acting purely from vague instinctive realization of what he must do. He dressed again, in dry clothes, and dropped at the table. After a while he sat up and it was dark, and he knew he had blacked out again. He lighted a light and nearly dropped it to the floor. Then he stumbled to the washbasin and splashed his face with cold water. Then he bathed his scalp, feeling tenderly of the lacerations there.

A boot with a California spur.

That was all he had seen. The tally book was gone, and a man wearing a new boot with a California-type spur, a large rowel, had taken it. He got coffee on, and while he waited for it he took his guns out and dried them painstakingly, wiping off each shell, and then replacing them in his belt with other shells from a box on a shelf.

He reloaded the guns, and then slipping into his slicker he went outside for his rifle. Between sips of coffee, he worked over his rifle until he was satisfied. Then he threw a small pack together and stuffed his slicker pockets with shotgun shells.

The shotgun was an express gun and short barreled. He slung it from a loop under the slicker. Then he took a lantern and went to the stable and saddled the claybank. Leading the horse outside into the driving rain, he swung into the saddle and turned along the road toward Basin.

There was no letup in the rain. It fell steadily and heavily, yet the claybank slogged along, alternating between a shambling trot and a fast walk. Allen Ring, his chin sunk in the upturned collar of his slicker, watched the drops fall from the brim of his Stetson and felt the bump of the shotgun under his coat.

He had seen little of the tally book, but sufficient to know that it would blow the lid off the very range war they were fearing. Knowing the Hazlitts, he knew they would bring fire and gunplay to every home even remotely connected with the death of their brother.

The horse slid down a steep bank and shambled across the wide wash. Suddenly, the distant roar that had been in his ears for some time sprang into consciousness and he jerked his head up. His horse snorted in alarm, and Ring stared, openmouthed, at the wall of water, towering all of ten feet high, that was rolling down the wash toward him.

With a shrill rebel yell he slapped the spurs to the claybank, and the startled horse turned loose with an astounded leap and hit the ground in a dead run. There was no time to slow for the bank of the wash, and the horse went up, slipped at the very brink, and started to fall back.

Ring hit the ground with both boots and scrambled over the brink, and even as the flood roared down upon them, he heaved on the bridle and the horse cleared the edge and stood trembling. Swearing softly, Ring kicked the mud from his boots and mounted again. Leaving the raging torrent behind him, he rode on.

Thick blackness of night and heavy clouds lay upon the town when he sloped down the main street and headed the horse toward the barn. He swung down and handed the bridle to the handyman.

"Rub him down," he said. "I'll be back."

He started for the doors and then stopped, staring at the three horses in neighboring stalls. The liveryman noticed his glance and looked at him.

"The Hazlitts. They come in about an hour ago, ugly as sin."

Allen Ring stood wide legged, staring grimly out the door. There was a coolness inside him now that he recognized. He dried his hands carefully.

"Bilton in town?" he asked.

"Sure is. Playin' cards over to the Mazatzal Saloon."

"He wear Mex spurs? Big rowels?"

The man rubbed his jaw. "I don't remember. I don't know at all. You watch out," he warned. "Folks are on the prod."

Ring stepped out into the street and slogged through the mud to the edge of the boardwalk before the darkened general store. He kicked the mud from his boots and dried his hands again, after carefully unbuttoning his slicker.

Nobody would have a second chance after this. He knew well enough that his walking into the Mazatzal would precipitate an explosion. Only, he wanted to light the fuse himself, in his own way.

He stood there in the darkness alone, thinking it over. They would all be there. It would be like tossing a match into a lot of fused dynamite. He wished then that he was a better man with a gun than he was or that he had someone to side him in this, but he had always acted alone and would scarcely know how to act with anyone else.

He walked along the boardwalk with long strides, his boots making hard sounds under the steady roar of the rain. He couldn't place that spur, that boot. Yet he had to. He had to get his hands on that book.

Four horses stood, heads down in the rain, saddles covered with slickers. He looked at them and saw they were of three different brands. The window of the Mazatzal was rain wet, yet standing at one side he glanced within.

The long room was crowded and smoky. Men lined the bar, feet on the brass rail. A dozen tables were crowded with cardplayers. Everyone seemed to have taken refuge here from the rain. Picking out the Hazlitt boys, Allen saw them gathered together at the back end of the room. Then he got Ross Bilton pegged. He was at a table playing cards, facing the door. Stan Brule was at this end of the bar, and Hagen was at a table against the wall, the three of them making three points of a flat triangle whose base was the door.

It was no accident. Bilton, then, expected trouble, and he was not looking toward the Hazlitts. Yet, on reflection, Ring could see the triangle could center fire from three directions on the Hazlitts as well. There was a man with his back to the door who sat in the game with Bilton. And not far from Hagen, Rolly Truman was at the bar.

Truman was toying with his drink, just killing time. Everybody seemed to be waiting for something.

Could it be he they waited upon? No, that was scarcely to be considered. They could not know he had found the book, although it was certain at least one man in the room knew, and possibly others. Maybe it was just the tension, the building up of feeling over his taking over of the place at Red Rock. Allen Ring carefully turned down the collar of his slicker and wiped his hands dry again.

He felt jumpy and could feel that dryness in his mouth that always came on him at times like this. He touched his gun butts and then stepped over and opened the door.

Everyone looked up or around at once. Ross Bilton held a card aloft, and his hand froze at the act of dealing, holding still for a full ten seconds while Ring closed the door. He surveyed the room again and saw Ross play the card and say something in an undertone to the man opposite him. The man turned his head slightly and it was Ben Taylor!

The gambler looked around, his face coldly curious, and for an instant their eyes met across the room, and then Allen Ring started toward him.

There was no other sound in the room, although they could all hear the unceasing roar of the rain of the roof. Ring saw something leap up in Taylor's eyes, and his own took on a sardonic glint.

"That was a good hand you dealt me down Texas way," Ring said. "A good hand!"

"You'd better draw more cards," Taylor said. "You're holdin' a small pair!"

Ring's eyes shifted as the man turned slightly. It was the jingle of his spurs that drew his eyes, and there they were, the large rowelled California-style spurs, not common here. He stopped beside Taylor so the man had to tilt his head back to look up. Ring was acutely conscious that he was now centered between the fire of Brule and Hagen. The Hazlitts looked on curiously, uncertain as to what was happening.

"Give it to me, Taylor," Ring said quietly. "Give it to me now."

There was ice in his voice, and Taylor, aware of the awkwardness of his position, got to his feet, inches away from Ring.

"I don't know what you're talking about," he flared.

"No?"

Ring was standing with his feet apart a little, and his hands were breast high, one of them clutching the edge of his raincoat. He hooked with his left from that position, and the blow was too short, too sudden, and too fast for Ben Taylor.

The crack of it on the angle of his jaw was audible, and then Ring's right came up in the gambler's solar plexus and the man's knees sagged. Spinning him around, Ring ripped open his coat with a jerk that scattered buttons across the room. Then from an inside pocket he jerked the tally book.

He saw the Hazlitts start at the same instant that Bilton sprang back from the chair, upsetting it.

"Get him!" Bilton roared. "Get him!"

Ring shoved Taylor hard into the table, upsetting it and causing Bilton to spring back to keep his balance, and at the same instant, Ring dropped to a half crouch and turning left he drew with a flash of speed and saw Brule's gun come up at almost the same instant, and then he fired!

Stan Brule was caught with his gun just level, and the bullet smashed him on the jaw. The tall man staggered, his face a mask of hatred and astonishment mingled, and then Ring fired again, doing a quick spring around with his knees bent, turning completely around in one leap, and firing as his feet hit the floor. He felt Hagen's bullet smash into him, and he tottered. Then he fired coolly, and swinging as he fired, he caugh Bilton right over the belt buckle.

It was fast action, snapping, quick, yet deliberate. The four fired shots had taken less than three seconds.

Stepping back, he scooped the tally book from the floor where it had dropped and then pocketed it. Bilton was on the floor, coughing blood. Hagen had a broken right arm and was swearing in a thick, stunned voice.

Stan Brule had drawn his last gun. He had been dead before he hit the floor. The Hazlitts started forward with a lunge, and Allen Ring took another step backward, dropping his pistol and swinging the shotgun, still hanging from his shoulder, into firing position.

"Get back!" he said thickly. "Get back or I'll kill the three of you! Back—back to where you stood!"

Their faces wolfish, the three stood lean and dangerous, yet the shotgun brooked no refusal, and slowly, bitterly and reluctantly, the three moved back, step by step.

Ring motioned with the shotgun. "All of you—along the wall!"

The men rose and moved back, their eyes on him, uncertain, wary, some of them frightened.

Allen Ring watched them go, feeling curiously lightheaded and uncertain. He tried to frown away the pain from his throbbing skull, yet there was a pervading weakness from somewhere else.

"My gosh!" Rolly Truman said. "The man's been shot! He's bleeding!"

"Get back!" Ring said thickly.

His eyes shifted to the glowing potbellied stove, and he moved forward, the shotgun waist high, his eyes on the men who stared at him, awed.

The sling held the gun level, his hand partly supporting it, a finger on the trigger. With his left hand he opened the stove and then fumbled in his pocket.

Buck Hazlitt's eyes bulged. "No!" he roared. "No, you don't!"

He lunged forward, and Ring tipped the shotgun and fired a blast into the floor, inches ahead of Hazlitt's feet. The rancher stopped so suddenly he almost fell, and the shotgun tipped to cover him.

"Back!" Ring said. He swayed on his feet. "Back!" He fished out the tally book and threw it into the flames.

Something like a sigh went through the crowd. They stared, awed as the flames seized hungrily at the opened book, curling around the leaves with hot fingers, turning them brown and then black and to ashes.

Half hypnotized the crowd watched. Then Ring's eyes swung to Hazlitt. "It was Ben Taylor killed him," he muttered. "Taylor, an' Bilton was with him. He—he seen it."

"We take your word for it?" Buck Hazlitt demanded furiously.

Allen Ring's eyes widened and he seemed to gather himself. "You want to question it? You want to call me a liar?"

Hazlitt looked at him, touching his tongue to his lips. "No," he said. "I figured it was them."

"I told you true," Ring said, and then his legs seemed to fold up under him and he went to the floor.

The crowd surged forward and Rolly Truman stared at Buck as Hazlitt neared the stove. The big man stared into the flames for a minute. Then he closed the door.

"Good!" he said. "Good thing! It's been a torment, that book, like a cloud hangin' over us all!"

The sun was shining through the window when Gail Truman came to see him. He was sitting up in bed and feeling better. It would be good to be back on the place again, for there was much to do. She came in, slapping her boots with her quirt and smiling.

"Feel better?" she asked brightly. "You certainly look better. You've shaved."

He grinned and rubbed his jaw. "I needed it. Almost two weeks in this bed. I must have been hit bad."

"You lost a lot of blood. It's lucky you've a strong heart."

"It ain't—isn't so strong any more," he said, "I think it's grown mighty shaky here lately."

Gail blushed. "Oh? It has? Your nurse, I suppose?"

"She is pretty, isn't she?"

Gail looked up, alarmed. "You mean, you—"

"No, honey," he said, "you!"

"Oh." She looked at him and then looked down. "Well, I guess—"

"All right?"

She smiled then, suddenly and warmly. "All right."

"I had to ask you," he said. "We had to marry."

"Had to? Why?"

"People would talk, a young, lovely girl like you over at my place all the time—would they think you were looking at the view?"

"If they did," she replied quickly, "they'd be wrong!"

"You're telling me?" he asked.

AUTHOR'S NOTE

HIS BROTHERS DEBT

Gun fighters were many, most of them not known out of their own particular area. The few who did win attention were those who followed the trail towns as gamblers or peace officers.

The so-called "bounty hunters" were almost unknown, and the few who did attempt to pursue that somewhat precarious trade worked at it only occasionally. Rewards were actually rare, difficult to collect, and usually the people of any particular area were only too glad to have a bad man leave the country. They did not want him brought back and they certainly did not want to pay for a killing when, if the situation demanded, they could do it themselves. In the few cases I know of the "bounty hunter" was despised, and no more popular than a rattle snake.

A gun fighter was no more than a man who was good with a gun and had the misfortune to get into a gun battle and the good fortune to win it. After a few such difficulties he became known. There were many such men whose names never got into the movies.

One such man was Johnny Owen, a slender, handsome man usually well-dressed. A man who gambled but neither smoked nor drank (there were many such men, but he was reputed to have killed twenty men, chiefly in self-defense as an officer of the law).

His Brother's Debt

You're yellow, Casady!" Ben Kerr shouted. "Yellow as saffron! You ain't got the guts of a coyote! Draw, curse you. Fill your hand so I can kill you! You ain't to live!" Kerr stepped forward, his big hands spread over his gun butts. "Go ahead, *reach!*"

Rock Casady, numb with fear, stepped slowly back, his face gray. To right and left were the amazed and incredulous faces of his friends, the men he had ridden with on the O Bar, staring unbelieving.

Sweat broke out on his face. He felt his stomach retch and twist within him. Turning suddenly, he plunged blindly through the door and fled.

Behind him, one by one, his shamefaced, unbelieving friends from the O Bar slowly sifted from the crowd. Heads hanging, they headed homeward. Rock Casady was yellow. The man they had worked with, sweated with, laughed with. The last man they would have suspected. Yellow.

Westward, with the wind in his face and tears burning his eyes, his horse's hoofs beating out a mad tattoo upon the hard trail, fled Rock Casady, alone in the darkness.

Nor did he stop. Avoiding towns and holding to the hills, he rode steadily westward. There were days when he starved and days when he found game, a quail or two, killed with unerring shots from a six-gun that never seemed to miss. Once he shot a deer. He rode wide of towns and deliberately erased his trail, although he knew no one was following him or cared where he went.

Four months later, leaner, unshaven, and saddle weary, he rode into the yard of the Three Spoke Wheel. Foreman

Tom Bell saw him coming and glanced around at his boss, big Frank Stockman.

"Look what's comin'. Looks like he's lived in the hills. On the dodge, maybe."

"Huntin' grub, most likely. He's a strappin' big man, though, an' looks like a hand. Better ask him if he wants a job. With Pete Vorys around, we'll have to be huntin' strangers or we'll be out of help!"

The mirror on the wall of the bunkhouse was neither cracked nor marred, but Rock Casady could almost wish that it was. Bathed and shaved, he looked into the tortured eyes of a dark, attractive young man with wavy hair and a strong jaw.

People had told him many times that he was a handsome man, but when he looked into his eyes he knew he looked into the eyes of a coward.

He had a yellow streak.

The first time—well, the first time but one—that he had faced a man with a gun he had backed down cold. He had run like a baby. He had shown the white feather.

Tall, strongly built, skillful with rope or horse, knowing with stock, he was a top hand in any outfit. An outright genius with guns, men had often said they would hate to face him in a shootout. He had worked hard and played rough, getting the most out of life until that day in the saloon in El Paso when Ben Kerr, gunman and cattle rustler, gambler and bully, had called him, and he had backed down.

Tom Bell was a knowing and kindly man. Aware that something was riding Casady, he told him his job and left him alone. Stockman watched him top off a bad bronc on the first morning and glanced at Bell.

"If he does everything like he rides, we've got us a hand!"

And Casady did everything as well. A week after he had hired out he was doing so much work as any two men. And the jobs they avoided, the lonely jobs, he accepted eagerly.

"Notice something else?" Stockman asked the ranch

owner one morning. "That new hand sure likes the jobs that keep him away from the ranch."

Stockman nodded. "Away from people. It ain't natural, Tom. He ain't been to Three Lakes once since he's been here."

Sue Landon looked up at her uncle. "Maybe he's broke!" she exclaimed. "No cowhand could have fun in town when he's broke!"

Bell shook his head. "It ain't that, Sue. He had money when he first come in here. I saw it. He had anyway two hundred dollars, and for a forty-a-month cowpoke, that's a lot of money!"

"Notice something else?" Stockman asked. "He never packs a gun. Only man on the ranch who doesn't. You'd better warn him about Pete Vorys."

"I did." Bell frowned. "I can't figure this hombre, Boss. I did warn him, and that was the very day he began askin' for all the bad jobs. Why, he's the only man on the place who'll fetch grub to Cat McLeod without bein' bullied into it!"

"Over in that Rock Canyon country?" Stockman smiled. "That's a rough ride for any man. I don't blame the boys, but you've got to hand it to old Cat. He's killed nine lions and forty-two coyotes in the past ninety days! If he keeps that up we won't have so much stock lost!"

"Two bad he ain't just as good on rustlers. Maybe," Bell grinned, "we ought to turn him loose on Pete Vorys!"

Rock Casady kept his palouse gelding moving steadily. The two packhorses ambled placidly behind, seemingly content to be away from the ranch. The old restlessness was coming back to Casady, and he had been on the Three Spoke only a few weeks. He knew they liked him, knew that despite his taciturn manner and desire to be alone, the hands liked him as well as did Stockman or Bell.

He did his work and more, and he was a hand. He avoided poker games that might lead to trouble and stayed away from town. He was anxiously figuring some way to be absent from the ranch on the following Saturday, for he knew the whole crowd was going to a dance and shindig in Three Lakes.

While he talked little, he heard much. He was aware

of impending trouble between the Three Spoke Wheel outfit and the gang of Pete Vorys. The latter, who seemed to ride the country as he pleased, owned a small ranch north of Three Lakes, near town. He had a dozen tough hands and usually spent money freely. All his hands had money, and while no one dared say it, all knew he was rustling.

Yet he was not the ringleader. Behind him there was someone else, someone who had only recently become involved, for recently there had been a change. Larger bunches of cattle were being stolen, and more care was taken to leave no trail. The carelessness of Vorys had given way to more shrewd operation, and Casady overheard enough talk to know that Stockman believed a new brain was directing operations.

He heard much of Pete Vorys. He was a big man, bigger than Rock. He was a killer with at least seven notches on his gun. He was pugnacious and quarrelsome, itching for a fight with gun or fists. He had, only a few weeks before, whipped Sandy Kane, a Three Spoke hand, within an inch of his life. He was bold, domineering, and tough.

The hands on the Three Spoke were good men. They were hard workers, willing to fight, but not one of them was good enough to tackle Vorys with either fists or gun.

Cat McLeod was scraping a hide when Rock rode into his camp in Blue Spring Valley. He got up, wiping his hands on his jeans and grinning.

"Howdy, son! You sure are a sight for sore eyes! It ain't no use quibblin', I sure get my grub on time when you're on that ranch! Hope you stay!"

Rock swung down. He liked the valley and liked Cat.

"Maybe I'll pull out, Cat." He looked around. "I might even come up here to stay. I like it."

McLeod glanced at him out of the corners of his eyes. "Glad to have you, son. This sure ain't no country for a young feller, though. It's a huntin' an' fishin' country, but no women here, an' no likker. Nothin' much to do, all said an' done."

* * *

Casady unsaddled in silence. It was better, though, than a run-in with Vorys, he thought. At least, nobody here knew he was yellow. They liked him and he was one of them, but he was careful.

"Ain't more trouble down below, is there? That Vorys cuttin' up much?" The old man noted the gun Rock was wearing for the trip.

"Some. I hear the boys talkin' about him."

"Never seen him yourself?" Cat asked quizzically. "I been thinkin' ever since you come up here, son. Might be a good thing for this country if you did have trouble with Vorys. You're nigh as big as him, an' you move like a catamount. An' me, I know 'em! Never seen a man lighter on his feet than you."

"Not me," Rock spoke stiffly. "I'm a peace-lovin' man, Cat. I want no trouble with anybody."

McLeod studied the matter as he worked over his hide. For a long time now he had known something was bothering Rock Casady. Perhaps this last remark, that he wanted no trouble with anybody, was the answer?

Cat McLeod was a student of mankind as well as the animals upon whom he practiced his trade. In a lifetime of living along the frontier and in the world's far places, he had learned a lot about men who liked to live alone and about men who sought the wilderness. If it was true that Rock wanted no trouble, it certainly was not from lack of ability to handle it.

There had been that time when Cat had fallen, stumbling to hands and knees. Right before him, not three feet from his face and much nearer his outstretched hands, lay one of the biggest rattlers Cat had ever seen. The snake's head jerked back above its coil, and then, with a gun's roar blasting in his ears, that head was gone and the snake was a writhing mass of coils, showing only a bloody stump where the head had been!

Cat had gotten to his feet gray faced and turned. Rock Casady was thumbing a shell into his gun. The young man grinned.

"That was a close one!" he had said cheerfully.

McLeod had dusted off his hands, staring at Casady.

"I've heard of men drawin' faster'n a snake could strike, but that's the first time I ever seen it!"

Since then he had seen that .44 shoot the heads off quail and he had seen a quick hip shot with the rifle break a deer's neck.

Now his mind reverted to their former topic. "If that Vorys is tied in with some smart hombre, there'll be hell to pay! Pete was never no great shakes for brains, but he's tough, tough as all get out! With somebody to think for him, he'll make this country unfit to live in!"

Later that night, McLeod looked over his shoulder from the fire. "You know," he said, "if I was wantin' a spread of my own an' didn't care much for folks, like you, I'd go down into the Pleasant Valley Outlet, south of here. Lonely, but she's sure grand country!"

Two days later Rock was mending a bridle when Sue Landon walked over to him. She wore jeans and a boy's shirt, and her eyes were bright and lovely.

"Hi!" she said brightly. "You're the new hand? You certainly keep out of the way. All this time on the ranch and I never met you before!"

He grinned shyly. "Just a quiet hombre, I reckon," he said. "If I had it my way I'd be over there with Cat all the time."

"Then you won't like the job I have for you!" she said. "To ride into Three Lakes with me, riding herd on a couple of pack horses."

"Three Lakes?" He looked up so sharply it startled her. "Into town? I never go into town, ma'am. I don't like the place. Not any town."

"Why, that's silly! Anyway, there's no one else, and Uncle Frank won't let me go alone with Pete Vorys around."

"He wouldn't bother a girl, would he?"

"You sure don't know Pete Vorys!" Sue returned grimly. "He does pretty much what he feels like, and everybody's afraid to say anything about it. Although," she added, "with this new partner he's got he's toned down some. But come on—you'll go?"

Reluctantly, he got to his feet. She looked at him curiously, not a little piqued. Any other hand on the ranch would have jumped at the chance, and here she had deliberately made sure there were no others available before going to him. Her few distant glimpses of Rock Casady had excited her interest, and she wanted to know him better.

Yet as the trail fell behind them, she had to admit she was getting no place. For shyness there was some excuse, although usually even the most bashful hand lost it when alone with her. Rock Casady was almost sullen, and all she could get out of him were monosyllables.

The truth was that the nearer they drew to Three Lakes the more worried Rock grew. It had been six months since he had been in a town, and while it was improbable he would see anyone he knew, there was always a chance. Cowhands were notoriously footlose and fancy free. Once the story of his backing out of a gunfight got around, he would be through in this country, and he was tired of running.

Yet Three Lakes looked quiet enough as they ambled placidly down the street and tied up in front of the general store. He glanced at Sue tentatively.

"Ma'am," he said, "I'd sure appreciate it if you didn't stay too long. Towns make me nervous."

She looked at him, more than slightly irritated. Her trip with him, so carefully planned, had thus far come to nothing, although she had to admit he was the finest-looking man she had ever seen, and his smile was quick and attractive.

"I won't be long. Why don't you go have a drink? It might do you good!" She said the last sentence a little sharply, and he looked quicky at her, but she was already flouncing into the store, as well as any girl could flounce in jeans.

Slowly he built a cigarette, studying the Hackamore Saloon over the way. He had to admit he was tempted, and probably he was foolish to think that he would get into trouble or that anyone would know him. Nevertheless, he sat down suddenly on the edge of the boardwalk and lighted his smoke.

He was still sitting there when he heard the sound of

booted heels on the boardwalk and then heard a raucous voice.

"Hey! Lookit here! One of them no 'count Three Spokers in town! I didn't think any of them had the sand!"

In spite of himself, he looked up, knowing instantly that this man was Pete Vorys.

He was broad in the shoulder, with narrow hips. He had a swarthy face with dark, brilliant eyes. That he had been drinking was obvious, but he was far from drunk. With him were two tough-looking hands, both grinning cynically at him.

Vorys was spoiling for a fight. He had never been whipped and doubted there lived a man who could whip him in a tooth-and-nail knockdown and drag-out battle. This Three Spoker looked big enough to be fun.

"That's a rawhide outfit, anyway," Vorys sneered. "I've a mind to ride out there sometime, just for laughs. Wonder where they hooked this ranny?"

Despite himself, Rock was growing angry. He was not wearing a gun, and Vorys was. He took the cigarette out of his mouth and looked at it. Expecting trouble, a crowd was gathering. He felt his neck growing red.

"Hey, you!" Vorys booted him solidly in the spine, and the kick hurt. At the same time, he slapped Casady with his sombrero. Few things are more calculated to enrage a man.

Rock came to his feet with a lunge. As he turned, with his right palm he grabbed the ankle of Vorys' boot, and with his left fist he smashed him in the stomach, jerking up on the leg. The move was so sudden, so totally unexpected, that there was no chance to spring back. Pete Vorys hit the boardwalk flat on his shoulder blades!

A whoop of delight went up from the crowd, and for an instant, Pete Vorys lay stunned. Then with an oath he came off the walk, lunging to his feet.

Rock sprang back, his hands wide. "I'm not packin' a gun!" he yelled.

"I don't need a gun!" Vorys yelled. It was the first time he had ever hit the ground in a fight and he was furious.

He stepped in, driving a left to the head. Rock was no

boxer. Indeed, he had rarely fought except in fun. He took that blow now, a stunning wallop on the cheekbone. At the same moment, he let go with a wicked right swing. The punch caught Vorys on the chin and rocked him to his heels.

More astonished than hurt, he sprang in and threw two swings for Rock's chin, and Casady took them both coming in. A tremendous light seemed to burst in his brain, but the next instant he had Pete Vorys in his hands. Grabbing him by the collar and the belt, he heaved him to arm's length overhead and hurled him into the street. Still dazed from the punches he had taken, he sprang after the bigger man, and seizing him before he could strike more than an ineffectual punch, swung him to arm's length overhead again, and slammed him into the dust!

Four times he grabbed the hapless bully and hurled him to the ground while the crowd whooped and cheered. The last time, his head clearing, he grabbed Vorys' shirt-front with his left hand and swung three times into his face, smashing his nose and lips. Then he lifted the man and heaved him into the water tank with such force that water showered around him.

Beside himself, Rock wheeled on the two startled men who had walked with Vorys. Before either could make a move, he grabbed them by their belts. One swung on Rock's face, but he merely ducked his head and heaved. The man's feet flew up and he hit the ground on his back. Promptly, Rock stacked the other atop him.

The man started to get up, and Rock swung on his face, knocking him into a sitting position. Then grabbing him, he heaved him into the water tank with Vorys, who was scrambling to get out. Then he dropped the third man into the pool and putting a hand in Vorys' face, shoved him back.

For an instant, then, while the street rocked with cheers and yells of delight, he stood, panting and staring. Suddenly, he was horrified. In his rage he had not thought of what this would mean, but suddenly he knew that they would be hunting him now with guns. He must face a shootout or skip the country!

Wheeling, he shoved through the crowd, aware that someone was clinging to his arm. Looking down, he saw Sue beside him. Her eyes were bright with laughter and pride.

"Oh, Rock! That was wonderful. Just *wonderful!*"

"Let's get out of town!" he said quickly. "Now!"

So pleased was she by the discomfiture of Pete Vorys and his hands by a Three Spoker that she thought nothing of his haste. His eye swelling and his nose still dripping occasional drops of blood, they hit the trail for the home ranch. All the way, Sue babbled happily over his standing up for the Three Spoke and what it meant, and all the while all he could think of was the fact that on the morrow Vorys would be looking for him with a gun.

He could not face him. It was far better to avoid a fight than to prove himself yellow, and if he fled the country now, they would never forget what he had done and always make excuses for him. If he stayed behind and showed his yellow streak, he would be ruined.

Frank Stockman was standing on the steps when they rode in. He took one look at Rock's battered face and torn shirt and came off the steps.

"What happened?" he demanded. "Was it that Pete Vorys again?"

Tom Bell and two other hands were walking up from the bunkhouse, staring at Rock. But already, while he stripped the saddles from the horses, Sue Landon was telling the story, and it lost nothing in the telling. Rock Casady of the Three Spoke had not only whipped Pete Vorys soundly, but he had ducked Pete and two of his tough hands in the Three Lakes's water tank!

The hands crowded around him, crowing and happy, slapping him on the back and grinning. Sandy Kane gripped his hand.

"Thanks, pardner," he said grimly, "I don't feel so bad now!"

Rock smiled weakly, but inside he was sick. It was going to look bad, but he was pulling out. He said nothing, but after supper he got his own horse, threw the saddle aboard, and then rustled his gear. When he was all packed, he drew a deep breath and walked toward the ranch house.

Stockman was sitting on the wide veranda with Bell and Sue. She got up when he drew near, her eyes bright. He avoided her glance, suddenly aware of how much her praise and happiness meant to him. In his weeks on the Three Spoke, while he had never talked to her before today, his eyes had followed her every move.

"How are you, son?" Stockman said jovially. "You've made this a red-letter day on the Three Spoke! Come up an' sit down! Bell was just talking here; he says he needs a segundo, an' I reckon he's right. How'd you like the job? Eighty a month?"

He swallowed. "Sorry, Boss. I got to be movin'. I want my time."

"You *what?*" Bell took his pipe from his mouth and stared.

"I got to roll my hoop," he said stiffly. "I don't want trouble."

Frank Stockman came quickly to his feet. "But listen, man!" he protested. "You've just whipped the best man around this country! You've made a place for yourself here! The boys think you're great! So do I! So does Tom! As for Sue here, all she's done is talk about how wonderful you are! Why, son, you came in here a drifter, an' now you've made a place for yourself! Stick around! We need men like you!"

Despite himself, Casady was wavering. This was what he had always wanted and wanted now, since the bleak months of his lonely riding, more than ever. A place where he was at home, men who liked him, and a girl. . . .

"Stay on," Stockman said more quietly. "You can handle any trouble that comes, and I promise you, the Three Spoke will back any play you make! Why, with you to head 'em we can run Pete Vorys' and that slick partner of his, that Ben Kerr, clean out of the country!"

Casady's face blanched. "*Who?* Did you say, *Ben Kerr?*"

"Why, sure!" Stockman stared at him curiously, aware of the shocked expression on Rock's face. "Ben Kerr's the hombre who come in here to side Vorys! He's the smart one who's puttin' all those fancy ideas in Pete's head! He's a brother-in-law of Vorys or something!"

Ben Kerr—here!

That settled it. He could not stay now. There was no time to stay. His mind leaped ahead. Vorys would tell his story, of course. His name would be mentioned, or if not his name, his description. Kerr would know, and he wouldn't waste time. Why, even now. . . .

"Give me my money!" Casady said sharply. "I'm movin' out right now! Thanks for all you've offered, but I'm ridin'! I want no trouble!"

Stockman's face stiffened. "Why, sure," he said, "if you feel that way about it!" He took a roll of bills from his pocket and coolly paid over the money; then abruptly he turned his back and walked inside.

Casady wheeled, his heart sick within him, and started for the corral. He heard running steps behind him and then a light touch on his arm. He looked down, his eyes miserable, into Sue's face.

"Don't go, Rock!" she pleaded gently. "Please don't go! We all want you to stay!"

He shook his head. "I can't, Sue! I can't stay. I want no gun trouble!"

There—it was out.

She stepped back, and slowly her face changed. Girl that she was, she still had grown up in the tradition of the West. A man fought his battles with gun or fist; he did not run away.

"Oh?" her amazed contempt cut him like a whip. "So that's it? You're afraid to face a gun? Afraid for your life?" She stared at him. "Why, Rock Casady," her voice lifted as realization broke over her, "you're *yellow*!"

Hours later, far back in the darkness of night in the mountains, her words rang in his ears. She had called him yellow! She had called him a coward!

Rock Casady, sick at heart, rode slowly into the darkness. At first he rode with no thought but to escape, and then as his awareness began to return, he studied the situation. Lee's Ferry was northeast, and to the south he was bottled by the Colorado Canyon. North it was mostly

Vorys' range, and west lay Three Lakes and the trails leading to it. East, the Canyons fenced him off also, but east lay a lonely, little-known country, ridden only by Cat McLeod in his wanderings after varmints that preyed upon Three Spoke cattle. In that wilderness he might find someplace to hole up. Cat still had plenty of supplies, and he could borrow some from him. . . . Suddenly he remembered the canyon Cat had mentioned, the Pleasant Valley Outlet.

He would not go near Cat. There was game enough, and he had packed away a few things in the grub line when he had rolled his soogan. He found an intermittent stream that trailed down a ravine toward Kane Canyon, and followed it. Pleasant Valley Outlet was not far south of Kane. It would be a good hideout. After a few weeks, when the excitement was over, he could slip out of the country.

In a lonely canyon that opened from the south wall into Pleasant Valley Canyon, he found a green and lovely spot. There was plenty of driftwood and a cave hollowed from the Kaibab sandstone by wind and water. There he settled down. Days passed into weeks, and he lived on wild game, berries, and fish. Yet his mind kept turning northwestward toward the Three Spoke, and his thoughts gave him no rest.

On an evening almost three weeks after his escape from the Three Spoke, he was putting his coffee on when he heard a slight sound. Looking up, he saw old Cat McLeod grinning at him.

"Howdy, son!" he chuckled. "When you head for the tall timber you sure do a job of it! My land! I thought I'd never find you! No more trail'n trout swimmin' upstream!"

Rock arose stiffly. "Howdy, Cat. Just put the coffee on." He averted his eyes and went about the business of preparing a meal.

Cat seated himself, seemingly unhurried and undisturbed by his scant welcome. He got out his pipe and stuffed it full of tobacco. He talked calmly and quietly about game and fish and the mountain trails.

"Old Mormon crossin' not far from here," he said. "I could show you where it is."

After they had eaten, McLeod leaned back against a rock. "Lots of trouble back at the Three Spoke. I reckon you was the smart one, pullin' out when you did."

Casady made no response, so McLeod continued. "Pete Vorys was some beat up. Two busted ribs, busted nose, some teeth gone. Feller name of Ben Kerr came out to the Three Spoke huntin' you. Said you was a yella dog an' he knowed you of old. He laughed when he said that, an' said the whole Three Spoke outfit was yella. Stockman, he wouldn't take that, so he went for his gun. Kerr shot him."

Rock's head came up with a jerk. "Shot Stockman? He killed him?" There was horror in his voice. This was his fault— *his*!

"No, he ain't dead. He's sure bad off, though. Kerr added injury to insult by runnin' off a couple of hunded head of Three Spoke stock. Shot one hand doin' it."

A long silence followed in which the two men smoked moodily. Finally, Cat looked across the fire at Rock.

"Son, there's more'n one kind of courage, I say. I seen many a dog stand up to a grizzly that would hightail it from a skunk. Back yonder they say you're yella. Me, I don't figure it so."

"Thanks, Cat," Rock replied simply, miserably. "Thanks a lot, but you're wrong. I am yellow."

"Reckon it takes pretty much of a man to say that, son. But from what I hear you sure didn't act it against Pete an' his riders. You walloped the tar out of them!"

"With my hands it's different. It's—it's—guns."

McLeod was silent. He poked a twig into the fire and relighted his pipe.

"Ever kill a man, son?" His eyes probed Rock's, and he saw the young rider's head nod slowly. "Who was it? How'd it happen?"

"It was—" he looked up, his face drawn and pale. "I killed my brother, Cat."

McLeod was shocked. His old eyes went wide. "You killed your brother? Your *own* brother?"

Rock Casady nodded. "Yeah," he said bitterly, "my

own brother. The one person in this world that really mattered to me!"

Cat stared, and then slowly his brow puckered. "Son," he said, "why don't you tell me about it? Get it out of your system, like."

For a long while Rock was silent. Then he started to speak.

"It was down in Texas. We had a little spread down there, Jack and me. He was only a shade older, but always protectin' me, although I sure didn't need it. The finest man who ever walked, he was.

"Well, we had us a mite of trouble, an' this here Ben Kerr was the ringleader. I had trouble with Ben, and he swore to shoot me on sight. I was a hand with a gun, like you know, an' I was ready enough to fight, them days. One of the hands told me, an' without a word to Jack, I lit into the saddle an' headed for town.

"Kerr was a gunslick, but I wasn't worried. I knew that I didn't have scarcely a friend in town an' that his whole outfit would be there. It was me against them, an' I went into town with two guns an' sure enough on the prod.

"It was gettin' late when I hit town. A man I knowed told me Ben was around with his outfit and that nobody was goin' to back me one bit, them all bein' scared of Ben's boys. He told me, too, that Ben Kerr would shoot me in the back as soon as not, he bein' that kind.

"I went huntin' him. Kidlike, an' never in no fight before, I was jumpy, mighty jumpy. The light was bad. All of a sudden, I saw one of Ben's boys step out of a door ahead of me. He called out, 'Here he is, Ben! Take him!' Then I heard runnin' feet behind me, heard 'em slide to a halt, an' I wheeled, drawin' as I turned, an' fired." His voice sank to a whisper.

Cat, leaning forward, said, "You shot? An' then . . . ?"

"It was Jack. It was my own brother. He'd heard I was in town alone, an' he come runnin' to back me up. I drilled him dead center!"

Cat McLeod stared up at the young man, utterly appalled. In his kindly old heart he could only guess at the horror that must hae filled Casady, then scarcely more than a boy, when he had looked down into that still, dead face and seen his brother.

"Gosh, son." He shook his head in amazed sympathy. "It ain't no wonder you hate gunfights! It sure ain't! But . . . ?" He scowled. "I still don't see. . . ." His voice trailed away.

Rock drew a deep breath. "I sold out then and left the country. Went to ridin' for an outfit near El Paso. One night I come into town with the other hands, an' who do I run into but Ben Kerr? He thought I'd run because I was afraid of him, an' he got tough. He called me—right in front of the outfit. I was goin' to draw, but all I could see there in front of me was Jack, with that blue hole between his eyes! I turned and ran."

Cat McLeod stared at Rock and then into the fire. It was no wonder, he reflected. He probably would have run, too. If he had drawn he would have been firing on the image of the brother. It would have been like killing him over again.

"Son," he said slowly, "I know how you feel, but stop a minute an' think about Jack, this brother of yours. He always protected you, you say. He always stood up for you. Now don't you suppose he'd understand? You thought you was all alone in that town. You'd every right in the world to think that was Ben Kerr behind you. I would have thought so, an' I wouldn't have wasted no time shootin', neither.

"You can't run away from yourself. You can't run no further. Someday you got to stand an' face it, an' it might as well be now. Look at it like this: Would your brother want you livin' like this? Hunted an' scared? He sure wouldn't! Son, ever' man has to pay his own debt an' live his own life. Nobody can do it for you, but if I was you, I'd sort of figure my brother was dead because of *Ben Kerr*, an' I'd stop runnin'!"

Rock looked up slowly. "Yeah," he agreed, "I see that plain. But what if when I stepped out to meet him, *I look up an' see Jack's face again*?"

His eyes dark with horror, Rock Casady turned and plunged downstream, stumbling, swearing in his fear and loneliness and sorrow.

* * *

At daylight, old Cat McLeod opened his eyes. For an instant, he lay still. Then he realized where he was and what he had come for, and he turned his head. Rock Casady, his gear and horse, were gone. Stumbling to his feet, McLeod slipped on his boots and walked out in his red flannels to look at the trail.

It headed south, away from Three Lakes, and away from Ben Kerr. Rock Casady was running again.

The trail south to the canyon was rough and rugged. The palouse was surefooted and had a liking for the mountains, yet seemed undecided, as though the feeling persisted that he was going the wrong way.

Casady stared bleakly ahead, but he saw little of the orange and red of the sandstone cliffs. He was seeing again Frank Stockman's strong, kindly face and remembering his welcome at the Three Spoke. He was remembering Sue's hand on his sleeve and her quick smile, and old Tom Bell, gnarled and worn with handling cattle and men. He drew up suddenly and turned the horse on the narrow trail. He was going back.

"Jack," he said suddenly aloud, "stick with me, boy. I'm sure goin' to need you now!"

Sandy Kane, grim lipped and white of face, dismounted behind the store. Beside him was Sue Landon.

"Miss Sue," he said, "you get that buyin' done fast. Don't let none of that Vorys crowd see you. They've sure taken this town over since they shot the boss."

"All right, Sandy." She looked at him bravely and then squeezed the older man's hand. "We'll make it, all right." Her blue eyes darkened. "I wish I'd been a man, Sandy. Then the boys would come in and clean up this outfit!"

"Miss Sue," he said gently, "don't fret none. Our boys are just honest cowhands. We don't have a gunfighter in the lot, nobody who could stand up to Kerr or Vorys. No man minds a scrap, but it would be plain suicide!"

The girl started to enter the store, but then caught the cowhand's hand.

"Sandy," she said faintly, "look!"

A tall man with broad shoulders had swung down before the store. He tied his horse with a slipknot and hitched his guns into place. Rock Casady, his hard young face bleak and desperate, stared carefully along the street.

It was only three blocks long, this street. It was dusty and warm with the noonday sun. The gray-fronted buildings looked upon the dusty canal that separated them, and a few saddled horses stamped lazily, flicking their tails at casual flies. It was like that other street, so long ago.

Casady pulled the flat brim of his black hat a little lower over his eyes. Inside he felt sick and faint. His mouth was dry. His tongue trembled when it touched his lips. Up the street a man saw him and got slowly to his feet, staring as if hypnotized. The man backed away and then dove into the Hackamore Saloon.

Rock Casady took a deep breath, drew his shoulders back, and started slowly down the walk. He seemed in a trance where only the sun was warm and the air was still. Voices murmured. He heard a gasp of astonishment, for these people remembered that he had whipped Pete Vorys, and they knew what he had come for.

He wore two guns now, having dug the other gun and belt from his saddlebags to join the one he had only worn in the mountains. A door slammed somewhere.

Ben Kerr stared at the face of the man in the door of the saloon.

"Ben, here comes that yellow-backed Casady! And he's wearin' a gun!"

"He is, is he?" Kerr tossed off his drink. "Fill that up, Jim! I'll be right back. This will only take a minute!"

He stepped out into the street. "Come to get it this time?" he shouted tauntingly. "Or are you runnin' again?"

Rock Casady made no reply. His footsteps echoed hollowly on the boardwalk, and he strode slowly, finishing his walk at the intersecting alley, stepping into the dust and then up on the walk again.

Ben Kerr's eyes narrowed slightly. Some sixth sense warned him that the man who faced him had subtly changed. He lifted his head a little and stared. Then he shrugged off the feeling and stepped out from the building.

"All right, yellabelly! If you want it!" His hand swept down in a flashing arc and his gun came up.

Rock Casady stared down the street at the face of Ben Kerr, and it was only the face of Kerr. In his ear was Jack's voice: "Go ahead, kid! Have at it!"

Kerr's gun roared and he felt the hot breath of it bite at his face. And then suddenly, Rock Casady laughed! Within him all was light and easy, and it was almost carelessly that he stepped forward. Suddenly the .44 began to roar and buck in his hand, leaping like a live thing within his grasp. Kerr's gun flew high in the air, his knees buckled, and he fell forward on his face in the dust.

Rock Casady turned quickly toward the Hackamore. Pete Vorys stood in the door, shocked to stillness.

"All right, Pete! Do you want it or are you leavin' town?"

Vorys stared from Kerr's riddled body to the man holding the gun.

"Why, I'm leavin' town!" Vorys said. "That's my roan, right there. I'll just . . ." As though stunned, he started to mount, and Rock's voice arrested him.

"No, Pete. You walk. You hoof it. And start now!"

The bully of Three Lakes wet his lips and stared. Then his eyes shifted to the body in the street.

"Sure, Rock," he said, taking a step back. "I'll hoof it." Turning, stumbling a little, he started to walk. As he moved, his walk grew swifter and swifter as though something followed in his tracks.

Rock turned and looked up, and Sue Landon was standing on the boardwalk.

"Oh, Rock! You came back!"

"Don't reckon I ever really left, Sue," he said slowly. "My heart's been right here all the time!"

She caught his arm, and the smile in her eyes and on her lips was bright. He looked down at her.

Then he said aloud. "Thanks, Jack!"

She looked up quickly. "What did you say?"

He grinned at her. "Sue," he said, "did I ever tell you about my brother? He was one grand hombre! Someday, I'll tell you." They walked back toward the horses, her hand on his arm.

AUTHOR'S NOTE
A STRONG LAND GROWING

So much has been written of the wild, roistering, gunfighting west that many have a distorted idea of just who came west and why. As a matter-of-fact most young men at the time had grown up attending church, of one denomination or another, and many of the organized companies heading for California banned drinking, gambling, and swearing. Also, they were committed to resting on the Sabbath wherever and whenever that was practical.

Many of the companies so organized had their own uniforms and a semimilitary arrangement. Often they paraded in the streets of Boston or wherever their point of origin was, making a fine show before heading west.

Stores offered supplies and equipment for the western journey to such an extent that many were over equipped with useless material that had to be discarded before covering the worst of the trail.

As most of these men kept diaries or wrote letters home, there is no doubt as to their feelings, ambitions, and plans. Many who began with such high hopes found only lonely graves beside the trail.

A Strong Land Growing

At eight o'clock Marshal Fitz Moore left his house and walked one block west to Gard's Saloon. It was already open, and Fitz could hear Gard's swamper sweeping up the debris from the previous night.

Crossing the street, the marshal paused at the edge of the boardwalk to rub out his cigar on top of the hitching rail. As he did, he turned his eyes but not his head, glancing swiftly up the narrow street alongside the saloon. The gray horse was gone.

Fitz Moore hesitated, considering this, estimating time and probabilities. Only then did he turn and enter the Eating House just ahead of him.

The Fred Henry gang of outlaws had been operating in this corner of the territory for more than two years, but this town of Sentinel had so far escaped their attentions. Fitz Moore, who had been marshal of Sentinel for more than half of that time, had taken particular care to study the methods of the Henry outfit. He had wanted to be ready for them—and now there was also a matter of self-protection. In several of the recent raids the town marshal had been slain, and in the last three the slaying had occurred within seconds after the raid had begun.

A persistent pattern of operation had been established, and invariably the timing of the raids had coincided with the availability of large sums of money. And such a time in Sentinel, Fitz Moore knew, was now.

So, unless all his reasoning was at fault, the town was

marked for a raid within two hours. And he was marked for death!

The marshal was a tall, spare man with a dark, narrow face and a carefully trimmed mustache. Normally his expression was placid, only his eyes seeming alive and aware.

As he entered the restaurant now he removed his flat-crowned black hat. His frock coat was unbuttoned, offering easy access to his Smith & Wesson .44 Russian. It was belted high and firmly on his left side just in front of his hip, butt to the right, the holster at a slight angle.

Three men and two women sat at the long community table in the Eating House, but only one of them murmured a greeting. Jack Thomas glanced up and said, "Morning, Marshal," his voice low and friendly.

Acknowledging the greeting, the marshal sat down at the far end of the table and accepted the cup of coffee brought from the kitchen by the Chinese cook.

With his mind closed to the drift of conversation from the far end of the table, he considered the situation that faced him. His days began in the same identical manner, with a survey of the town from each of the six windows of his house. This morning he had seen a gray horse tied behind Peterson's unused corral, where it would not be seen by a casual glance.

With field glasses the marshal had examined the horse. It was streaked with the salt of dried sweat, evidence of hard riding. There were still some dark, damp spots, implying that the horse had been ridden not long before, and the fact that it was still bridled and saddled indicated that it would soon be ridden again. The brand was a Rocking R, not a local iron.

When Fitz Moore had returned to his living room, he had seated himself and opened his Plutarch. For an hour he read quietly and with genuine pleasure, finally rising to glance from the back window. The gray horse had not been moved.

At eight, when he had left for breakfast, the horse was still there, but by the time he had walked a block, it was gone. And there lingered in the air a faint dust.

Down the arroyo, of course, in the access to canyons,

forest, and mountains, there was concealment and water. Taking into consideration the cool night, the sweat-marked horse—not less than six miles to the point of rendezvous. The rider of the gray obviously had been making some final check with a local source of information. To get back to the rendezvous, discuss the situation and return, he had two hours, perhaps a little more. He would deal in minimums.

The marshal lighted a cigar, accepted a fresh cup of coffee from the Chinese, and leaned back in his chair. He was a man of simple tastes and many appreciations. He knew little of cattle and less of mining, but two things he did know. He knew guns and he knew men.

He was aware of the cool gray eyes of the young woman, the only person present whom he did not know. There was about her a nagging familiarity that disturbed him. He tasted his coffee and glanced out the window. Reason warned him that he should be suspicious of any stranger in town at this time, yet instinct told him this girl warranted no suspicion.

The Emporium Bank would be open in approximately an hour. A few minutes later Barney Gard would leave his saloon and cross the street with the Saturday and Sunday receipts. It would be a considerable sum.

The Emporium safe would be unlocked by that time, and since they had been accepting money from ranchers and dust from miners, there would be plenty of ready cash there. In one hour there would be twenty thousand in spendable cash within easy reach of grasping fingers and ready guns.

And the Henry gang, had taken steps that had made them aware of this! The marshal realized this now.

He did not know the name of the stranger who had played poker with the Catfish Kid last week. He had known the face. It had been that of a man who had been in Tascosa with the bandit leader, Fred Henry, two years ago. Tied to this was the fact that the Rocking R brand was registered to one Harvey Danuser, alias Dick Mawson, the fastest gunhand in the Henry outfit.

He was suddenly aware that a question had been

addressed to him. "What would you do, Marshal," Jack Thomas was saying, "if the Henry gang raided Sentinel?"

Fitz Moore glanced at the burning end of his cigar. Then he looked up, his eyes level and appraising. "I think," he said mildly, "I should have to take steps."

The marshal was not a precipitate man. Reputed to be fast with a gun, that speed had yet to be proved locally. Once a few years ago, he had killed the wrong man. He hoped never to make that mistake again.

So far he had enforced the peace in Sentinel by shrewd judgment of character, appreciation of developing situations, and tactical moves that invariably left him in command. Authorized to employ an assistant, he had not done so. He preferred to work alone, as he lived alone.

He was, he acknowledged—but only to himself—a lonely man. If he possessed any capacity for affection or friendship it had not been obvious to the people of Sentinel. Yet this was an added strength. No one presumed to take him lightly or to expect favoritism.

Long ago he had been considered a brilliant conversationalist, and even in a time when a cowhand's saddlebags might carry a volume of Shakespeare as often as one by Ned Buntline, he was a widely read man. He had been a captain in the cavalry of the United States, a colonel in a Mexican revolution, a shotgun messenger for Wells Fargo, and a division superintendent on the Butterfield Stage Line.

Naturally, he knew considerable about the Henry gang. The outlaws had been operating for several years, but only of late had exhibited a tendency to shoot first and talk later. This seemed to indicate that at least one of the gang had become a ruthless killer.

All three of the marshals who had recently been killed had been shot in the back. An indication that a modus operandi had been established. First kill the marshal, then rob the town. With the marshal dead, resistance was unlikely before the bandits could make their escape.

Fitz Moore dusted the ash from his cigar. He thought that gray horse had been standing long enough for the sweat to dry, which meant he had been ridden into town before daybreak. At that hour everything was closed, and he saw no one on the street, which indicated that the rider went inside somewhere. And that indicated he not only knew where to go at that hour but was sure he would be welcomed.

The Henry gang had an accomplice in Sentinel. When the rider of the gray horse had left town that accomplice undoubtedly had been awake, and with a raid imminent it was unlikely he would go back to sleep. What place more likely for him to be than in this cafe? Here he could see who was around and have a chance to judge the marshal's temper.

Had anyone entered just before he had arrived? Fitz Moore knew everyone in the room except the girl with the gray eyes. She was watching him now.

Each of the others had a reason to be here at this hour. Barney Gard had opened his saloon and left it to the ministrations of the swamper. Jack Thomas directed the destinies of the livery stable. Johnny Haven, when he wasn't getting drunk and trying to tree the town, was a hardworking young cowhand and thoroughly reliable.

The older of the two women present was Mary Jameson, a plump and gossipy widow, the town's milliner, dressmaker, and Niagara of conversation. When she finished her breakfast she would walk three doors down the street and open her shop.

But the girl with the gray eyes! Her face was both delicate and strong, her hair dark and lovely, and she had a certain air of being to the manor born. Perhaps it was because she did possess that air, like someone from the marshal's own past, that she seemed familiar. And because she was the sort of girl—

But it was too late for that now. He was being a fool.

Yet there was a definite antagonism in her eyes when she looked at him, and he could not account for it. He was accustomed to the attention of women—something he had always had—but not antagonistic attention.

Disturbed by this and by that haunting familiarity, as of a forgotten name that hangs upon the lips yet will not be spoken, he shook off these questions to consider his more immediate problem.

The marshal glanced thoughtfully at Johnny Haven. The young cowboy was staring sourly at his plate, devoting his attention almost exclusively to his coffee. Over his right temple was a swelling and a cut, and this, coupled with his hangover, had left Johnny in a disgruntled mood. Last night had seen the end of his monthly spree, and the cut was evidence of the marshal's attention.

Johnny caught the marshal's glance and scowled irritably. "You sure leave a man with a headache, Marshal. Did you have to slug me with that gun?"

Fitz Moore once more dusted the ash from his cigar. "I didn't have an ax handle, and nothing else seemed suitable for the job." He added casually, "Of course, I might have shot you."

Johnny Haven was aware of this. He knew perfectly well that most marshals would have done just that, but coming from Fitz Moore it was almost an explanation.

"Is it so easy to kill men?" It was the girl with the gray eyes who spoke, in a voice that was low and modulated, but also in it contempt was plain.

"That depends," Fitz Moore replied quietly, "on the man doing the shooting and upon the circumstances."

"I think"—her eyes seemed to blaze momentarily—"that you would find it easy to kill. You might even enjoy killing. That is, if you were able to feel anything at all."

The depth of feeling in her voice was so apparent that even Johnny turned to look at her. She was dead white, her eyes large.

The marshal's expression did not change. He knew that Johnny Haven understood, as any Westerner would. Johnny himself had given cause for shooting on more than one occasion. He also knew that what Marshal Moore had just said was more of an explanation than he had ever given to any other man. Fitz Moore had arrested Johnny Haven six times in as many months, for after every payday Johnny came to town hunting trouble.

The girl's tone and words had in them an animosity for which none of them could account, and it left them uneasy.

Barney Gard got to his feet and dropped a dollar on the table. Johnny Haven followed him out, and then the milliner left. Jack Thomas loitered over his coffee.

"That Henry bunch has got me worried, Marshal," he said. "Want me to get down the old scattergun, just in case?"

Fitz Moore watched Barney Gard through the window. The saloonman had paused on the walk to talk to Johnny Haven. Under the stubble of beard, Johnny's face looked clean and strong, reminding the marshal again, as it had before, of the face of another boy, scarcely older.

"It won't be necessary," Moore replied. "I'll handle them in my own way, in my own time. It's my job, you know."

"Isn't that a bit foolish? To refuse help?"

The contempt still in the girl's voice stirred him, but his expression revealed nothing. He nodded gravely.

"Why, I suppose it might be, ma'am, but it's the job they hired me to do."

"Figured I'd offer," Thomas said, unwilling to let the matter drop. "You tell me what you figure to do, and I'll be glad to help."

"Another time." The marshal tasted his coffee again and looked directly at the girl. "You are new in Sentinel. Will you be staying long?"

"Not long."

"You have relatives here?"

"No."

He waited, but no explanation was offered. Fitz Moore was puzzled, and he studied her out of the corners of his eyes. There was no sound but the ticking of the big old-fashioned clock on the shelf.

The girl sat very still, the delicate line of her profile bringing to him a faint, lost feeling, a nostalgia from his boyhood when there was perfume in the air, bluegrass, picket fences . . .

And then he remembered!

Thomas got to his feet. He was a big, swarthy man, always untidy, a bulge of fat pushing his wide belt. "You need my help, Marshal," he said, "you call on me."

Fitz Moore permitted himself one of his rare smiles. "If there is trouble, Jack," he said, as he glanced up. "You'll be among the first to know."

The clock ticked off the slow seconds after the door closed, and then the marshal spoke into the silence.

"Why have you come here? What can you do in this place?"

She looked down at her hands. "All I have is here—a little further west. I left the stage only to hire a rig. . . . And then I heard your name, and I wanted to see what manner of man it would be who could kill his best friend."

He got to his feet. At this moment he knew better than ever beore what loneliness meant.

"You must not judge too quickly," he said quietly. "Each man deserves to be judged against the canvas of his time and his country."

"There is only one way to judge a killer."

"Wait. You will know what I mean if you will wait a little while. And stay off the street today." He walked to the door and stopped with his hand upon the latch. "He used to tell me about you. We talked of you, and I came to feel that I knew you well. I had hoped—before it happened—that we could meet. But in a different way than this. What will happen today I want you to see. I do not believe you lack the courage to watch what happens, nor to revise your opinions if you feel you have been mistaken. Your brother, as you were advised in my letter, was killed by accident."

"But you shot him! You were in a great hurry to kill."

"He ran up behind me."

"To help you."

"I had seen him a hundred miles from there. It was—quick. At such a time one does not think. One acts."

"Kill first," she said bitterly, "and look afterward."

His face was stiff. "I am afraid that is just what one does. I am sorry, Julia."

He lifted the latch. "When you see what is done today, try to think how else it might have been handled. If you cannot see this as I do, then before night comes you will think me more cruel than you have before. But if you understand . . . where there is understanding there is no hate."

Outside the door he paused and surveyed the street with care. Not much longer now.

Across from him was Gard's Saloon. One block down the street, his own office and his home, and across from it, just a little beyond, an abandoned barn. He studied it thoughtfully and then glanced again at Gard's and at the bank, diagonally across, beyond the milliner's shop.

It would happen here, upon this dusty street, between these buildings. Here men would die, and it was his mission to be sure the right man lived and the bad died. He was expendable, but which was he? Good or bad?

Fitz Moore knew every alley, every door, every corner in this cluster of heat-baked, alkali-stamped buildings that soon would be an arena for life and death. His eyes turned thoughtfully again to the abandoned barn. It projected several feet beyond the otherwise carefully lined buildings. The big door through which hay had once been loaded gaped wide.

So little time!

He knew what they said about him. "Ain't got a friend in town," he had overheard Mrs. Jameson say. "Stays to hisself in that long old house. Got it full of books, folks say. But kill you quick as a wink, he would. He's cold—mighty cold."

But was he? Was he?

When he had first come to this town he found it a shambles, wrecked by a passing trail-herd crew. He had found it terrorized by the two dozen gunmen and looted by card sharks and thieves. Robbery had been the order of the day, and murder all too frequent. It had been six months now since there had been a robbery of any kind, and more than nine months since the last killing. Did that count for nothing at all?

He took out a cigar and bit off the end. What was the matter with him today? He had not felt like this in years. Was it, as they say happens to a drowning man, that his life was passing before his eyes just before the end? Or was it seeing Julia Heath, the sum total of all he had ever wanted in a girl? And, realizing who she was, knew how impossible all he had ever longed for had become?

They had talked of it, he and Tom Heath, and he knew Tom had written to Julia, suggesting she come west because he had found the man for her. And two weeks later Tom had been dead with his, with Fitz Moore's, bullet in his heart!

The marshal walked on along the street of false-fronted, weather-beaten buildings. Squalid and dismal as they looked, crouching here where desert and mountains met, the town was changing. It was growing with the hopes of the people, with their changing needs. This spring, for the first time, flowers had been planted in the yard of the house beyond the church, and in front of another house a tree had been trimmed.

From being a haphazard collection of buildings, catering to the transient needs of a transient people, the town of Sentinel was becoming vital, acquiring a consciousness of the future, a sense of belonging. A strong land growing, a land which would give birth to strong sons who could build and plant and harvest.

Fitz Moore turned into the empty alley between the Emporium and the abandoned barn, which was a relic of overambition during a boom. And thoughts persisted. With the marshal dead, and the town helpless—

But how had the outlaw gang planned to kill him? For that it had been planned was to him a certainty. And it must be done and done quickly when the time came.

The loft of the barn commanded a view of the street. The outlaws would come into town riding toward the barn, and somewhere along that street, easily covered by a rifleman concealed in the barn, he, the marshal of Sentinel, would be walking.

He climbed the stairs to the loft. The dust on the steps had been disturbed. At the top a board creaked under his feet, and a rat scurried away. The loft was wide and empty. Only dust and wisps of hay.

From that wide door the raid might be stopped, but this was not the place for him. His place was down there in that hot, dusty street, where his presence might count. There was much to do. And now there was only a little time.

Returning to his quarters, Fitz Moore thrust an extra gun into his pocket and belted on a third. Then he put two shotguns into his wood sack. Nobody would be surprised to see him with the sack, for he always carried firewood in it that he got from the pile in back of Gard's.

He saw Jack Thomas sitting in a chair before the livery stable. Barney Gard came from the saloon, glanced at the marshal, and then went back inside. Fitz Moore paused, relighting his dead cigar.

The topic of what would happen here if the Henry gang attempted a raid was not a new one. He had heard much speculation. Some men, like Thomas, had brought it up before, trying to feel him out, to discover what he thought, what *he* would do.

Jack Thomas turned his big head on his thick neck and glanced toward the marshal. He was a good-natured man, but too inquisitive, too dirty.

Johnny Haven, sitting on the steps of the saloon porch, looked at the marshal and grinned. He was a powerful, aggressive young man.

"How's the town clown?" he asked.

Moore paused, drawing deep on his cigar, permitting himself a glance toward the loft door, almost sixty yards away and across the street. Deliberately he had placed himself in line with the best shooting position.

"Johnny," he said, "if anything happens to me, I want you to have this job. If nothing does happen to me, I want you for my deputy."

Young Haven could not have been more astonished, but he also was deeply moved. He looked up as if he believed the marshal had been suddenly touched by the heat. Aside from the words, the very fact that Marshal Moore had ventured a personal remark was astonishing.

"You're twenty-six, Johnny, and it's time you grew up. You've played at being a bad man long enough. I've looked the town over, and you're the man I want."

Johnny . . . Tom. He avoided thinking of them together, yet there was a connection. Tom once had been a good man, too, but now he was a good man gone. Johnny was a good man, much like Tom, though walking the hairline of the law.

Johnny Haven was profoundly impressed. To say that he admired and respected this tall, composed man was no more than the truth. After his first forcible arrest by Fitz Moore, Johnny had been furious enough to beat him up or kill him, but each time he had come to town he had found himself neatly boxed and helpless.

Nor had Fitz Moore ever taken unfair advantage, never striking one blow more than essential and never keeping the young cowhand in jail one hour longer than necessary. And Johnny Haven was honest enough to realize that he never could have handled the situation as well.

Anger had resolved into reluctant admiration. Only his native stubbornness and the pride of youth had prevented him from giving up the struggle. "Why pick on me?" He spoke roughly to cover his emotion. "You won't be quitting."

There was a faint suggestion of movement from the loft. The marshal glanced at his watch. Two minutes to ten.

"Johnny—" The sudden change of tone brought Johnny's head up sharply. "When the shooting starts, there are two shotguns in this sack. Get behind the end of the water trough and use one of them. Shoot from under the trough. It's safer."

Two riders walked their mounts into the upper end of the street, almost a half block away. Two men on powerful horses, better horses than would be found on any cow ranch.

Three more riders came from a space between the buildings, from the direction of Peterson's Corral. One of them was riding a gray horse. They were within twenty yards when Barney Gard came from the saloon carrying two canvas bags. He was headed for the bank when one of the horsemen swung his mount to a route that would cut across Barney's path.

"Shotgun in the sack, Gard." The Marshal's voice was conversational.

* * *

Then, as sunlight glinted on a rifle barrel in the loft door, Fitz Moore took one step forward, drawing as he moved, and the thunder of the rifle merged with the bark of his own gun. Then the rifle clattered, falling, and an arm lay loosely in the loft door.

The marshal had turned instantly. "All right, Henry!" His voice rang like a trumpet call in the narrow street. "You're asking for it! *Take* it!"

There was no request for surrender. The rope awaited these men, and death rode their guns and hands.

As one man they drew, and the marshal sprang into the street, landing flat footed and firing. The instant of surprise had been his. And his first shot, only a dancing second after the bullet that had killed the man in the loft, struck Fred Henry over the belt buckle.

Behind and to the marshal's right a shotgun's deep roar blasted the sunlit morning. The man on the gray horse died falling, his gun throwing a useless shot into the hot, still air.

Horses reared, and a cloud of dust and gunpowder arose, stabbed through with crimson flame and the hoarse bark of guns.

A rider leaped his horse at the marshal, but Fitz Moore stood his ground and fired. The rider's face seemed to disintegrate under the impact of the bullet.

And then there was silence. The roaring was gone and only the faint smells lingered—the acrid tang of gunpowder, of blood in the dust, of the brighter crimson scent of blood on a saddle.

Johnny Haven got up slowly from behind the horse trough. Barney Gard stared around as if he had just awakened, his hands gripping a shotgun.

There was a babble of sound then, of people running into the street. And a girl with gray eyes was watching. Those eyes seemed to reach across the street and into the heart of the marshal.

"Only one shot!" Barney Gard exclaimed. "I got off only one shot and missed that one!"

"The Henry gang wiped out!" yelled an excited citizen. "Wait'll Thomas hears of this!"

"He won't be listenin," somebody else said. "They got him."

Fitz Moore turned like a duelist. "I got him," he said flatly. "He was their man. Tried all morning to find out what I'd do if they showed up. . . ."

An hour later Johnny Haven followed the marshal into the street. Four men were dead and two were in jail.

"How did you know, Marshal?"

"You learn, Johnny. You learn or you die. That's your lesson for today. Learn to be in the right place at the right time and keep your own counsel. You'll be getting my job." His cigar was gone. He bit the end from a fresh one and went on, "Jack Thomas was the only man the rider of the gray horse I told you I saw could have reached without crossing the street. He wouldn't have left the horse he'd need for a quick getaway on the wrong side of the street. Besides, I'd been doubtful of Thomas. He was prying too much."

When he entered the Eating House, Julia Heath was at the table again. She was white and shaken. He spoke to her.

"I'm sorry, Julia, but now you see how little time there is for a man when guns are drawn. These men would have taken the money honest men worked to get, and they would have killed as they have killed before. Such men know only the law of the gun." He placed his hands on the table. "I should have known you at once, but I never thought—after what happened—that you would come, even to settle the estate. He was proud of you, Julia, and he was my best friend."

"But you killed him."

Marshal Moore gestured toward the street. "It was like that. Guns exploding, a man dying under my gun, and then running feet behind me in a town where I had no friends. I thought Tom was on his ranch in Colorado. I killed the man who was firing at me, turned, and fired toward the running feet. And killed my friend, your brother."

She knew then how it must have been for this man, and she was silent.

"And now?" she murmured.

"My job will go to Johnny Haven, but I'm going to stay here and help this town grow, help it become a community of homes, use some of the things I know that have nothing to do with guns. This"—he gestured toward the street—"should end it for a while. In the breathing space we can mature, settle down, change the houses into homes, and bring some beauty into this makeshift."

She was silent again, looking down at the table. At last she spoke, her voice barely audible. "It—it's worth doing."

"It will be." He looked at his unlighted cigar. "You'll be going to settle Tom's property. When you come back, if you want to, you might stop off again. If you do, I'll be waiting to see you."

She looked at him, seeing beyond the coldness, seeing the man her brother must have known. "I think I shall. I think I'll stop—when I come back."

Out in the street a man was raking dust over the blood. Back of the old barn a hen cackled, and somewhere a pump started to complain rustily, drawing clear water from a deep, cold well.

AUTHOR'S NOTE

THE TURKEYFEATHER RIDERS

James B. Gillett was a Texas Ranger form 1875 to 1881. In his book Six Years With the Texas Rangers *he says that a ranger could "keep a constant stream of fire pouring from his carbine when his horse is going at top speed and hit his mark nine times out of ten."*

Speaking later of the Horrell faction, who figured in the Horrell-Higgins feud, he says: "having grown up with firearms in their hands, they were quick as lighting with either Winchester or pistol."

Later, speaking of the ranger company of which he was a member, with Lieutenant Reynold in command, he says: "Nearly every member of the company had more or less experience as an officer and all were exceedingly fine marksmen."

In the years 1889–90, the Texas Rangers, according to Gillette, arrested 579 persons, among them 76 murderers.

Gillette's book is one of the best on the Texas Rangers, not a history of the force but a good account of his service with them.

The Turkeyfeather Riders

Jim Sandifer swung down from his buckskin and stood for a long minute staring across the saddle toward the dark bulk of Bearwallow Mountain. His was the grave, careful look of a man accustomed to his own company under the sun and in the face of the wind. For three years he had been riding for the B Bar, and for two of those years he had been ranch foreman. What he was about to do would bring an end to that, an end to the job, to the life here, to his chance to win the girl he loved.

Voices sounded inside, the low rumble of Gray Bowen's bass and the quick, light voice of his daughter, Elaine. The sound of her voice sent a quick spasm of pain across Sandifer's face. Tying the buckskin to the hitch rail, he ducked under it and walked up the steps, his boots sounding loud on the planed boards, his spurs tinkling lightly.

The sound of his steps brought instant stillness to the group inside and then the quick tattoo of Elaine's feet as she hurried to meet him. It was a sound he would never tire of hearing, a sound that had brought gladness to him such as he had never known before. Yet when her eyes met his at the door her flashing smile faded.

"Jim! What's wrong?" Then she noticed the blood on his shoulder and the tear where the bullet had ripped his shirt, and her face went white to the lips. "You're hurt!"

"No—only a scratch." He put aside her detaining hand. "Wait. I'll talk to your dad first." His hands dropped to hers, and as she looked up, startled at his touch, he said gravely and sincerely, "No matter what happens now, I want you to know that I've loved you since the day we met. I've thought of little else, believe that." He dropped her hands then and stepped past her into the huge room where Gray Bowen waited, his big body relaxed in a homemade chair of cowhide.

Rose Martin was there, too, and her tall, handsome son, Lee. Jim's eyes avoided them for he knew what their faces were like; he knew the quiet serenity of Rose Martin's face, masking a cunning as cold and calculating as her son's flaming temper. It was these two who were destroying the B Bar, they who had brought the big ranch to the verge of a deadly range war by their conniving. A war that could have begun this morning, but for him.

Even as he began to speak he knew his words would put him right where they wanted him, that when he had finished, he would be through here, and Gray Bowen and his daughter would be left unguarded to the machinations of this woman and her son. Yet he could no longer refrain from speaking. The lives of men depended on it.

Bowen's lips thinned when he saw the blood. "You've seen Katrishen? Had a run-in with him?"

"No!" Sandifer's eyes blazed. "There's no harm in Katrishen if he's left alone. No trouble unless we make it. I ask you to recall, Gray, that for two years we've lived at peace with the Katrishens. We have had no trouble until the last three months." He paused, hoping the idea would soak in that trouble had begun with the coming of the Martins. "He won't give us any trouble if we leave him alone!"

"Leave him alone to steal our range!" Lee Martin flared.

Sandifer's eyes swung. "*Our* range? Are you now a partner in the B Bar?"

Lee smiled, covering his slip. "Naturally, as I am a friend of Mr. Bowen's, I think of his interests as mine."

Bowen waved an impatient hand. "That's no matter! What happened?"

Here it was, then. The end of all his dreaming, his planning, his hoping. "It wasn't Katrishen. It was Klee Mont."

"*Who?*" Bowen came out of his chair with a lunge, veins swelling. "Mont shot *you*? What for? Why, in heavens' name?"

"Mont was over there with the Mello boys and Art Dunn. He had gone over to run the Katrishens off their Iron Creek holdings. If they had tried that, they would have started a first-class range war with no holds barred. I stopped them."

Rose Martin flopped her knitting in her lap and glanced up at him, smiling smugly. Lee began to roll a smoke, one eyebrow lifted. This was what they had wanted, for he alone had blocked them here. The others the Martins could influence, but not Jim Sandifer.

Bowen's eyes glittered with his anger. He was a choleric man, given to sudden bursts of fury, a man who hated being thwarted and who was impatient of all restraint.

"You stopped them? Did they tell you whose orders took them over there? Did they?"

"They did. I told them to hold off until I could talk with you, but Mont refused to listen. He said his orders had been given him and he would follow them to the letter."

"He did right!" Bowen's voice boomed in the big room. "Exactly right! And you stopped them? *You* countermanded my orders?"

"I did." Sandifer laid it flatly on the line. "I told them there would be no burning or killing while I was foreman. I told them they weren't going to run us into a range war for nothing."

Gray Bowen balled his big hands into fists. "You've got a gall, Jim! You know better than to countermand an order of mine! And you'll leave me to decide what range I need! Katrishen's got no business on Iron Creek, an' I told him so! I told him to get off an' get out! As for this range war talk, that's foolishness! He won't fight!"

"Putting them off would be a very simple matter,"

Lee Martin interposed quietly. "If you hadn't interfered, Sandifer, they would be off now and the whole matter settled."

"Settled nothin'!" Jim exploded. "Where did you get this idea that Bill Katrishen could be pushed around? The man was an officer in the Army during the war, an' he's fought Indians on the plains."

"You must be a great friend of his," Rose Martin said gently. "You know so much about him."

The suggestion was there, and Gray Bowen got it. He stopped in his pacing, and his face was like a rock. "You been talkin' with Katrishen? You sidin' that outfit?"

"This is my outfit. I ride for the brand," Sandifer replied. "I know Katrishen, of course. I've talked to him."

"And to his daughter?" Lee suggested, his eyes bright with malice. "With his pretty daughter?"

Out of the tail of his eye Jim saw Elaine's head come up quickly, but he ignored Lee's comment. "Stop and think," he said to Bowen. "When did this trouble start? When Mrs. Martin and her son came here! You got along fine with Katrishen until then! They've been putting you up to this!"

Bowen's eyes narrowed. "That will be enough of that!" he said sharply. He was really furious now, not the flaring, hot fury that Jim knew so well, but a cold, hard anger that nothing could touch. For the first time Jim realized how futile any argument was going to be. Rose Martin and her son had insinuated themselves to much and too well into the picture of Gray Bowen's life.

"You wanted my report," Sandifer said quietly. "Mont wouldn't listen to my arguments for time. He said he had his orders and would take none from me. I told him then that if he rode forward it was against my gun. He laughed at me, then reached for his gun. I shot him."

Gray Bowen's widened eyes expressed his amazement. "You shot *Mont*? You beat him to the draw?"

"That's right. I didn't want to kill him, but I shot the gun out of his hand and held my gun on him for a minute to let him know what it meant to be close to death. Then I started them back here."

Bowen's anger was momentarily swallowed by his astonishment. He recalled suddenly that in the three years Sandifer had worked for him there had been no occasion for him to draw a gun in anger. There had been a few brushes with Apaches and one with rustlers, but all rifle work. Klee Mont was a killer with seven known killings on his record and had been reputed to be the fastest gunhand west of the Rio Grande.

"It seems peculiar," Mrs. Martin said composedly, "for you to turn your gun on men who ride for Mr. Bowen, taking sides against him. No doubt you meant well, but it does seem strange."

"Not if you know the Katrishens," Jim replied grimly. "Bill was assured he could settle on that Iron Creek holding before he moved in. He was told that we made no claim on anything beyond Willow and Gilita creeks."

"Who," Lee insinuated, "assured him of that?"

"I did," Jim said coolly. "Since I've been foreman, we've never run any cattle beyond that boundary. Iron Mesa is a block that cuts us off from the country south of there, and the range to the east is much better and is open for us clear to Beaver Creek and south to the Middle Fork."

"So you decide what range will be used? I think for a hired hand you take a good deal of authority. Personally, I'm wondering how much your loyalty is divided. Or if it is divided. It seems to me you act more as a friend of the Katrishens—or their daughter."

Sandifer took a step forward. "Martin," he said evenly, "are you aimin' to say that I'd double-cross the boss? If you are, you're a liar!"

Bowen looked up, a chill light in his eyes that Sandifer had never seen there before. "That will be all, Jim. You better go."

Sandifer turned on his heel and strode outside.

When Sandifer walked into the bunkhouse, the men were already back. The room was silent, but he was aware of the hatred in the cold, blue eyes of Mont as he lay sprawled in his bunk. His right hand and wrist were bandaged. The Mello boys snored in their bunks, while Art Dunn idly shuffled cards at the table. These were the new hands, hired since the coming of the Martins. Only three of the older hands were in, and none of them spoke.

"Hello—lucky." Mont rolled up on his elbow. "Lose your job?"

"Not yet," Jim said shortly, aware that his remark brought a fleeting anger to Mont's eyes.

"You will!" Mont assured him. "If you are in the country when this hand gets well, I'll kill you!"

Jim Sandifer laughed shortly. He was aware that the older hands were listening, although none would have guessed it without knowing them.

"You called me lucky, Klee. It was you who were lucky in that I didn't figure on killin' you. That was no miss. I aimed for your gunhand. Furthermore, don't try pullin' a gun on me again. You're too slow."

"*Slow?*" Mont's face flamed. He reared up in his bunk. "Slow? Why, you two-handed bluffer!"

Sandifer shrugged. "Look at your hand," he said calmly. "If you don't know what happened, I do. That bullet didn't cut your thumb off. It doesn't go up your hand or arm; the wound runs *across* your hand."

They all knew what he meant. Sandifer's bullet must have hit his hand as he was in the act of drawing and before the gun came level, indicating that Sandifer had beaten Mont to the draw by a safe margin. That Klee Mont realized the implication was plain, for his face darkened and then paled around the lips. There was pure hatred in his eyes when he looked up at Sandifer.

"I'll kill you!" he said viciously. "I'll kill you!"

As Sandifer started outside, Rep Dean followed him. With Grimes and Sparkman, he was one of the older hands.

"What's come over this place, Jim? Six months ago there wasn't a better spread in the country."

Sandifer did not reply, and Dean built a smoke. "It's that woman," he said. "She twists the boss around her little finger. If it wasn't for you, I'd quit, but I'm thinkin' that there's nothin' she wouldn't like better than for all of the old hands to ask for their time."

Sparkman and Grimes had followed them from the bunkhouse. Sparkman was a lean-bodied Texan with some reputation as an Indian fighter.

"You watch your step," Grimes warned. "Next time Mont will backshoot you!"

They talked among themselves, and as they conversed, he ran his thoughts over the developments of the past few months. He had heard enough of Mrs. Martin's sly, insinuating remarks to understand how she had worked Bowen up to ordering Katrishen driven off, yet there was no apparent motive. It seemed obvious that the woman had her mind set on marrying Gray Bowen, but for that it was not essential that any move be made against the Katrishens.

Sandifer's limitation of the B Bar range had been planned for the best interests of the ranch. The range they now had in use was bounded by streams and mountain ranges and was rich in grass and water, a range easily controlled with a small number of hands and with little danger of loss from raiding Indians, rustlers, or varmints.

His willingness to have the Katrishens move in on Iron Creek was not without the B Bar in mind. He well knew that range lying so much out of the orbit of the ranch could not be long held tenantless, and the Katrishens were stable, honest people who would make good neighbors and good allies. Thinking back, he could remember almost to the day when the first rumors began to spread, and most of them had stemmed from Lee Martin himself. Later, one of the Mello boys had come in with a bullet hole in the crown of his hat and a tale of being fired on from Iron Mesa.

"What I can't figure out," Grimes was saying, "is what that no-account Lee Martin would be doin' over on the Turkeyfeather.

Sandifer turned his head. "On the Turkeyfeather? That's beyond Iron Mesa! Why, that's clear over the other side of Katrishen's!"

"Sure enough! I was huntin' that brindle steer who's always leadin' stock off into the canyons when I seen Martin fordin' the Willow. He was ridin' plumb careful, an' he sure wasn't playin' no tenderfoot then! I was right wary of him, so I took in behind an' trailed him over to that rough country near Turkeyfeather Pass. Then I lost him."

The door slammed up at the house, and they saw Lee Martin come down the steps and start toward them. It was dusk, but still light enough to distinguish faces. Martin walked up to Sandifer.

"Here's your time." He held out an envelope. "You're through!"

"I'll want that from Bowen himself," Sandifer replied stiffly.

"He doesn't want to see you. He sent this note." Martin handed over a sheet of the coarse brown paper on which Bowen kept his accounts. On it, in Bowen's hand, was his dismissal.

> I won't have a man who won't obey orders. Leave tonight.

Sandifer stared at the note, which he could barely read in the dim light. He had worked hard for the B Bar, and this was his answer.

"All right," he said briefly. "Tell him I'm leaving. It won't take any great time to saddle up."

Martin laughed. "That won't take time, either. You'll walk out. No horse leaves this ranch."

Jim turned back, his face white. "You keep out of this, Martin. That buckskin is my own horse. You get back in your hole an' stay there!"

Martin stepped closer. "Why, you cheap bigmouth!"

The blow had been waiting for a long time, but it came fast now. It was a smashing left that caught Martin on the chin and spilled him on his back in the dust. With a muttered curse, Martin came off the ground and rushed, but Sandifer stepped in, blocking a right and whipping his own right into Lee's midsection. Martin doubled over, and Jim straightened him with a left uppercut and then knocked him crashing into the corral fence.

Abruptly, Sandifer turned and threw the saddle on the buckskin. Sparkman swore. "I'm quittin', too!" he said.

"An' me!" Grimes snapped. "I'll be doggoned if I'll work here now!"

Heavily, Martin got to his feet. His white shirt was bloody, and they could vaguely see a blotch of blood over the lower part of his face. He limped away, muttering.

"Sparky," Jim said, low voiced, "don't quit. All of you stay on. I reckon this fight ain't over, an' the boss may need a friend. You stick here. I'll not be far off!"

Sandifer had no plan, yet it was Lee Martin's ride to the Turkeyfeather that puzzled him most, and almost of its own volition, his horse took that route. As he rode he turned the problem over and over in his mind, seeking for a solution, yet none appeared that was satisfactory. Revenge for some old grudge against the Katrishens was considered and put aside; he could not but feel that whatever the reason for the plotting of the Martins, there had to be profit in it somewhere.

Certainly, there seemed little to prevent Rose Martin from marrying Gray Bowen if she wished. The old man was well aware that Elaine was a lovely, desirable girl. The cowhands and other male visitors who came to call for one excuse or another were evidence of that. She would not be with him long, and if she left, he was faced with the dismal prospect of ending his years alone. Rose Martin was a shrewd woman and attractive for her years, and she knew how to make Gray comfortable and how to appeal to him. Yet obviously there was something more in her mind than this, and it was that something more in which Sandifer was interested.

Riding due east Jim crossed the Iron near Clayton and turned west by south through the broken country. It was very late, and vague moonlight filtered through the yellow pine and fir that guarded the way he rode with their tall columns. Twice he halted briefly, feeling a strange uneasiness, yet listen as he might he could detect no alien sound, nothing but the faint stirring of the slight breeze through the needles of the pines and the occasional rustle of a blown leaf. He rode on, but now he avoided the bright moonlight and kept more to the deep shadows under the trees.

After skirting the end of the Jerky Mountains, he headed for the Turkeyfeather Pass. Somewhere off to his left, lost against the blackness of the ridge shadow, a faint sound came to him. He drew up, listening. He did not hear it again, yet his senses could not have lied. It was the sound of a dead branch scraping along leather, such a sound as might be made by a horseman riding through brush.

Sliding his Winchester from its scabbard, he rode forward, every sense alert. His attention was drawn to the buckskin, whose ears were up and who, when he stopped, lifted its head and stared off toward the darkness. Sandifer started the horse forward, moving easily.

To the left towered the ridge of Turkeyfeather Pass, lifting all of five hundred feet above him, black, towering, ominous in the moonlight. The trees fell away, massing their legions to right and left, but leaving before him an open glade, grassy and still. Off to the right Iron Creek hustled over the stones, whispering wordless messages to the rocks on either bank. Somewhere a quail called mournfully into the night, and the hoofs of the buckskin made light whispering sounds as they moved through the grass at the edge of the glade.

Jim drew up under the trees near the creek and swung down, warning the buckskin to be still. Taking his rifle he circled the glade under the trees, moving like a prowling wolf. Whoever was over there was stalking him, watching a chance to kill him or perhaps only following to see where he went. In any case, Jim meant to know who and why.

Suddenly he heard a vague sound before him, a creak of saddle leather. Freezing in place, he listened and heard it again, followed by the crunch of gravel. Then he caught the glint of moonlight on a rifle barrel and moved forward, shifting position to get the unseen man silhouetted against the sky. Sandifer swung his rifle.

"All right," he said calmly, "drop that rifle and lift your hands! I've got you dead to rights!"

As he spoke, the man was moving forward, and instantly the fellow dived headlong. Sandifer's rifle spat fire, and he heard a grunt, followed by a stab of flame. A bullet whipped past his ear. Shifting ground on cat feet, Jim studied the spot carefully.

The man lay in absolute darkness, but listening he could hear the heavy breathing that proved his shot had gone true. He waited, listening for movement, but there was none. After a while the breathing grew less and he took a chance.

"Better give up!" he said. "No use dyin' there!"

There was silence and then a slight movement of gravel. Then a six-shooter flew through the air to land in the open space between them.

"What about that rifle?" Sandifer demanded cautiously.

"Lost . . . for God's sake, help . . . me!"

There was no mistaking the choking sound. Jim Sandifer got up and holding his rifle on the spot where the voice had sounded, crossed into the shadows. As it was, he almost stumbled over the wounded man before he saw him. It was Dan Mello, and the heavy slug had torn into his body but seemed not to have emerged.

Working swiftly, Jim got the wounded man into an easier position and carefully pulled his shirt away from the wound. There was no mistaking the fact that Dan Mello was hit hard. Jim gave the wounded man a drink and then hastily built a fire to work by. His guess that the bullet had not emerged proved true, but moving his hand gently down the wounded man's back he could feel something hard near his spine. When he straightened, Mellow's eyes sought his face.

"Don't you move," Sandifer warned. "It's right near your spine. I've got to get a doctor."

He was worried, knowing little of such wounds. The man might be bleeding internally.

"No, don't leave me!" Mello pleaded. "Some varmint might come!" The effort of speaking left him panting.

Jim Sandifer swore softly, uncertain as to his proper course. He had little hope that Mello could be saved, even if he rode for a doctor. The nearest one was miles away, and movement of the wounded man would be very dangerous. Nor was Mello's fear without cause, for there were mountain lions, wolves, and coyotes in the area, and the scent of blood was sure to call them.

"Legs—gone," Mello panted. "Can't feel nothing."

"Take it easy," Jim advised. The nearest place was Bill Katrishen's, and Bill might be some hand with a wounded man. He said as much to Mello. "Can't be more'n three, four miles," he added. "I'll give you back your gun an' build up the fire."

"You—you'll sure come back?" Mello pleaded.

"What kind of coyote do you think I am?" Sandifer asked irritably. "I'll get back as soon as ever I can." He looked down at him. "Why were you gunnin' for me? Mont put you up to it?"

Mello shook his head. "Mont, he—he ain't—bad. It's that Martin—you watch. He's pizen—mean."

Leaving the fire blazing brightly, Jim returned to his buckskin and jumped into the saddle. The moon was higher now, and the avenues through the trees were like roads, eerily lighted. Touching a spur to the horse, Jim raced through the night, the cool wind fanning his face. Once a deer scurried from in front of him and then bounded off through the trees, and once he thought he saw the lumbering shadow of an old grizzly.

The Katrishen log cabin and pole corrals lay bathed in white moonlight as he raced his horse into the yard. The drum of hooves upon the hard-packed earth and his call brought movement and an answer from inside: "Who is it? What's up?"

Briefly, he explained, and after a minute the door opened.

"Come in, Jim. Figured I heard a shot a while back. Dan Mello, you say? He's a bad one."

Hurrying to the corral, Jim harnessed two mustangs and hitched them to the buckboard. A moment later Bill Katrishen, tall and gray haired, came from the cabin, carrying a lantern in one hand and a black bag in the other.

"I'm no medical man," he said, "but I fixed a sight of bullet wounds in my time." He crawled into the buckboard, and one of his sons got up beside him. Led by Sandifer they started back over the way he had come.

Mello was still conscious when they stopped beside him. He looked unbelievingly at Katrishen.

"You come?" he said. "You knowed who—who I was?"

"You're hurt, ain't you?" Katrishen asked testily. Carefully, he examined the man and then sat back on his heels. "Mello," he said, "I ain't one for foolin' a man. You're plumb bad off. That bullet seems to have slid off your hip bone an' tore right through you. If we had you down to the house, we could work on you a durned sight better, but I don't know whether you'd make it or not."

The wounded man breathed heavily, staring from one to the other. He looked scared, and he was sweating, and under it his face was pale.

"What you think," he panted, "all right—with me."

"The three of us can put him on them quilts in the back of the buckboard. Jim, you slide your hands under his back."

"Hold up," Mello's eyes wavered and then focused on Jim. "You watch—Martin. He's plumb—bad."

"What's he want, Mello?" Jim said. "What's he after?"

"G—old," Mellow panted, and then suddenly he relaxed.

"Fainted," Katrishen said. "Load him up."

All through the remainder of the night they worked over him. It was miles over mountain roads to Silver City and the nearest doctor, and little enough that he could do. Shortly before the sun lifted, Dan Mello died.

Bill Katrishen got up from beside the bed, his face drawn with weariness. He looked across the body of Dan Mello at Sandifer.

"Jim, what's this all about? Why was he gunning for you?"

Hesitating only a moment, Jim Sandifer explained the needling of Gray Bowen by Rose Martin, the undercover machinations of her and her tall son, the hiring of the Mellos at their instigation and of Art Dunn and Klee Mont. Then he went on to the events preceding his break with the B Bar. Katrishen nodded thoughtfully, but obviously puzzled.

"I never heard of the woman, Jim. I can't figure why she'd have it in for me. What did Mello mean when he said Martin was after gold?"

"You've got me. I know they are money hungry, but the ranch is—" He stopped, and his face lifted, his eyes narrowing. "Bill, did you ever hear of gold around here?"

"Sure, over toward Cooney Canyon. You know, Cooney was a sergeant in the Army, and after his discharge he returned to hunt for gold he located while a soldier. The Apaches finally got him, but he had gold first."

"Maybe that's it. I want a fresh horse, Bill."

"You get some sleep first. The boys an' I'll take care of Dan. Kara will fix breakfast for you."

The sun was high when Jim Sandifer rolled out of his bunk and stumbled sleepily to the door to splash his face in cold water poured from a bucket into the tin basin. Kara heard him moving and came to the door, walking carefully and lifting her hand to catch the door jam.

"Hello, Jim? Are you rested? Dad an' the boys buried Dan Mello over on the knoll."

Jim smiled at her reassuringly.

"I'm rested, but after I eat I'll be ridin', Kara." He looked up at the slender girl with the rusty hair and pale freckles. "You keep the boys in, will you? I don't want them to be where they could be shot at until I can figure a way out of this. I'm going to maintain peace in this country or die tryin'!"

"You're a good man, Jim," the girl said. "This country needs more like you."

Sandifer shook his head somberly. "Not really a good man, Kara, just a man who wants peace and time to build a home. I reckon I've been as bad as most, but this is a country for freedom and a country for things to be done. We can't do it when we are killin' each other."

The buckskin horse was resting, but the iron gray that Katrishen had provided was a good mountain horse. Jim Sandifer pulled his gray hat low over his eyes and squinted against the sun. He liked the smell of pine needles, the pungent smell of sage. He moved carefully, searching the trail for the way Lee Martin's horse had gone the day Grimes followed him.

Twice he lost the trail and then found it only to lose it finally in the sand of a wash. The area covered by the sand was small, a place where water had spilled down a steep mountainside, eating out a raw wound in the cliff, yet there the trail vanished. Dismounting, Sandifer's careful search disclosed a brushed-over spot near the cliff and then a chafed spot near the cliff and then a chafed place on a small tree. Here Lee Martin had tied his horse, and from here he must have gone on foot.

It was a small rock, only half as big as his fist, that was the telltale clue. The rock showed where it had lain in the earth but had been recently rolled aside. Moving close, he could see that the stone had rolled from under a clump of brush, the clump rolled easily under his hand. Then he saw that although the roots were still in the soil, at some time part of it had been pulled free, and the clump had been rolled over to cover an opening no more than a couple of feet wide and twice as high. It was a man-made tunnel, but one not recently made.

Concealing the gray in the trees some distance off, Sandifer walked back to the hole, stared around uneasily, and then ducked his head and entered. Once he was inside, the tunnel was higher and wider, and then it opened into a fair-sized room. Here the ore had been stoped out, and he looked around, holding a match high.

The light caught and glinted upon the rock, and moving closer he picked up a small chunk of rose quartz seamed with gold!

Pocketing the sample, he walked further in until he saw a black hole yawning before him, and beside it lay a notched pole such as the Indians had used in Spanish times to climb out of mine shafts. Looking over into the hole, he saw a longer pole reaching down into the darkness. He peered over and then straightened. This, then, was what Dan Mello had meant! The Martins wanted gold.

The match flickered out, and standing there in the cool darkness, he thought it over and understood. This place was on land used, and probably claimed, by Bill Katrishen, and it could not be worked unless they were driven off. But could he make Gray Bowen believe him? What would Lee do if his scheme was exposed? Why had Mello been so insistent that Martin was dangerous?

He bent over and started into the tunnel exit and then stopped. Kneeling just outside were Lee Martin, Art Dunn, and Jay Mello. Lee had a shotgun pointed at Jim's body. Jim jerked back around the corner of stone even as the shotgun thundered.

"You dirty, murderin' rat!" he yelled. "Let me out in the open and try that!"

Martin laughed. "I wouldn't think of it! You're right where I want you now, an' you'll stay there!"

Desperately, Jim stared around. Martin was right. He was bottled up now. He drew his gun, wanting to chance a shot at Martin while yet there was time, but when he stole a glance around the corner of the tunnel, there was nothing to be seen. Suddenly, he heard a sound of metal striking stone, a rattle of rock, and then a thunderous crash, and the tunnel was filled with dust, stifling and thick. Lee Martin had closed off the tunnel mouth, and he was entombed alive!

Jim Sandifer leaned back against the rock wall of the stope and closed his eyes. He was frightened. He was frightened with a deep, soul-shaking fear, for this was something against which he could not fight, these walls of living rock around him, and the dead debris of the rock-choked tunnel. Had there been time and air, a man might work out an escape, but there was so little time, so little air. He was buried alive.

Slowly, the dust settled from the heavy air. Saving his few matches, he got down on his knees and crawled into the tunnel, but there was barely room enough. Mentally, he tried to calculate the distance out, and he could see that there was no less than fifteen feet of rock between him and escape—not an impossible task if more rock did not slide down from above. Remembering the mountain, he knew that above the tunnel mouth it was almost one vast slide.

He could hear nothing, and the air was hot and close. On his knees he began to feel his way around, crawling until he reached the tunnel and the notched pole. Here he hesitated, wondering what the darkness below would hold.

Water, perhaps? Or even snakes? He had heard of snakes taking over old mines, and once, crawling down the ladder into an old shaft, he had seen an enormous rattler, the biggest he had ever seen, coiled about the ladder just below him. Nevertheless, he began to descend—down, down into the abysmal blackness below him. He seemed to have climbed down an interminable distance when suddenly his boot touched rock.

Standing upright, one hand on the pole, he reached out. His hand found rock on three sides, on the other, only empty space. He turned in that direction and ran smack into the rock wall, knocking sparks from his skull. He drew back, swearing, and found the tunnel. At the same time, his hand touched something else, a sort of ledge in the corner of the rock, and on the ledge—his heart gave a leap!

Candles!

Quickly, he got out a match and lit the first one. Then he walked into the tunnel. Here was more of the rose Quartz, and it was incredibly seamed with gold. Lee Martin had made a strike. Rather, studying the walls, he had found an old man, perhaps an old Spanish working, although work had been done here within the last few weeks. Suddenly Jim saw a pick and he grinned. There might yet be a way out. Yet a few minutes of exploration sufficed to indicate that there was no other opening. If he was to go out, it must be by the way he came.

Taking the candles with him he climbed the notched pole and stuck a lighted candle on a rock. Then, with a pick at his side, he started to work at the debris choking the tunnel. He lifted a rock and moved it aside, then another.

An hour later, soaked with sweat, he was still working away, pausing each minute or so to examine the hanging wall. The tunnel was cramped, and the work moved slowly ahead, for every stone removed had to be shoved back into the stope behind him. He reached the broken part overhead, and when he moved a rock, more slid down. He worked on, his breath coming in great gasps, sweat dripping from his face and neck to his hands.

A new sound came to him, a faint tapping. He held still, listening, trying to quiet his breathing and the pound of his heart. Then he heard it again, an unmistakable tapping!

Grasping his pick, he tapped three times, then an interval, then three times again. The he heard somebody pull at the rocks of the tunnel, and his heart pounded with exultation. He had been found!

How the following hours passed Sandifer never quite knew, but working feverishly, he fought his way through the border of time that divded him from the outer world and the clean, pine-scented air. Suddenly, a stone was moved and an arrow of light stabbed the darkness, and with it came the cool air he wanted. He took a deep breath, filling his lungs with air so liquid it might almost be water, and then he went to work, helping the hands outside to enlarge the opening. When there was room enough, he thrust his head and shoulders through and then pulled himself out and stood up, dusting himself off—and found he was facing, not Bill Katrishen or one of his sons, but Jay Mello!

"You?" he was astonished. "What brought you back?"

Jay wiped his thick hands on his jeans and looked uncomfortable.

"Never figured to bury no man alive," he said. "That was Martin's idea. Anyway, Katrishen told me what you done for Dan."

"Did he tell you I'd killed him? I'm sorry, Jay. It was him or me."

"Sure. I knowed that when he come after you. I didn't like it nohow. What I meant, well—you could've left him lie. You didn't need to go git help for him. I went huntin' Dan, when I found you was alive, an' I figured it was like that, that he was dead. Katrishen gave me his clothes, an' I found this—"

It was a note, scrawled painfully, perhaps on a rifle stock or a flat rock, written, no doubt, while Jim was gone for help.

> Jay:
>
> Git shet of Marten. Sandfer's all right. He's gone for hulp to Katrisshn. I'm hard hit. Sandfer shore is wite. So long, Jay, good ridin.
>
> Dan.

"I'm sorry, Jay. He was game."

"Sure." Jay Mello scowled. "It was Martin got us into this, him an' Klee Mont. We never done no killin' before, maybe stole a few hosses or run off a few head of cows."

"What's happened? How long was I in there?" Jim glanced at the sun.

"About five, six hours. She'll be dark soon." Mello hesitated, "I reckon I'm goin' to take out—light a shuck for Texas."

Sandifer thrust out his hand. "Good luck, Jay. Mabye we'll meet again."

The outlaw nodded. He stared at the ground, and then he looked up, his tough, unshaven face strangely lonely in the late-afternoon sun.

"Sure wish Dan was ridin' with me. We always rode together, him an' me, since we was kids." He rubbed a hard hand over his lips. "What d'you know? That girl back to Katrishen's? She put some flowers on his grave! Sure enough!"

He turned and walked to his horse, swung into the saddle, and walked his horse down the trail, a somber figure captured momentarily by the sunlight before he turned away under the pines. Incongruously, Jim noticed that the man's vest was split up the back, and the crown of his hat was torn.

The gray waited patiently by the brush, and then Jim Sandifer untied him and swung into the saddle. It was a fast ride he made back to the ranch on Iron Creek. There he swapped saddles, explaining all to Katrishen. "I'm riding," he said. "There's no room in this country for Lee Martin now."

"Want us to come?" Bill asked.

"No. They might think it was war. You stay out of it, for we want no Pleasant Valley War here. Leave it lay. I'll settle this."

He turned from the trail before he reached the B Bar, riding through the cottonwoods and sycamores along the creek. Then he rode up between the buildings and stopped beside the corral. The saddle leather creaked when he swung down, and he saw a slight movement at the corner of the corral.

"Klee? Is that you?" It was Art Dunn. "What's goin' on up at the house?"

Jim Sandifer took a long step forward. "No, Art," he said swiftly, "it's me!"

Dunn took a quick step back and grabbed for his gun, but Jim was already moving, expecting him to reach. Sandifer's left hand dropped to Art's wrist, and his right smashed up in a wicked uppercut to the solar plexus.

Dunn grunted and his knees sagged. Jim let go of his wrist then and hooked sharply to the chin, hearing Dunn's teeth click as the blow smashed home. Four times more Jim hit him, rocking his head on his shoulders; then he smashed another punch to the wind and grabbing Dunn's belt buckle, jerked his gun belt open.

The belt slipped down and Dunn staggered and went to his knees. The outlaw pawed wildly, trying to get at Jim, but he was still gasping for the wind that had been knocked out of him.

The bunkhouse door opened and Sparkman stepped into the light. "What's the matter?" he asked. "What goes on?"

Sandifer called softly, and Sparkman grunted and came down off the steps. "Jim! You here? There's the devil to pay up at the house, man! I don't know what came off up there, but there was a shootin'! When we tried to go up, Mont was on the steps with a shotgun to drive us back."

"Take care of this hombre. I'll find out what's wrong fast enough. Where's Grimes an' Rep?"

"Rep Dean rode over to the line cabin on Cabin Creek to round up some boys in case of trouble. Grimes is inside."

"Then take Dunn an' keep your eyes open! I may need help. If I yell, come loaded for bear an' huntin' hair!"

Jim Sandifer turned swiftly and started for the house. He walked rapidly, circling as he went toward the little-used front door, opened only on company occasions. That door, he knew, opened into a large, old-fashioned parlor that was rarely used. It was a showplace, stiff and uncomfortable, and mostly gilt and plush. The front door was usually locked, but he remembered that he had occasion to help move some furniture not long before and the door had been left unlocked. There was every chance that it still was, for the room was so little used as to be almost forgotten.

Easing up on the veranda, he tiptoed across to the door and gently turned the knob. The door opened inward, and he stepped swfitly through and closed it behind him. All was dark and silent, but there was light under the intervening door and a sound of movement. With the thick carpet muffling his footfalls, he worked his way across the room to the door.

"How's the old man?" Martin was asking.

His mother replied. "He's all right. He'll live."

Martin swore. "If that girl hadn't bumped me, I'd have killed him and we'd be better off. We could easy enough fix things so that Sandifer would get blamed for it."

"Don't be in such a hurry," Rose Martin intervened. "You're always in such a fret. The girl's here, an' we can use her to help. As long as we have her, the old man will listen, and while he's hurt, she'll do as she's told."

Martin muttered under his breath. "If we'd started by killing Sandifer like I wanted, all would be well," he said irritably. "What he said about the Katrishen trouble startin' with our comin' got the old man to thinkin. Then I figure Bowen was sorry he fired his foreman."

"No matter!" Rose Martin was brusque. "We've got this place, and we can handle the Katrishens ourselves. There's plenty of time now Sandifer's gone."

Steps sounded. "Lee, the old man's comin' out of it. He wants his daughter."

"Tell him to go climb a tree!" Martin replied stiffly. "You watch him!"

"Where's Art?" Klee protested. "I don't like it, Lee! He's been gone too long. Somethin's up!"

"Aw, forget it! Quit cryin'! You do more yelpin' than a mangy coyote!"

Sandifer stood very still, thinking. There was no sound of Elaine, so she must be a prisoner in her room. Turning, he tiptoed across the room toward the far side. A door there, beyond the old piano, opened into Elaine's room. Carefully, he tried the knob. It held.

At that very instant a door opened abruptly, and he saw light under the door before him. He heard a startled gasp from Elaine and Lee Martin's voice, taunting, familiar.

"What's the matter? Scared?" Martin laughed. "I just came in to see if you was all right. If you'd kept that pretty mouth of yours shut, your dad would still be all right! You tellin' him Sandifer was correct about the Katrishens an' that he shouldn't of fired him!"

"He shouldn't have," the girl said quietly. "If he was here now, he'd kill you. Get out of my room."

"Maybe I ain't ready to go?" he taunted. "An' from now on I'm goin' to come an' go as I like."

His steps advanced into the room, and Jim tightened his grip on the knob. He remembered that lock, and it was not set very securely. Suddenly, an idea came to him. Turning, he picked up an old glass lamp, large and ornate. Balancing it momentarily in his hand, he drew it back and hurled it with a long overhand swing through the window!

Glass crashed on the veranda, and there lamp hit, went down a step, and stayed there. Inside the girls' room, there was a startled exclamation, and he heard running footsteps from both the girl's room and the old man's. Somebody yelled, "What's that? What happened?" And he hurled his shoulder against the door.

As he had expected, the flimsy lock carried away and he was catapulted through the door into Elaine's bedroom. Catching himself, he wheeled like a cat and sprang for the door that opened into the living room beyond. He reached it just as Mont jerked the curtain back, but not wanting to endanger the girl, he swung hard with his fist instead of drawing his gun.

The blow came out of a clear sky to smash Mont on the jaw, and he staggered back into the room. Jim Sandifer sprang through, legs spread, hands wide.

"You, Martin!" he said sharply. "Draw!"

Lee Martin was a killer, but no gunman. White to the lips, his eyes deadly, he sprang behind his mother and grabbed for the shotgun.

"Shoot, Jim!" Elaine cried. "Shoot!"

He could not. Rose Martin stood between him and his target, and Martin had the shotgun now and was swinging it. Jim lunged, shoving the table over, and the lamp shattered in a crash. He fired and then fired again. Flame stabbed the darkness at him, and he fell back against the wall, switching his gun. Fire laced the darkness into a stabbing crimson crossfire, and the room thundered with sound and then died to stillness that was the stillness of death itself.

No sound remained, only the acrid smell of gunpowder mingled with the smell of coal oil and the faint, sickish-sweet smell of blood. His guns ready, Jim crouched in the darkness, alert for movement. Somebody groaned and then sighed deeply, and a spur grated on the floor. From the next room, Gray Bowen called weakly. "Daughter? Daughter, what's happened? What's wrong?"

There was no movement yet, but the darkness grew more familiar. Jim's eyes became more accustomed to it. He could see no one standing. Yet it was Elaine who broke the stillness.

"Jim? Jim, are you all right? Oh, Jim—are you safe?"

Maybe they were waiting for this.

"I'm all right," he said.

"Light your lamp, will you?" Deliberately, he moved, and there was no sound within the room—only outside, a running of feet on the hard-packed earth. Then a door slammed open, and Sparkman stood there, gun in hand.

"It's all right, I think," Sandifer said. "We shot it out."

Elaine entered the room with a light and caught herself with a gasp at the sight before her. Jim reached for the lamp.

"Go to your father," he said swiftly. "We'll take care of this."

Sparkman looked around, followed into the room by Grimes. "Good grief!" he gasped. "They are all dead! All of them!"

"The woman, too?" Sandifer's face paled. "I hope I didn't—"

"You didn't," Grimes said. "She was shot in the back by her own son. Shootin' in the dark, blind an' gun crazy."

"Maybe it's better," Sparkman said. "She was an old hellion."

Klee Mont had caught his right at the end of his eyebrow, and a second shot along the ribs. Sandifer walked away from him and stood over Lee Martin. His face twisted in a sneer, the dead man lay sprawled on the floor, literally shot to doll rags.

"You didn't miss many," Sparkman said grimly.

"I didn't figure to," Jim said. "I'll see the old man and then give you a hand."

"Forget it." Grimes looked up, his eyes faintly humorous. "You stay in there. An' don't spend all your time with the old man. We need a new setup on this here spread, an' with a new son-in-law who's a first-rate cattleman, Gray could set back an' relax!"

Sandifer stopped with his hand on the curtain. "Maybe you got something there," he said thoughtfully. "Maybe you have!"

"You can take my word for it," Elaine said, stepping into the door beside Jim. "He has! He surely has!"

AUTHOR'S NOTE

LIT A SHUCK FOR TEXAS

In the old days, when a man was going through the brush to another campfire or another cabin he lit a handful of cornshucks to light his way. So he "lit a shuck," which became the phrase used to say somebody was going or had gone.

And many times when a man went west they just wrote after his name "GTT," which meant "gone to Texas," which was as good as saying he'd gone completely out of the known world, that he had vanished into limbo, and many did disappear in just that way.

A lot of men were picking up and leaving. In fact, the expression "gone west" was one way of saying a man was dead, although a lot of those who went west did not die, and a lot of them did not go home, either. They just kept on lighting a shuck for somewhere else. The West was a wandering man's country. There was always something to be seen just around the bend or over the hill, and all a man had to do to get there was get onto the middle of a horse and keep looking between its ears.

Lit a Shuck for Texas

The Sandy Kid slid the roan down the steep bank into the draw and fast walked it over to where Jasper Wald sat his big iron-gray stallion. The Kid, who was nineteen and new to this range, pulled up a short distance from his boss. That gray stallion was mighty near as mean as Wald himself.

"Howdy, Boss! Look what I found back over in that rough country east of here."

Wald scowled at the rock the rider held out. "I ain't payin' yuh to hunt rocks," he declared. "You get back there in the breaks roundin' up strays like I'm payin' yuh for."

"I figgered yuh'd be interested. I reckon this here's gold."

"Gold?" Wald's laugh was sardonic, and he threw a contemptuous glance at the cowhand. "In this country? Yuh're a fool!"

The Sandy Kid shoved the rock back in his chaps pocket and swung his horse back toward the brush, considerably deflated. Maybe it was silly to think of finding gold here, but that rock sure enough looked it, and it was heavy. He reckoned he'd heard somewhere that gold was a mighty heavy metal.

When he was almost at the edge of the badlands, he saw a steer heading toward the thick brush, so he gave the roan a taste of the diggers and spiked his horse's tail after the steer. That old ladino could run like a deer, and it headed out for those high rocks like a tramp after a chuck wagon, but when it neared the rocks, the mossyhorn ducked and, head down, cut off at right angles, racing for the willows.

Beyond the willows was a thicket of brush, rock, and cactus that made riding precarious and roping almost suicidal, and once that steer got into the tangle beyond he was gone.

The Kid shook out a loop and hightailed it after the steer, but it was a shade far for good roping when he made his cast. Even at that, he'd have made it, but just as his rope snagged the steer, the roan's hoof went into a gopher hole, and the Sandy Kid sailed right off over the roan's ears.

As he hit the ground all in a lump, he caught a glimpse of the ladino. Wheeling around, head down with about four or five feet of horn, it started for him.

With a yelp, the Kid grabbed for his gun, but it was gone, so he made a frantic leap for a cleft in the ground. Even as he rolled into it, he felt the hot breath of the steer, or thought he did.

The steer went over the cleft, scuffling dust down on the cowboy. When the Kid looked around, he saw he was lying in a crack that was about three feet wide and at least thirty feet deep. He had landed on a ledge that all but closed off the crack for several feet.

Warily he eased his head over the edge and then jerked back with a gasp, for the steer was standing, red-eyed and mean, not over ten feet away and staring right at him.

Digging out the makings, the Kid rolled a cigarette. After all, why get cut up about it? The steer would go away after a while, and then it would be safe to come out. In the meantime it was mighty cool here and pleasant enough, what with the sound of falling water and all.

The thought of water reminded the Kid that he was thirsty. He studied the situation and decided that with care he could climb to the bottom without any danger. Once down where the water was, he could get a drink. He was not worried, for when he had looked about he had seen his horse, bridle reins trailing, standing not far away. The roan would stand forever that way.

His six-gun, which had been thrown from his holster when he fell, also lay up there on the grass. It was not over twenty feet from the rim of the crevice, and once it was in his hand, it would be a simple thing to knock off that steer. Getting the pistol was quite another thing. With that steer on the prod, it would be suicide to try.

When he reached the bottom of the crevice he peered around in the vague light. At noon, or close to that, it would be bright down here, but at any other time it would be thick with shadows. Kneeling by the thin trickle of water, the Kid drank his fill. Lifting his face from the water, he looked downstream and almost jumped out of his skin when he saw a grinning skull.

The Sandy Kid was no pilgrim. He had fought Apaches and Comanches, and twice he had been over the trail to Dodge. But seeing a skull grinning at him from a distance of only a few feet did nothing to make him feel comfortable and at ease.

"By grab, looks like I ain't the first to tumble into this place," he said. "That hombre must have broken a leg and starved to death."

Yet when he walked over and examined the skeleton, he could see he was wrong. The man had been shot through the head.

Gingerly, the Kid moved the skull. There was a hole on the other side, too, and a bullet flattened against the rock.

He was astonished.

"Well, now! Somebody shot this hombre while he laid here,' the Kid decided.

Squatting on his haunches, the Sandy Kid puffed his cigarette and studied the situation. Long experience in reading sign had made it easy for his eyes to see what should be seen. A few things he noticed now. This man, already wounded, had fallen or been pushed into the crack, and then a man with a gun had leaned over the edge above and shot him through the head!

There was a notch in his belt that must have been cut by a bullet, and one knee had been broken by a bullet, for the slug was still there, embedded in the joint.

The Kid was guessing about the notch, but from the

look of things and the way the man was doubled up, it looked like he had been hurt pretty bad aside from the knee.

The shirt was gone except for a few shreds, and among the rocky debris there were a few buttons, an old pocketknife, and some coins. The boots, dried and stiff, were not a horseman's boots, but the high-topped, flat-heeled type that miners wear. A rusted six-shooter lay a bit further downstream, and the Kid retrieved it. After a few minutes he determined that the gun was still fully loaded.

"Prob'ly never got a shot at the skunk," the Sandy Kid said thoughtfully. "Well, now! Ain't this a purty mess?"

When he studied the skeleton further, he noticed something under the ribs that he had passed over, thinking it a rock. Now he saw it was a small leather sack which the dead man had evidently carried inside his shirt. The leather was dry and stiff, and it ripped when he tried to open it. Within were several fragments of the same ore the Kid had himself found!

Tucking the samples and the remnants of the sack under a rocky ledge, the Kid stuck the rusty six-shooter in his belt and climbed back to the ledge, where a cautious look showed that the ladino was gone.

The roan pricked up its ears and whinnied, not at all astonished that this peculiar master of his should come crawling out of the ground. The Kid had lost his rope, which was probably still trailing from the steer's horns, but he was not thinking of that. He was thinking of the murdered man.

When he awakened the next morning he rolled over on his side and stared around the bunkhouse. Everyone was still asleep, and then he realized that it was Sunday.

Wald was nowhere around when the Kid headed for the cookshack. Smoke was rising slowly, for Cholly Cooper, the best cook on that range, was conscientious. When you wanted breakfast you got it, early or late. The Sandy Kid was glad that Wald was not around, for he had no love for his morose, quick-to-anger boss.

It was not a pleasant outfit to ride for, Cooper being the only friendly one in the bunch. Jasper Wald never spoke, except to give an order or to criticize in a dry, sarcastic voice. He was about forty, tough and hard-bitten. Rumor had it that he had killed more than one man. His two permanent hands were Jack Swarr, a burly Kansas man, always unshaven, and Dutch Schweitzer, a lean German who drank heavily.

"Hi, Sandy." Cholly waved a fork at him. "Set yoreself down and I'll get some coffee. Up early, ain't you?"

"Uh-huh." The Kid pulled the thick cup toward him. "Sort of reckoned I'd ride up to the Forks. Few things I need. Shirts and stuff."

Cholly dished out a couple of thick slabs of beef and four eggs. "Better eat," he said. "I wouldn't want yuh pourin' them shirts onto an empty stomach."

While Cholly refilled the Kid's cup, he said in a low voice, "What did you all do to the boss? He was shore riled up when he came in and saw yuh hadn't showed up with the rest of the hands."

"Reckon he was just sore. I tied in with an old mossyhorn up in the breaks and lost my rope. Durned steer had one horn, looked long enough for two steers, and a stub on the other end."

Cooper chuckled. "You ain't the first who lost a rope on Ol' Stob! You were lucky not to get killed."

"Rough country, over thataway," the Sandy Kid suggested. "Ever been over there?"

"No further'n the creek, and I don't aim to. Only one man ever knowed that country, unless it was the Apaches, and that was Jim Kurland. He always claimed there was gold over there, but most folks just laughed at him."

"Rancher?"

"No, sort of a prospector. He mined some, I guess, afore he came here. Dead now, I reckon. He headed off into that country about a year ago and nobody ever saw hide nor hair of him again. His wife, she died about three, four months ago, and his daughter works down to Wright's Store. She handles the post office in there, mostly."

Jim Kurland. It was a name to remember. The Sandy

Kid knew he was walking on dangerous ground. The killer of Kurland, if it was his skeleton the Kid had found, was probably still around, and any mention of Kurland's name might lead to trouble. It would be wise to proceed with caution.

The Sandy Kid was no hero. He had never toted a badge, and like most cowhands of his day, he looked upon the law as a nuisance originated mainly to keep riders from having a good time. He went his own way, and if someone made trouble for him, he figured to handle it himself. He would be ashamed to ask for help and figured all sheriffs were the same.

He was interested in gold. If there was a mine as rich as that ore seemed to indicate, he wanted it. Why, with a little gold a man could buy a spread of his own and stock it with those new whiteface cattle that carried so much more beef than a longhorn. A man could do right well with a little money to go on. . . .

When he rode into the Forks he headed right for the store. He was not planning on doing any drinking this day. It was Sunday, but Sim Wright kept his store open seven days a week the year 'round. The Sandy Kid, who was a lean six feet and with a shock of sandy hair and mild gray eyes, swung down from the roan and crossed the boardwalk to the store.

At first he thought it was empty. Then he saw the girl who stood behind the counter, her eyes on him.

He jerked his hat from his head and went toward her. "Ma'am," he said, "I better get me a couple of shirts. Yuh got anything with checks in it?"

"Big checks?" She smiled at him.

"Uh-huh, that's right."

She shoved him the shirts, one of them with black and white checks as big as those on a checkerboard.

He fingered them thoughtfully. Then he said, "Ma'am, is yore name Kurland?"

"That's my last name. My first name is Betty."

"Mine's Sandy," he told her. "They call me the Sandy Kid."

He hesitated and then slid a hand into his pocket and took out the pocketknife and laid it on the shirts.

Her face went white as she caught it up. She looked at the Kid. "Where did you get this?"

Slowly, carefully, he told her. As he talked, she stared at him with wide eyes. "You think," she asked when he had finished, "that he was murdered? But why?"

"He had gold samples, ma'am. Folks will do a powerful lot for gold. I would, myself. I sort of figured I'd keep quiet about this, and sort of hunt that claim myself, and when I found it, I'd stake her out. Then I heard about you, an' I figgered yuh'd like to know about yore pappy and have him buried proper."

"Who killed him?"

"That I don't know. I reckon if a body was to try, he could find out, but you'd have to keep still about findin' him for a while."

"If I keep still, will you find the murderer? If you do, I'll give you that claim."

"No, ma'am, I couldn't take yore claim. Menfolks in my family wasn't raised no such way. But I don't have a particle of use for a coyote that would murder a man like that, so if yuh want, I'll have a look around in my spare time."

Her eyes were large and dark. It was nice looking into them. The Sandy Kid reckoned he had never looked into eyes that were like hers. And her lips—she had right nice lips. Not too full and not thin, either. He liked that. Her neck was sure white— She was smiling at him, amused.

He flushed a deep red. "Reckon yuh must think I never saw a girl before," he said. "Well, I reckon mebbe I never did really look at one. Somehow, they never sort of called themselves to mind."

"Thank you, Sandy."

All the way back to the ranch he was thinking how nice that name sounded from her lips.

The Bar W lay like an ugly sore in the bottom of the flat. There were three adjoining pole corrals, an unpainted frame bunkhouse, and a ranch house of adobe. The cookshack was also adobe, and there was smoke coming from the chimney when he rode in with his shirts.

It was still quite early, for the ranch was only a short

piece from town. He unsaddled the roan and walked back toward the cookshack for coffee. They were all there. Nobody said anything when he came in, but Cholly threw him a warning glance. The Kid got a cup and filled it with coffee. Then he sat down.

"What happened to yuh last night?" Wald demanded, glaring at him across the table.

"Me? I had me a run-in with that Old Stob horned ladino. Lost my rope."

"You still got that rock?"

"That?" The Sandy Kid shrugged carelessly. "No. I throwed it away. Reckon it was just iron pyrites or somethin'."

Nothing more was said, but he felt uncomfortable. He had found Jasper Wald an unpleasant man to work for, and the sooner he got himself another job the better off he would be. There was something in Wald's baleful glance that disturbed him.

"In the mornin'," Wald said after a few minutes, "you work that Thumb Butte country."

The Kid nodded, but made no comment. The Thumb Butte area was six miles across the valley from the badlands where he'd had the run-in with Old Stob, that red-eyed mossyhorn. Was it accident or design that had caused Wald to send him to the other side of the ranch?

Yet the next day he realized that his new working ground had advantages of its own. He worked hard all morning and rounded up and turned into a mountain corral forty head of cattle that he had combed out of the piñons.

Switching his saddle to a bay pony, he took off into the draws that led south and west, away from the ranch. An hour's riding brought him to the Argo trail, and he cantered along to the little town at Argo Springs. Here was the only land office within two hundred miles or more where a mining claim could be registered.

A quick check of the books, offered him by an obliging justice of the peace who also served in five or six other capacities, showed him that no mining claim had been located in the vicinity of the badlands. Hence, if the killer of Jim Kurland had found the claim, he was working it on the sly. He did some further checking, but the discovery he made was by accident. It came out of a blue sky when Pete Mallinger, at the Wells Fargo office, noticed his brand.

"Bar W, eh? You bring one of them boxes over here? The ones Wald's been shippin' to El Paso?"

"Me? No, I just rode over to get myself some smokin'." He grinned confidentially. "The boss doesn't even know I'm gone."

"I wouldn't let him ketch yuh. He's a tough one, that Jasper Wald is. Throw a gun on a man soon's look at him. Got money, too, he has. He's buyin' up most of that Agua Dulce Canyon country."

The Sandy Kid rolled a smoke and listened, his eyes sweeping the narrow street with its hitching rails and clapboarded buildings. Jasper Wald was not making enough on the Bar W to buy any land, not even with all his free-and-easy branding operations. Nothing you could really complain about, but nevertheless the Bar W brand was showing up on almost everything on the range that came within sight of a Bar W hand.

Before he left, the Kid managed to get his hands on the address in El Paso. The boxes were being shipped to Henry Wald, a brother of Jasper, and they were notably heavy.

The Sandy Kid strolled thoughtfully away from the door of the Wells Fargo office and crossed the dusty street to the saloon. He might as well have a drink while he was here. He pushed through the swinging doors into the bare, untidy barroom. Dutch Schweitzer was leaning an below on the bar, staring at him.

"Howdy." The Sandy Kid strolled up to the bar and ordered a drink. "Looks like we've both strayed on the same mornin'."

Dutch looked at him with sullen eyes, "No, I'm on the job. The boss sent me over here. He didn't send you."

"Shore he didn't. I rounded up enough stock for a full day in that country where I'm workin'. It's dry work, so I ambled over for a drink."

"At the Wells Fargo office?"

The Kid shrugged. He picked up his glass and tossed

off his drink. "I'm on my way back," he said and turned to go. Schweitzer's voice halted him.

"Wait."

The Sandy Kid turned. Suddenly, he felt cold. He had never met a man in a gun battle, but there was cold deadliness in the big German's eyes. The Kid stood with his feet apart a little, and his mouth felt dry. He felt sure Dutch meant to kill him.

Schweitzer had been drinking but was not drunk. The man had an enormous capacity for liquor, yet he rarely drank to the point where he was unsteady or loose talking. Only, when he drank he grew mean and cruel.

"You're a smart kid. Too blamed smart," he said meaningly.

Two men in the back of the room got up and eased out through the rear door. The Sandy Kid could see that the bartender was obviously frightened.

Curiously, the Kid was not. He watched Dutch carefully, aware that the man was spoiling for trouble, that he had a fierce, driving urge for brutality. Some inner canker gnawed at him, some bitter hatred that he seemed to nurse for everything and everybody. The Sandy Kid knew it was not personal animosity. It was simply that in these moods Dutch Schweitzer was a killer, and only the tiniest spark was needed to touch him off.

In that mental clarity that comes in moments of great stress, the kid found himself aware of many things—a wet ring on the bar where his glass had stood, the half-empty bottle near Schweitzer, the two empty tables in the back of the room. He saw the sickly pallor on the bartender's flabby face and the yellow hairs on the backs of Schweitzer's hands.

"You stick your nose into trouble." Schweitzer lifted the bottle with his left hand to pour a drink. Then his face suddenly twisted with blind, bitter fury, and he jerked the bottle up to throw it at the Kid.

Afterward, the Kid could never remember any impulse or feeling. He simply drew and fired without any thought or plan, and he fired at the bottle.

It exploded in a shower of glass and drenched

Schweitzer with whiskey. He sprang back, amazed, and when he looked up at the Kid he was cold sober.

Slowly, his eyes wide and his face pale, Schweitzer lifted his hands in a gesture of surrender. "I ain't drawin'," he said, astonishment making his voice thick. "I ain't makin' a move."

"See that yuh don't!" The Sandy Kid said flatly. He glared at the bartender and then backed through the swinging doors and holstered his gun. With a wary eye on the saloon, he crossed to his horse, mounted, and rode out of town.

He moved in a sort of daze. He was no gunfighter and had never fancied himself as such. He was only a drifting cowhand who dreamed of someday owning his own spread. He had never found any occasion for split-second drawing, although he had practiced, of course.

He had been wearing a six-gun for years, and he practiced throwing it hour after hour, but more to ease the monotony of long nights on night guard than from any desire for skill. It had been something to do, like riffling cards, playing solitaire, or juggling stones.

Like all Texas men of his time he had done his share of fighting and he had done a lot of shooting. He knew he was a good shot and that he nearly always got what he went after, but shooting as quickly and accurately as he had done in the saloon had never been considered.

Out of town, he did not ride away. When Dutch Schweitzer returned he would tell Jasper Wald what had happened. There would be trouble then, the Kid knew, and the least he could expect would be to be fired. Yet there was something he would do before he left town. Riding around the town in the juniper-clad hills, he dismounted and seated himself for a long wait.

He saw Dutch ride out a short time later. He saw the streets become less peopled, and he saw the sun go down. When it was dark, he moved down to the Wells Fargo office. When Dutch left he had been driving a buckboard, and that meant something to the Kid.

Using his knife, he cut away the putty around a pane

of glass and then reached through and unfastened the window. Raising it, he crawled in.

For an instant he stood still, listening. There was no sound, so he struck a match and shielding it in his hands, looked around for the box. He identified it quickly enough by the address. It was not large but was strongly built. With a hammer he found lying on a shelf, he pried up one of the top boards. He struck another match and peered into the box. Inside, wrapped in sacking, was a lot of the same ore he had found in the leather bag under the skeleton of Jim Kurland!

He blew out the match and then pushed the board back in place, hitting it a couple of light taps with the hammer. Then he went out, closed the window, and replaced the pane of glass, using some slivers of wood to hold the pane in place.

Jasper Wald, then, had killed Jim Kurland and found the claim. Or perhaps he had found the claim first. The ore was extremely rich, and he was shipping it, a very little at a time, to El Paso, where his brother was probably having it milled.

A slow process, certainly, but it was high-grade ore, and no doubt Wald had made plans to file on the claim when there would be no danger of Kurland's disappearance being linked with the proceedings. Everyone from the Forks to the Stone Tree Desert and Agua Dulce Canyon knew Kurland was the only mining man around and also that he regularly penetrated the badlands of the Stone Tree.

The Sandy Kid took to the trail and put the roan to a fast trot. He was foolish, he told himself, to be mixing into something that was no concern of his. It would have been wiser to forget what he had seen after he came out of that crack in the mountain. Even now, he reflected, it was not too late to travel to some far-off place like the Blue Mountains or maybe that Grand Canyon country of Arizona, which he had never seen but had heard cowhands lying about.

Little as he knew about gold, he could tell that the ore he had seen was fabulously rich, for the rock had been lined and threaded with it, and being so heavy, it had to be rich ore. Such a boxful as he had seen in the express office might be worth two or three thousand dollars.

Now that he thought about it, he had an idea where that claim was located. Not more than a half mile from where he had jumped into the crack to escape the steer, the plateau broke sharply off in a sheer cliff, some fifty or sixty feet high, that overhung the waterless, treeless waste of Stone Tree Desert and could even open upon the desert itself. That rupture, obviously the result of volcanic disturbance, could have exposed the vein from which the ore had come.

Pure speculation, of course, but the Sandy Kid had an idea he was nosing along the right trail. Also, he was aware that his interest did not arise from chivalry. He was not going into this to help a lady in distress. Trouble with Jasper Wald and his two hard-bitten henchmen was not lightly to be invited, and if he did go into it knowing what he was facing, it was only partly because of the way Betty Kurland had looked at him that he was following through.

It was a fool thing, he told himself. He had no particular urge to get money. Much as he'd like a ranch, he didn't want to have his head shot off getting it. He admitted to himself that if it had not been for Betty, he would never have gone all the way into this fight.

"The devil with it!" he said viciously. "I'll go back to the Bar W an' roll my soogan an' hit the trail!"

But when he came to the last forks, he kept on toward the mountains. He circled when he hit the willows and let the pony take its own gait. He was just edging out toward the cliff edge where he could see over into the Stone Tree when a rifle bullet hit the fork of his saddle with a wicked thwack, and then the bullet whined off ahead of him. It was a wonder it hadn't glanced back into his stomach or hit the pony's head.

The echo of the report drifted over him as he hit the ground running, and he grabbed the bridle and swung the bay pony back into the brush. Then he slid his Winchester .44 out of the saddle scabbard and Injun crawled toward the cliff edge.

That shot meant that somebody wasn't fooling, so the

Kid wasn't planning on fun himself. He was some shakes with a Winchester, and when he got to cover where he could see out, he looked around, trying to locate the spot the varmint had shot from. There was nobody in sight.

The Sandy Kid was not a trusting soul. His past dealings with Comanches had not been calculated to inspire any confidence in the serene and untrammeled appearance of woods or mountains. So after a long look, he left the bay pony tethered to a bush and crawled to the very lip of the cliff. When he glanced over, he could see something that looked like a pile of waste and rock taken from a mine tunnel, but he wasn't looking for that. All in good time he could have an interest in the gold.

Then, in the rocks further along the rim of the cliff, he detected a slight movement. He looked again, widening and then squinting his eyes. It looked like a boot heel. Not much of a mark at that distance, and not much damage could be done if he hit it.

"We'll scare the daylights out of yuh, anyway!" he said, and lifting the Winchester, he nestled his cheek affectionately against the stock and squeezed off a shot.

Dust obscured the spot for a moment, but no dust could blot out the startled yell he heard. Somebody lunged into view then, and the Sandy Kid's jaw dropped. It was Betty Kurland! She was wearing a man's trousers and a man's shirt and limping with one boot heel gone, but that hair could belong to nobody else!

He got up, waving his arms, and ran out to meet her. She turned on him, and her own rifle was coming hip high when she got a better look and recognized him. She came on a couple of steps and then stopped, her eyes flashing with indignation.

"I thought you were my friend!" she flared at him. "Then you shoot at me!"

"You shot at me!" he declared. "How was I to know?"

"That's different!"

Such feminine logic was so amazing that he gulped and swallowed. "Yuh shouldn't have come out here," he protested. 'It isn't safe!"

"I wanted to find my father," she said. "Where is he?"

He led her to the lip of the cliff, and they found a way down. The Kid wanted a look at that desert, first. They came around in full sight of the mine tunnel and were just in time to see a man climbing out of a hole.

"I'll go get what's left of Kurland," they heard the man say. "They'll never find him here!"

The Sandy Kid was cursing softly, for he had been so preoccupied with the girl that he had walked around unthinking and now found himself looking into a gun held by Jasper Wald. The rancher had seen him, even if Jack Swarr, climbing from the freshly dug grave, had not.

"Well, now!" Wald said. "If this ain't nice! You and that girl walkin' right up on us!"

"Don't you try nothin'," the Kid said. "This girl is known to be here. If she doesn't show up you'll have the law around."

Wald chuckled. "No, we won't. Not for long, anyway. I'll just tell them this Kurland girl showed up to meet you, and you two took off to get married, over to Lordsburg or somewheres. They'll figger yuh eloped and never even think of lookin' for yuh!"

Swarr grinned. "Hey, that's a good idea, Boss! An' we can pile 'em in the same hole with her pa!"

"If I were you," the Sandy Kid said, "I'd guess again. I just come from Argo Springs. I know all about that gold ore you've been shippin' to El Paso, and I ain't the only one."

Jasper Wald hesitated. His idea for getting rid of the two had been a sudden inspiration and a good one, but the thought that the Kid might have mentioned the gold to someone in Argo Springs disturbed him. It would mean he would have to move slowly, or worse, that he was already suspected.

Suddenly there was a clatter of stones, and they looked up. Only Wald, who held the gun on the Kid did not shift his eyes. The newcomer was Dutch Schweitzer.

"Watch that hombre, Boss!" the German said hoarsely. "He's gun slick!"

"Him?" Swarr was incredulous. "That kid?"

"How old was Bill Bonney?" Dutch asked sarcastically. "He flashed a gun on me today so fast I never even saw his hand move!"

Angered and worried, Jasper Wald stared at the Kid. Quickly, Swarr explained.

"Aw, Boss," Dutch said, "he's lyin'. I nosed around town after he left. After he left me, I mean. He never talked to nobody."

"How did I find out about the gold in that box yuh brought in? Addressed to Henry Wald, in El Paso?" The Kid asked him.

"He must have seen the box," Dutch protested.

The Sandy Kid's mind was running desperately ahead, trying to find a way out. "Also" he added, "I checked on this claim. You never filed on it, so I did."

"What?" Wald's shout was a bellow of fury. His face went dark with blood. "You filed on this claim? Why, you—" Rage drove all caution from his mind. "I'll shoot yuh, blast yuh, and let yuh die right out in the sun! You—"

"Boss!" Swarr shouted. "Hold it! Mebbe he's lyin'! Mebbe he didn't file! Anyway," he added craftily, "why kill him until he signs the claim over to us?"

Wald's rage died. He glanced at Swarr. "You're right," he said. "We can get possession that way."

The Sandy Kid chuckled. "You'll have no cinch gettin' me to sign anything."

"It'll be easy," Wald said sharply. "We'll just start by tyin' up that girl and takin' her boots off. By the time she gets a litle fire on her feet, yuh'll sign!"

Dutch Schweitzer glanced at his chief. Then he helped Jack Swarr tie the girl. Swarr knelt and pulled off her boots. He drew deeply on his cigarette and thrust it toward her foot.

Dutch stared at them, his eyes suddenly hardening. "None of that!" he said. "I thought yuh were bluffin'! Cut it out!"

"Bluffin'?" Swarr looked up. "I'll show yuh if I'm bluffin'!" He jammed the cigarette forward, and Betty screamed.

Dutch Schweitzer's face went pale, and with an oath,

he grabbed for a gun. At the same time, Jasper Wald swung his gun toward the German. That was all the break the Sandy Kid needed. His right hand streaked for his gun butt, and he was shooting with the first roar from Wald's gun.

The Kid's first shot took Jack Swarr in the stomach as the big man lunged upward, clawing for his pistol. Dutch had a gun out and was firing. The Kid saw his body jerk with the impact of Wald's bullet, and he swung his own gun. Wald faced him at the same instant.

For one unbelieving instant, the Sandy Kid looked over the stabbing flame of his own Colt into the flaring muzzle of Wald's six-shooter. He triggered his gun fast at almost point-blank range.

He swayed on his feet, his legs spread wide, and saw Jasper Wald's cruel face turn white before his eyes. The rancher's knees sagged, and he went to the ground, glaring bitterly at the Sandy Kid. He tried then to lift his gun, but the Kid sprang forward and knocked it from his grasp. Wald slumped over on the sand, his face contorted.

Swarr, the Kid saw at a glance, was dead. Yet it had not been only his bullet, for the German must have got in at least one shot. Swarr's face and head were bloody.

Schweitzer lay on his back, his face upturned to the sun. The Sandy Kid knelt beside him, but a glance told him there was nothing he or anyone could do.

Dutch stared at him. "Never was no hand to abuse women," he said, "never—no hand."

The Sandy Kid turned to Betty Kurland, who stood staring down at Dutch. "He was a strange man," she said.

"Let's get out of here," the Kid said. Taking her by the hand, he led her toward the path down which Schweitzer had come.

On the cliff top, they stood for a moment together. Betty's face was white now, and her eyes seemed unusually large and dark. He noticed then that she hadn't limped.

"Was yore foot burned badly?" he asked. "I didn't think to help yuh."

"It wasn't burned at all!" she told him. "I jerked my foot back as he thrust the cigarette at it."

"But you screamed?" he protested.

"Yes, I know," she said, looking at him. "You had to have your chance to draw, and they hadn't taken away your guns. And I knew about Dutch Schweitzer."

"Knew about him? What?"

"The Apaches killed his wife. They burned her. I thought, maybe— That was why he drank so much, I guess."

When they were on the trail toward the Forks, he looked at her and then glanced quickly away. "Well, yuh've got yore claim," he said. "All yuh've got to do is stake it out and file on it. I never did. Yuh found yore pa, too. Looks like yuh're all set. I reckon I'll hug the rawhide and head out of the country. A loose horse is always huntin' new pastures!"

"I'll need a good man to ramrod that mine for me!" she protested. "Wouldn't you do that? I promised you half, too!"

"Ma'am"—the Sandy Kid was growing red around the gills and desperate, for she was sure enough a pretty girl—"I reckon I never was made to stay no place. I'm packin' my duffle and takin' the trail out of here. If anybody comes around askin' for the Sandy Kid, you tell 'em he lit a shuck and went to Texas!"

He turned his horse at the forks of the road and headed for the Bar W. His own horse was there, and since Wald wouldn't be needing this bay pony, he might need him out West there, Arizona way. He sure did aim to see that Grand Canyon down which flowed the Colorado. A mile deep, they said. Of course, that was a durned lie, but she might be pretty deep, at that.

Once, he glanced back over his shoulder. The girl was only a dim figure on the skyline.

"First thing we know," he said to the bay pony, "she'd have me a-settin' in church a-wearin' a fried shirt. I'd shore be halter broke."

The bay pony switched his tail and picked up its feet in an Injun trot, and the Sandy Kid broke into song, a gritty baritone that made the bay lay back its ears.

Oh, there was a young cowhand who used to go
riding,

There was a young cowhand named Johnny
Go-day!
He rode a black pony an' never was lonely,
For a girl never said to him, "Johnny, go 'way!"

AUTHOR'S NOTE

THE NESTER AND THE PIUTE

Value has a lot to do with time and location. There's been many a man who would give his shirt for a good cup of coffee, so if you steal something from a man you'd better have some idea of the value he sets on it.

A man gets things set in his mind. When he's got his teeth ready for hot biscuits and sourwood honey, you take it from him at some risk.

The Nester and the Piute

He was ridin' loose in the saddle when we first saw him, and he was wearing a gun, which was some unusual for the Springs these days. Out on the range where a man might have a run-in with a locoed steer or maybe a rattler, most of the boys carried guns, but around town Sheriff Todd had sort of set up a rulin' against it.

It was the second time I'd seen him, but he looked some different this mornin', and it took me a minute or two to decide what it was made the difference, and then I decided it was partly the gun and partly that look in his eyes.

He reined in that yellow horse in front of Green's and hooked one long leg around the saddle horn.

"Howdy."

"Howdy." Hatcher was the only one who anwered, only the rest of us sort of looked up at him. He dug in his shirtpocket for the makin's and started to build a smoke.

Nobody said anything, just sort of waitin' to see what was on his mind. He had an old carbine in a saddle scabbard, and the scabbard wasn't under his leg, but with the muzzle pointed down and the stock close to his hand. A man ridin' thataway ain't rightly figurin' on usin' a rope on no stock. That rifle would be in the way, but if he was figurin' on needin' a rifle right quick, it would be a plumb handy way to carry it.

When he had his smoke built he lit it with his left hand, and I got a good glimpse of his eyes, kind of cold and gray, and them lookin' us over.

Nobody here was friendly to him, yet nobody was unfriendly, neither. All of us had been around the Springs for years, all but him. He was the nester from Squaw Rock, an' nesters aren't right popular around cow range. However, the times was a changin' an' we all knowed it, so it wasn't like it might have been a few years before, when the country was new.

"Seen a tall-like hombre on a black horse?"

He asked the question like maybe it was a formality that he wanted to get over with, and not like he expected an answer.

"What sort of man?"

It was Hatcher who had started the talkin', as if he was ridin' point for the rest of us.

"Maybe two hundred pounds, sort of limp in his right leg, maybe. Rides him a black horse, long-gaited crittur, and he wears two guns, hangin' low."

"Where'd you see him?"

"Ain't never seed him. I seen his sign."

Yanell, who lived over nigh to Squaw Rock himself, looked up from under his hat brim and spat into the dust. What he was thinkin' we was all thinkin'. If this nester read sign that well and trailed the Piute clean from Squaw Rock, he was no pilgrim.

That description fitted the Piute like a glove, and nobody amongst us had any love for the Piute. He'd been livin' in the hills over toward White Hills for the last six years, ever since he come back to the country after his trouble. The Piute had done a bit of horse stealin' and rustlin' from time to time and we all knowed it, but none of us were right anxious to trail him down.

Not that we were afraid. Only, none of us had ever caught him in the act, so we just left it up to Sheriff Todd, who wanted it that way. This here nester seemed to have some ideas of his own.

"No," Hatcher said, "I ain't seen nobody like that. Not lately."

The nester—his name was Bin Morley—nodded like he'd expected nothin' else. "Reckon I'll ride along," he said. "Be seein' you!"

He swung his leg back over the saddle and kicked his toe into a stirrup. The yellow horse started to walk like it was a signal for something, and we sat there watchin' him fade out down toward the cottonwoods at the end of the town.

Hatcher bit off a hunk of chewing and rolled it in his jaws. "If he meets up with the Piute," he said, "he's askin' for trouble."

Yanell spat into the dust. "Reckon he'll handle it," he said drily. "Somethin' tells me the Piute rustled cows off the wrong hombre."

"Wonder what Sheriff Todd'll say?" Hatcher wanted to know.

"This here Morley, now," Yanell said, "he sort of looks like a man who could do his own lawin'. He's one of them hombres what ain't felt the civilizin' influences of Sheriff Todd's star, nor he ain't likely to!"

The nester's yellow horse ambled casually out over the trail toward White Hills. From time to time Bin Morley paused to study the trail, but from here it was much easier. He knew the look of the big black's track now, and from what was said later, I reckon the Piute wasn't really expectin' no trouble. Me, I was plumb curious. My pappy always did tell me my bump of curiosity was too big for my britches, but after a few minutes I got up off the porch and walked around to where my steeldust was standin' three legged in the dust. I throwed a leg over him and trailed out after the nester.

Maybe I'd been listenin' too much to the old-timers around tellin' of cattle drives and Injun fightin'. You listen to the stories a mite and you get to honin' to see some of them fracases yourself.

Now I knowed the Piute. Actually, he was only part Piute, and the rest was some brand of white, but whatever it was, the combination had resulted in pure-D poison. That was one reason everybody was plenty willin' to accept Sheriff Todd's orders to leave law enforcement to him. I will say, he done a good job. He done a good job until it come to the Piute.

It was understandable about the Piute. That Injun left no more trail than a snake goin' over a flat rock, and no matter how much we suspected, nobody could ever get any evidence on him. Sheriff Todd had been on his trail a dozen times, but each time he lost it. I knew what Yanell was thinkin' just as well as if it was me. Anybody who could trail the Piute plumb from Squaw Creek wasn't likely to holler calf rope for any Injun rustler without smokin' things up a mite.

Me, I was just curious enough and ornery enough to want to see what would happen when this nester cornered the Piute.

He was a big, sullen brute, the Piute was. Rumor had it he'd killed a half dozen men, and certainly there was several that started out huntin' him that never showed up until somebody found 'em dead, but there'd never been evidence to prove a thing. He could sling a gun, and when we had the turkey shoot around about Thanksgiving, he used to fetch his guns down, and nine times out of ten, he got himself a turkey—and he used a six-gun. You take a man that moves around over the hills like a ghost, Injun footin' it over the rocks an' through the brush, and who shoots like that, and you get an idea why nobody was just too worried about gettin' him in a corner.

Six miles out I got a glimpse of the nester. The yellow horse was amblin' along, takin' it easy in a sort of loose-jointed trot that didn't look like much but seemed to eat up the country right fast.

The day wore on and I kept to the brush, not knowing how Morley would take it if he knew I was trailin' him. Then all of a sudden I saw him swing the yellow horse off the trail and drop to the ground. He was there for a minute, and ridin' closer, I could see he was bendin' over the body of a man. Then he swung back into the saddle and moseyed off down the trail.

When he went over the next rise I turned my horse down the hill. Even before I rode up, I knew who the dead man was. I could see his horse lying in the cactus off to one side, and only one man in that country rode a bay with a white splash on the shoulder. It was Sheriff Todd.

There was a sign around, but I didn't need more than a glance at it to tell me what had happened. Sheriff Todd had run into the Piute unexpectedlike and caught him flat-footed with stolen stock, the first time he had ever had that chance. Only from the look of it, Todd had been caught flat-footed himself. His gun was out, but unfired, and he had been shot twice in the stomach.

Lookin' down at that body, I felt something change inside me. I knowed right then, no matter how the nester come out, I was goin' to foller on my own hook. For Sheriff Todd was still alive when he hit the ground, and that Piute had bent over him, put a pistol to the side of his head, and blowed half his head off! There were powder burns around that hole in his temple where the bullet went in. It had been cold-blooded murder.

Swinging a leg over that gelding, I was startin' off when I happened to think of a gun, and turned back and recovered the one Sheriff Todd had worn. I also got his saddle gun out of the scabbard and started off, trailin' the nester.

From now on the sign was bad. The Piute knowed he was up against it now. He was takin' time to blot his tracks, and if it hadn't been for Morley, I'd never have trailed him half as far as I did.

We hadn't gone more than a few miles further before I saw something that turned me plumb cold inside. The Piute had turned off at the Big Joshua and was headin' down the trail toward Rice Flats!

That scared me, because Rice Flats was where my girl lived down there in a cabin with her kid brother and her ma, and they had lived there alone ever since her dad fell asleep and tumbled off his spring wagon into the canyon. The Piute had been nosin' around the flats long enough to scare Julie some, but I reckon it was the sheriff who had kept him away.

Now Sheriff Todd was gone, and the Piute knowed he was on the dodge from here on. He would know that killin' Sheriff Todd was the last straw, and he'd have to get clean out of the country. Knowin' that, he'd know he might's well get hung for one thing as another.

As my gelding was a right fast horse, I started him movin' then. I jacked a shell into the chamber of the sheriff's carbine and I wasn't thinkin' much about the nester. Yet by the time I got to the cabin on the flats, I knowed I was too late.

My steel-dust came into the yard at a dead run and I hit the dust and went for that house like a saddle tramp for a chuck wagon. I busted inside and took a quick look around. Ma Frank was lyin' on the bed with a big gash in her scalp, but she was conscious.

"Don't mind me!" she said. "Go after that Injun! He has taken out with Julie on her black!"

"What about you?" I asked, although goodness knows I was wantin' nothin' more than to be out and after Julie.

" 'Brose'll be back right soon. He rid over to Elmer's after some side meat."

'Brose was short for Ambrose, her fourteen-year-old boy, so knowin' he'd be back, I swung a leg over that saddle and headed out for the hills. My steel-dust knowed somethin' was in the wind and he hustled his hocks for those hills like he was headin' home from a trail drive.

The Piute had Julie and he was a killin' man, a killin' man who knowed he was up the crick without a paddle now, and if he was got alive he'd be rope meat for sure. No man ever bothered a woman or killed a man as well liked in that country as Sheriff Todd without ridin' under a cottonwood limb. Me, I'm a plumb peaceable sort of hand, but when I seen the sheriff back there I got my dander up. Now that Piute had stole my girl, I was a wild man.

Ever see that country out toward the White Hills? God must have been cleanin' up the last details of the job when He made that country, and just dumped a lot of the slag and wastin's down in a lot of careless heaps. Ninety percent of that country stands on end, and what doesn't stand on end is dryer than a salt desert and hotter than a bronc on a hot rock.

The Piute knowed every inch of it, and he was showin' us all he knowed. We went down across a sunbaked flat where weird dust devils danced like crazy in a world where there was nothin' but heat and dust and misery for man and beast. No cactus there, not even salt grass or yeso. Nothin' growed there, and the little winds that stirred along the dusty levels made you think of snakes glidin' along the ground.

My gelding slowed to a walk an' we plodded on, and somewhere miles ahead, beyond the wall of sun dancin' heat waves, there was a column of dust, a thin, smoky trail where the nester rode ahead of me. Right then, I began to have a sight of respect for that long-legged yellow horse he was ridin' because he kept on goin' an' even gained ground on my steel-dust.

Finally we got out of that hell's valley and took a trail along the rusty edge of some broken rock, windin' higher toward some sawtooth ridges that gnawed at the sky like starvin' coyotes in a dry season. That trail hung like an eyebrow to the face of the cliff we skirted, an' twice, away up ahead, I heard shots. I knowed they was shots from the Piute, because I'd seen that carbine the nester carried. It was a Spencer .56.

Never seen one? Mister, all they lack is wheels! A caliber .56 with a bore like a cannon, and, them shootin' soft nosed lead bullets. What they do to a man ain't pretty, like you'll know. I knowed well enough it wasn't the nester shootin' because when you unlimber a Spencer .56 she has a bellow like a mad bull in a rock canyon.

Sundown came and then the night, an' little breezes picked up and blew cool and pleasant down from the hills. Stop? There was no time for stoppin'. I knew my gelding would stand anything the Piute's horse would, and I knowed by the shootin' that the Piute knowed the nester was on his trail. He wasn't goin' to get nary a chance to cool his heels with that nester tailin' him down them draws and across the bunch-grass levels.

The Piute? I wasn't worried so much about Julie now. He might kill her, but that I doubted as long as he had a prayer of gettin' away with her. He was goin' to have to keep movin' or shoot it out.

The longer I rode, the more respect I got for Bin Morley. He stuck to that Piute's trail like a cocklebur to a sheep, and that yellow horse of his just kept his head down and kept moseyin' along those trails like he was born to 'em, and he probably was.

The stars come out and then the moon lifted, and they kept on goin'. My steel-dust was beginnin' to drag his heels, and so I knowed the end was comin'. At that, it was most mornin' before it did come.

How far we'd come or where we were I had no idea. All I knew was that up ahead of me was the Piute with my girl, and I wanted a shot at him. Nobody needed to tell me I was no hand to tie in a gun battle with the Piute with him holdin' a six-gun. He was too slick a hand for me.

Then all of a sudden as the sky was turnin' gray and the hills were losin' their shadows, I rounded a clump of cottonwoods and there was that yellow horse, standin' three footed, croppin' absently at the first green grass in miles.

The nester was nowhere in sight, but I swung down and with the carbine in hand, started down through the trees, catfootin' in along with no idea what I might see or where they could have gone. Then all of a sudden I come out on the edge of a cliff and looked down at a cabin in a grassy basin, maybe a hundred feet below and a good four hundred yards away.

Standin' in front of that cabin were two horses. My face was pretty pale, an' my stomach felt sick, but I headed for the trail down, when I heard a scream. It was Julie!

Then, in front of the cabin, I heard a yell, and that durned nester stepped right out in plain sight and started walking up to the cabin, and he wasn't more than thirty yards away from it.

That fool nester knowed he was askin' for it. The Piute might have shot from behind the door jamb or from a window, but maybe the nester figured I was behind him and he might draw him out for my fire. Or maybe he figured his comin' out in the open would make him leave the girl alone. Whatever his reason, it worked. The Piute stepped outside the door.

Me? I was standin' up there like a fool, just a-gawkin', while there, right in front of my eyes, the Piute was goin' to kill a man. Or was he?

He was playin' big Injun right then. Maybe he figured Julie was watchin' or maybe he thought the nester would scare. Mister, that nester wouldn't scare a copper cent.

The Piute swaggered about a dozen steps out from the cabin and stood there, his thumbs in his belt, sneerin'. The nester, he just moseyed along kind of lazylike, carryin' his old Spencer in his right hand like he'd plumb forgot about his hand gun.

Then, like it was on a stage, I seen it happen. That Piute went for his guns and the nester swung up his Spencer. There was two shots—then a third.

It's a wonder I didn't break my neck gettin' down that trail, but when I run up, the Piute was lyin' there on his back with his eyes glazin' over. I took one look an' then turned away, and you can call me a pie-eatin' tenderfoot, but I was sick as I could be. Mister, did you ever see a man who'd been hit by two soft-nosed .56 caliber bullets? In the stummick?

Bin Morley come out with Julie, and I straightened up an she run over to me and began askin' how Ma was. She wasn't hurt none, as the nester got there just in time.

We took the horses back, and then I fell behind with the nester. I jerked my head toward the Piute's body.

"You goin' to bury him?" I asked.

He looked at me like he thought I was soft in the head.

"What fur? He picked the place hisself, didn't he?"

We mounted up.

"Besides," he said, "I've done lost two whole days as it is, and gettin' behind on my work ain't goin' to help none." He was stuffin' something in his slicker on the back of his horse.

"What's that?" I asked.

"A ham," he said grimly, "a whole ham. I brung it clean from Tucson, an' that durned Piute stole it off me. Right out of my cabin. Ma, she was out pickin' berries when it happend."

"You mean," I said, "you trailed the Piute clean over here just for a ham?"

"Mister," the nester spat, "you durned right I did! Why Ma and me ain't et no hawg meat since we left Missoury, comin' three year ago!"

The steel-dust started to catch up with Julie's pony, but I heard the nester sayin', "Never was no hand to eat beef, nohow. Too durned stringy. Gets in my teeth!"

AUTHOR'S NOTE

BARNEY TAKES A HAND

From the beginning it was imperative that men marching west shoot well. Surgeon John Gale, of the Missouri Expedition in 1819 tells of training given to the soldiers on the western march. They were firing ball cartridges.

"Those who hit a circle of three inches diameter off-hand at fifty yards three times in six are raised from the awkward squad to second class. Those who hit the same mark at one hundred yards three times in six are raised to first class. They make rapid improvement. There are but few who are not in the first class."

Barney Takes a Hand

Blinding white sun simmered above the thick, flourlike dust of the road, and the ragged mesquite beside the trail was gray with that same dust. Between the ranch and the distant purple hills, there was nothing but endless flats and sagebrush, dusty and dancing with heat waves.

Tess Bayeux stood in the doorway and shaded her eyes against the sun. The road was empty, empty to the horizon beyond which lay the little cow town of Black Mesa.

With a little sigh of hopelessness, she turned away. It was too soon. Even if Rex Tilden had received her note and decided to come, he could never come so quickly.

After an hour, during which she forced herself not to look even once, she returned to the door. The road was still empty, only white dust and heat. Then her eyes turned the other way, and she looked out across the desert, out to where the road dwindled off to a miserable trail into the badlands where nothing lived. For an instant then, she thought the heat played tricks with her eyes, for between her and the distant cliffs was a tiny figure.

Struck by curiosity, she stood in the doorway, watching. She was a slender girl with a pert, impudent little nose above a friendly mouth and lips that laughed when her eyes did.

She was still there, much later, when the figure took shape and became a man. The man wore no hat. His shaggy black hair was white with dust, his heavy woolen shirt was open at the neck, and his hairy chest was also dusty.

The man's face was unshaven, and his jaw was heavy, almost brutal under the beard and dust.

The jeans he wore were strange to the cow country, and his feet wore the ragged remains of what had been sneakers. His jeans were belted with a wide leather belt, curiously carved.

He wore no gun.

Several times the man staggered, and finally, when he turned from the road and stopped at the gate, he grasped the top with his big hands and stared at Tess Bayeux.

For a long time he stared while she tried to find words, and then one of the big hands dropped and he fumbled for the latch. He came through the gate and closed it behind him. It was a small thing, yet in his condition it told her something.

The man came on toward the house, and when she saw his face she caught her breath. Sunburn had cracked the skin until it had bled, and the blood had dried. The face was haggard, a mask of utter weariness from which only the eyes glowed and seemed to be alive.

Brought to herself suddenly, she ran inside for water. She tried to pick up the dipper, but dropped it. Then she carried the bucket to the man, and he seized it in his two big hands and lifted it to his mouth. She put out a hand to stop him, but he had merely taken a mouthful and then held it away, sloshing the water about in his mouth.

He looked at her wisely, and suddenly she had a feeling that this man knew everything, that he was afraid of nothing, that he could do anything with himself. She knew how his whole body must be crying for water, yet he knew the consequences of too much too soon and held the bucket away, his face twisted as though in a sneer at his fervid desire for its cool freshness.

Then he swallowed a little, and for a moment his face twisted again. He straightened it with an effort and picking up the washbasin beside the door, filled it and began to bathe his face and hands, slowly, tenderly. In all this time he said nothing, made no explanation.

A long time ago Tess had ridden with her brother into the badlands beyond the desert. It was a waterless horror, a nightmare of gigantic stones and gnarled cacti, a place where nothing lived.

How far had this man come? How could he have walked all that distance across the desert? That he had walked was obvious, for his sneakers were in tatters and there was some blood on the ground where he stood.

He shook the water from his eyes and then, without speaking, stepped up on the porch and entered the house. Half frightened, she started to speak, but he merely stretched out upon the floor in the cool interior and almost at once was asleep.

Again she looked at the road. And still it was empty. If Rex Tilden were to come in time, he must come soon. Judge Barker had told her that as long as she had possession, there was a chance.

If she lost possession before he returned from Phoenix, there was little chance that anything could be done.

It was sundown when she saw them coming. It was not Rex Tilden, for he would come alone. It was the others.

It was Harrington and Clyde, the men Tess feared.

They rode into the yard at a canter and reined in at the edge of the veranda.

"Well, Miss Bayeux"—George Clyde's silky voice was underlined with malice—"you are ready to leave?"

"No."

Tess stood very still. She knew there was little Clyde wouldn't stoop to if he could gain an end. Harrington was brutal, rough. Clyde was smooth. It was Clyde she feared most, yet Harrington would do the rough work.

He was a big man and cruel.

"Then I am afraid we will have to move you," said Clyde. "We have given you time. Now we can give you only ten minutes more to get what you want and get out on the road."

"I'm not going." Tess held her head high.

Clyde's mouth tightened. "Yes, you are. Of course"—he crossed his hands on the saddle horn—"if you want to come to my place, I think I could make you comfortable there. If you don't come to my place, there will be nothing in Black Mesa for you."

"I'll stay here."

Tess stood facing them. She couldn't win. She knew that in her heart. Rex was too late now, and the odds were against her. Still, where would she go? She had no money; she had no friends who dared help her. There had been only Tilden.

"All right, Harrington," Clyde said grimly. "You move her. Put her outside the gate."

Harrington swung down from the saddle, his face glistening with evil. He stepped up on the porch.

"Stay where yuh are!" a voice said from behind her.

Tess started. She had forgotten the stranger, and his voice was peculiar. It was low, ugly with some fierceness that was only just covered by an even tone.

"You come a step further and I'll kill yuh!" he said.

Harrington stood flatfooted. George Clyde was quicker.

"Tess Bayeux, who is this man?"

"Shut up!" The man walked out on the porch, and his feet were catlike in their movements. "And get movin'."

"Listen, my friend," Clyde said, "you're asking for trouble. You're a stranger here and you don't know what you're saying."

"I know a skunk by the smell." The stranger advanced to the edge of the porch, and his red-rimmed eyes glared at Clyde. "Get goin'!"

"Why, you—"

Harrington reached for him.

He reached, but the stranger's left hand shot out and seized Harrington by the throat and jerked him to his tiptoes. Holding him there, the stranger slapped him twice across the face. Slapped him only, but left him with a trickle of blood at the corner of his mouth. Then, setting him down on his heels, the stranger shoved, and big Deek Harrington sprawled at full length in the dust.

Clyde's face was deadly. He glanced at Harrington and then at the stranger, and then his hand shot for his gun. But the stranger was quicker. He seized the bridle and jerked the horse around and, catching Clyde by his gunarm, whipped him from the saddle to throw him into the dust.

Clyde's gun flew free, and the stranger caught it deftly and thrust it into his own waistband.

"Now," he said, "start walkin'. When yuh're over the horizon, I'll turn yore hosses loose. Until then, walk!"

Harrington staggered to his feet, and Clyde got up more slowly. His black coat was dusty. The stranger looked at Harrington.

"You still wear a gun," he said coolly. "Want to die? If yuh do, why don't yuh try drawin' it."

Harrington wet his lips. Then his eyes fell and he turned away.

"That goes for later," the stranger said. "If yuh want to try a shot from up the road, do it. I haven't killed a snake in a week!"

The two men stumbled from the yard, and the stranger stood there, watching them go. Then he picked up the bucket and drank, for a long time. When the two recent visitors were growing small toward the horizon, he turned the horses loose, hitting each a ringing slap on the haunches.

They would never stop short of town if he knew Western horses.

"I'm going to get supper," Tess told him. "Would you like to eat?"

"You know I would." He looked at her for a moment. "Then yuh can tell me what this is all about."

Tess Bayeux worked swiftly, and when she had the coffee on and the bacon frying, she turned to look at the man who had come to her rescue. He was slumped in a chair at the table. Black hair curled in the V of his shirt, and there was black hair on his forearms.

"You aren't a Western man?" she asked him.

"I was—once," he answered. "but that was a long time ago. I lived in Texas, in Oklahoma, then in Utah. Now I'm back in the West to stay."

"You have a home somewhere?"

"No. Home is where the heart is, they say, and my heart is here"—he touched his chest—"for now. I'm still a dreamer, I reckon. Still thinkin' of the one girl who is somewhere."

"You've had a hard time," she said, looking at him again.

She had never seen so much raw power in a man, never seen so much sleeping strength as in the muscles that rolled beneath his shirt.

"Tell me about you," he said. "Who are them two men that was here?"

"Harrington and Clyde," she told him. "The H and C Cattle Company. They moved in here two years ago, during the drouth. They bought land and cattle. They prospered. They aren't big, but then, nobody else is either.

"The sheriff doesn't want trouble. Clyde outtalks those who dislike him. My father did, very much, and he wasn't outtalked. He died, killed by a fall from a bad horse, about a year ago. It seems he was in debt. He was in debt to Nevers, who runs the general store in Black Mesa. Not much, but more than he could pay. Clyde bought up the notes from Nevers.

"Wantrell, a lawyer in Phoenix who knew my father, is trying to get it arranged so we will have water here. If we do, we could pay off the notes in a short time. If we had water I could borrow money in Prescott. There is water on government land above us, and that's why Clyde wants it. He tried to get me to move away for the notes. Then he offered to pay me five hundred dollars and give me the notes.

"When I refused, he had some of his men dam the stream and shut off what water I had. My cattle died. Some of my horses were run off. Then he came in with some more bills and told me I'd have to leave or pay. He has some sort of a paper on the place. It says that my father promised to give Nevers the place if he didn't pay up or if anything happened to him."

"No friends?" asked the man.

"Yes, a man named Rex Tilden," Tess said. "He rode for Dad once and then started a ranch of his own. He's good with a gun, and when I wrote to him, he said he would come. He's five days late now."

The stranger nodded. "I know." He took a small wallet from his pocket. "That his?"

She caught it up, her face turning pale. She had seen it many times.

"Yes! You know him? You have seen him?"

"He's dead. Dry-gulched. He was killed near Santos three days ago."

"You knew him?" Tess repeated.

"No. I got kicked off a train I was ridin'. I found him dyin'. He told me about you, asked me to help. There was nobody else around, so I came."

"Oh, thank you! But Rex! Rex Tilden dead. And because of me!"

His face didn't change. "Mebbe." He brought out the gun he had taken from Clyde and checked it. "Mebbe I'll need this. Where's that dam?"

"Up there, on the ridge. But they have it guarded."

"Do they?" He didn't look interested.

She put the bacon on his plate and poured coffee. He ate in silence, and when he had finished, it was dark. He got up suddenly.

"You got a gun?" he asked.

"Just a small rifle, for rabbits."

"Use it. If anything moves, shoot."

"But it might be you!" she protested. "When you come back, I mean!"

He smiled, and his whole face seemed to lighten.

"When anything moves, shoot. It won't be me. When I come back yuh won't hear me."

"Who are you?" It was the first time she had asked that.

He hesitated, looking at the ground and then at her, and his eyes glinted with humor.

"My name is Barney Shaw," he said then. "That mean anything to yuh?"

She shook her head.

"Should it?"

"No, I reckon not."

He ate for a while in silence and then looked up at her.

"A few years ago I was punchin' cows. Then I worked in the mines. A man saw me in a fight once and trained me. In two years I was one of the best. Then I killed a man in a dice game and got two years for it. He was cheatin', I accused him, he struck at me.

"When the two years was up—I'd been sentenced to ten, but they let me out after two—I went to sea. I was at sea for four years. Then I decided to come back and find a place for myself, here in the West. But first, a job."

Tess looked at him understandingly.

"I need a man," she said, "but I haven't the money to pay."

He looked at his plate. "How about a workin' share?"

"All right. Fifty-fifty." She smiled ruefully. "But it isn't much. I think Clyde will win, after all."

"Not if I can help it. How much do yuh owe?"

"A thousand dollars. It might as well be a million. We don't have more than fifty head of cattle on the place, and only four saddle horses."

He went out the back door and vanished. Or so it seemed. Tess, glancing out a moment later, could see nothing. She should have told him about Silva, the guard at the dam. Silva was a killer and quick as a snake.

She turned again to the house and began putting things in order. First, she barricaded the front door and then opened the window a slit at the bottom. She got out her rifle, checked it, and laid out some ammunition.

Barney Shaw had seen the draw when he approached the house by the road, so when he left the house he hit it fast. It was deep enough by a head, and he started away. Fortunately, it led toward the dam. It was the old stream bed.

From the shadow of a gigantic boulder, he looked up

at the dam. Largely brush, logs, and earth, it was a hasty job and homemade. He watched for twenty minutes before he saw the guard. Silva, a Mexican, had found a place for himself where he could command all the approaches to the dam.

In the moonlight, a rock cedar made a heavy shadow. Barney Shaw moved, and then as Silva's head moved, he froze. He was out in the open, but he knew the light was indistinct. For a long time he stood still, and then as Silva's head moved again, Shaw glided forward to the shelter of the rock cedar.

He was no more than a dozen feet from the guard now, and through a hole in the bushy top of the cedar he could see Silva's long, lantern jaw, and even the darkness seemed to mark the thin mustache the man wore.

When Silva stood up, Shaw could see that the man was tall, yet feline in his movements. Silva stretched and then turned and came toward the cedar, walking carelessly. He had put his rifle aside and walked with the aimlessness of a man without care. Yet something in that very carelessness struck Shaw as the guard moved closer.

Silva stepped past the tree and then whirled and dived straight at Shaw, his knife flashing in the moonlight!

Only that sense of warning saved Barney Shaw. He stepped back, just enough, and whipped a left hook for Silva's chin. It landed, a glancing blow, and the Mexican dropped.

But catlike he was on his feet and, teeth bared, he lunged again. Shaw stepped in, warding off the knife, and slashed with the edge of his hand for the Mexican's neck. The blow was high and took the man across the temple and ear.

Silva went to his knees and lost his hold on the knife. Barney stepped in, and as the Mexican came up, he hit him once, twice. The blows cracked like whips in the still air, and the guard dropped to his face.

Dragging him roughly into the open, Shaw hastily bound him hand and foot. Then he walked over and picked up the guard's rifle. It was a Winchester and a good one.

Rustling around, he found an ax and a pick. Without so much as a glance toward the guard, he dropped down the face of the dam and, setting himself, sank the ax into one of the key posts. When he had cut through the posts and the timbers back of them, he was sweating profusely. He was aware, too, that the ax was making a ringing sound that would carry for at least a mile in that still air.

Putting the ax down, he took the pick and began digging at the dirt and rock that were piled on the water side of the dam. In a few minutes there was a trickle of water coming through, then a fair-sized stream.

Carrying the rifle, he went back to the edge of the draw where the timbers had been fitted into notches cut into the rock with a double jack and drill. It took him more than an hour, but he cut two timbers loose.

Dropping his tools he walked over to look at Silva. The Mexican was conscious, and his eyes blazed when Shaw looked at him, grinning.

"Don't worry," Barney said grimly. "Yuh're safe up here, and when the dam goes out they'll be up here in a hurry."

He turned and started away, keeping to the shadows of the cedars. And before he had walked a hundred yards he heard a whoosh and then the rustle of rushing water.

It was a small stream, and the water wasn't much, but it would more than fill the pools down below where Tess Bayeux's cattle came to drink.

There was no warning, and he was still some distance from the girl's cabin when he saw a rifle flash. Simultaneously something struck him a terrific blow alongside the head and he tumbled, face downward, into the gravel. He felt his body sliding head first, and then he lost consciousness.

When Barney Shaw opened his eyes it was daylight.

He tried to move his head, and pain shot through him like a burning iron. For an instant then he lay still, gathering the will to try again. The side of his head and face that was uppermost was caked with dried blood, and his hair was matted with it. That the morning was well along he knew, for his back was hot with sun, and from the feel, the sun was high.

Shaw moved his head and, despite the pain, forced himself to his knees. His head swimming, he peered about.

He lay on a rocky hillside. Below him, half hidden by a clump of cedar, and almost two miles away, was the house of Tess Bayeux. At his right he could hear water running, and that meant the stream he had released had not yet been stopped.

His rifle and pistol were still with him. Gingerly he felt his head. It was badly swollen, and the scalp was furrowed by a bullet. He had bled profusely, and he decided that if his dry-gulchers had looked at him they had decided the bullet had entered his skull.

What about Tess? Had they thrown her out? Or was she still holding the place? The silence was ominous, and obviously hours had passed.

Whoever had shot him had no doubt left him for dead and had also freed Silva. How many enemies were there? He had no way of knowing, and Tess had told him nothing. Harrington, Silva, and Clyde were three, and of them all, George Clyde was the most dangerous because he was the most intelligent.

From a position behind some boulders and cedar Shaw studied the small ranch house. There was no evidence of activity, nothing to indicate how the tide of battle had gone.

Then a door banged at the house and he saw a man come out, walking toward the corral. He roped two horses, and in a few minutes two riders started off to town. One of them was Silva.

It took Barney Shaw a half hour of painstaking effort to get to the wall of the house without being seen. He edged along to the corner and then stopped. Cautiously, he peered around. Not ten feet away a man was sitting on the edge of the porch, a rifle on his knees.

He was a short man, but square jawed and tough. As Barney looked, the man put the rifle against the post, took out a pipe, and began to fill it. Shaw made a quick calculation of his chances and decided against it. With Harrington, perhaps. Not this jasper. This hombre was different.

Suddenly Barney Shaw saw a slim piece of pipe, and it gave him an idea. Picking it up, he glanced to see if it was clear and then looked around for some pebbles. He selected a half dozen. In school, too many years ago, he had been an artist with a beanshooter.

The man on the porch had a beak of a nose that jutted out above his heavy jaw like the prow on a ship. Taking careful aim, Shaw, blew the first pebble. It missed.

The man glanced in the direction of the sound where the pebble hit the ground and then turned back, puffing contentedly at his pipe. Then Barney fired a second pebble.

It was a direct hit. The pebble, fired from the beanshooter with force, hit him right on the nose!

With a cry of pain, the man leaped to his feet, one hand grasping his nose. His pipe had fallen to the ground.

Instantly, Barney was around the corner. The man, holding his nose, his eyes watering, never saw him coming. It was only when Barney, picking up the rifle, knocked it against the porch, that the man whirled about. And Shaw slapped him alongside the head with the butt of the rifle, swinging it freehanded.

The fellow went down, grabbing for his gun, but Shaw stepped in and kicked it from his hand. Then as the fellow started to rise, Shaw slapped him across the temple with a pistol barrel. The man went down and out.

Coolly Barney shouldered the fellow and, walking with him to the barn, tied him securely and dropped him into a feed bin. Then he went outside and roped a horse. When it was saddled he led it to the house, left it ground hitched, and took a quick look. There was no sign of Tess Bayeux. Hiding the extra rifle, he swung into the saddle and started at a canter for town.

He was a tough-looking figure when he rode into town. His shock of black hair was still thick with dust, and his face was stained with blood. The two pistols were thrust into his waistband, and he carried a rifle in his hands.

He was cantering up the street when he saw Silva.

The Mexican had come to the door of the saloon, and when he saw Barney he swore and dropped a hand for a gun. Shaw swung the rifle and fired across the pommel of the saddle.

The first shot knocked the gun from Silva's hand, the second slammed him back into the wall. It was a shoulder shot. Silva stood there, staring stupidly.

Swinging down, Barney tied the horse and walked along the boardwalk. A dozen people had rushed out at the sound of a shot, but he ignored them. He merely walked to Silva and stopped. For a long time he looked at him.

"Next time I'll kill yuh!" he said, and walked inside.

Three men were in the bar besides the bartender. One of them was a powerfully built man with big hands and a flat nose. Behind the bar were some photos of him, posed like a boxer.

"You a fighter?" Shaw demanded. "If yuh are, I can lick yuh!"

The man looked at him, his eyes hard.

"I fight for money," he said.

"So do I," Shaw said. He looked at the bartender. "I'll fight this hombre, winner take all, skintight kid gloves, to a finish!"

The bartender's face whitened and then turned red.

"Yuh know who this is?" he demanded. "This is the Wyoming Slasher!"

"All right. Line up the fight." Shaw hesitated. "One thing—it must be one thousand dollars for the purse."

The bartender laughed.

"Yuh'll get that, easy. If yuh win. The boys like to see the Slasher fight!"

Barney Shaw nodded and walked out.

"Who was that?" Harrington demanded as he burst in from the back room. "Who was that man?"

"Some gent with his face all bloody, dusty as sin, wantin' to fight the Slasher for a thousand dollars!"

"The Slasher? A thousand dollars?" Harrington's eyes hardened. "Why, I'll fix his clock!"

"No you won't." Clyde walked into the room. "Let it ride. The Slasher will kill him. That will settle everything!"

Barney Shaw walked to the hotel, carrying his rifle in the hollow of his arm. He was going up the steps when he saw Tess. Her eyes widened.

"I thought—you were dead or gone!" she exclaimed.

"No." He looked at her. "What happened?"

"They surprised me, just before morning. The sheriff was with them, and he made me leave. They had some papers, and they said I had to leave. If I can pay in ten days I can go back."

"In ten days yuh'll pay," he promised and walked past her to the desk. "I want a room and a telegraph blank," he told the clerk.

The clerk shook his head.

"We don't have any rooms."

Barney Shaw reached over the desk and caught the clerk behind the neck and dragged him half over the desk.

"Yuh heard me," he said harshly. "I want a room and a telegraph blank! Yuh never sold this hotel out since it was built! Now get me that room!"

"Yes, sir!" The clerk swallowed and turned the register. "I just remembered. There is a room left."

He put a blank on the desk, and Barney wrote hastily, "Now is the time for all good men to come to the aid of their party." Then he signed his name. He told the clerk to send the message to the depot and have the agent get it off at once.

Tess came over and stood beside him.

"What are you going to do?" she asked.

"Fight the Slasher for a thousand dollars," he said. "That will pay off for yuh."

"The Slasher?" Her face paled. "Oh, not him, Barney! He's awful! He killed a man in a fight! And those men with him! That Dirk Hutchins, McCluskey, and the rest. They are awful!"

"Are they?" Barney smiled at her. "I'm goin' to wash up, then sleep." He turned and walked upstairs.

A man got up from across the room and walked over to the desk.

"What do yuh think, Martin?" he asked.

Martin Tolliver, the clerk, looked up and his face was grim.

"This one's different, Joe. I'm goin' to bet on him."

"I think I will, too," Joe said. "But we'll be the only ones."

"Yes," Martin agreed. "But he took hold of me. Joe, that hombre's got a grip like iron! It was like bein' taken in a vise! I was never so scared in my life!"

By noon the day of the fight, punchers were in from the ranches and miners from the mines. The ring had been pitched in the center of the big corral. Martin Tolliver, the hotel clerk, and Joe Todd were betting. They were getting odds.

A little after noon the train came in. By that time everyone was at the corral waiting for the fight to start, and only Silva saw the men get off the train. There were nine of them who got out of the two passenger coaches. Four were cattlemen, one was a huge, bearded man with blue anchors tatooed on his hands, and the other four were nondescripts in caps and jerseys.

The Wyoming Slasher was first in the ring. He came down, vaulted the ropes, and stood looking around. His hair was cropped short and he wore a black John L. Sullivan mustache. His eyes were blue and hard, and his face looked like stained oak.

Harrington and another man were in his corner. The sheriff had been selected as the referee.

Barney Shaw came from the hotel, walking across the street wearing an old slicker. As he stepped through the ropes a stocky man in a checked suit and a black jersey stepped up behind him and put a professional hand on his shoulder.

They got into the ring and walked to the center. The Slasher was half a head taller than Shaw and heavier. His wide cheekbones and beetling brows made him look fierce. The back of his head slid down into a thick neck.

Shaw's hair had been cut, and it was black and curly.

He looked brown, and when he turned and walked to his corner, there was an unexpected lightness in his step.

The Wyoming Slasher dropped his robe, and there was a gasp from the crowd who looked at the rolling muscles of his mighty shoulders and arms. He was built like a wrestler, but his weight was in his gigantic shoulders and deep chest.

He strode to the scratch, skintight gloves pulled on. The sheriff motioned, the slicker slid from Barney's shoulders, and he turned and came to scratch. His broad shoulders were powerful and tapered to narrow hips and slim, powerful legs. The Slasher put up his hands and Barney hit him, a quick left that tapped the blood at his thin lips. The Slasher lunged, and Barney slid away, rapping a quick right to the body.

The Slasher strode in, and Barney tried a left to the head that missed, and the Slasher grabbed him by the waist and hurled him to the ground. Shaw lit in a pile of dust, and the sheriff sprang in. "Round!" he shouted.

Shaw walked to his corner.

"He's strong," he said. He waved away the water bottle.

"Them new Queensbury rules would be better for you," his second said out of the corner of his mouth. "London Prize Ring rules was never no good. Yuh hurt a man and if he goes down the round is over."

They started again at the call of time, and Barney walked out quickly. The Slasher rushed, and Barney lanced the fellow's lips with another left and then stepped around and jabbed with the left again. There was a mix-up. Then Barney stepped away, and the Slasher hit him.

It was a hard right, and it shook Shaw to his heels, but he stepped away. He was skillfully, carefully feeling the bigger man out. Instinctively he knew it would be a hard fight. The other man was like iron, big and very, very strong. It would take time to down him. Barney was trying each punch, trying to find out what the big man would do.

All fighters develop habits. Certain ways of blocking lefts, ducking or countering. By trying each punch a few times Barney Shaw was learning the pattern of the Slasher's fighting, getting a blueprint in his mind.

When the second round had gone four minutes, he took a glancing left to the head and went down, ending the round.

When the minutes was up, he went out with a rush. The Slasher put up his hands and without even stopping his rush, Barney dropped low and thrust out his left. It caught the Slasher in the midriff and set him back on his heels.

Instantly Barney was upon him. Hitting fast, he struck the Slasher five times in the face with a volley of blows before the bigger man was brought up by the ropes. Then setting himself, he whipped a hard right to the Slasher's ribs!

The crowd was yelling wildly, and the Slasher came off the ropes and swung. Barney went under it and whipped a right to the heart. Then the Slasher's left took him and he rolled over on the ground!

He was badly shaken. In his corner, "Turkey Tom" Ryan, his second, grinned.

"Watch it," he said. "He can hit, the beggar!"

They had wiped the blood from the Slasher's face, and the big man looked hard. Near the Slasher's corner Barney could see George Clyde.

Barney Shaw went up to scratch and as the Wyoming Slasher rushed he stabbed a left to the mouth, parried a left himself, and hit hard to the body. Inside, he hammered away with both hands. He took a clubbing right to the head that cut his forehead and showered him with blood. But suddenly he knew that his time had come, and instead of backing away, he set himself and began slugging with everything he had.

The Slasher was caught off balance. He tried to get set, but he was too heavy. He struck several ponderous blows, but Barney was knifing his face with those skintight gloves. Jabbing a left, he turned his fist as it struck and ripped the Slasher's face. Then he stepped in and threw a wicked uppercut to the body. Then another and still another.

The Slasher started to fall, but Shaw caught him under the chin with the heel of his glove and shoved him erect against the ropes. Stepping back, he smashed both hands to the chin.

With the crowd roaring, Shaw leaped away and the Wyoming Slasher rolled off the ropes and fell flat on his face!

Instantly his seconds were over the ropes and swarming over him. Harrington rushed across the ring and seized one of Barney Shaw's hands, shouting something about his fists being loaded.

Turkey Tom shoved him away, and Shaw took off the glove and showed him his bare fist. Harrington snarled something, and Shaw slugged him in the ribs. As the big man started to fall, one of his friends stepped up, and instantly the ring was a bedlam of shouting, fighting men.

It was ten minutes before the ring was cleared, and then the Slasher was able to get to the scratch. He rushed immediately, and Shaw ducked, but as he ducked he slipped and the Slasher hit him and knocked him to his knees. He started to get up, and the Slasher rushed and struck him another ponderous blow. He went down hard. And the round ended.

He was barely on his second's knee when the call of "time" came again and, groggy, he went to scratch. The Wyoming Slasher charged. Shaw ducked, went into a clinch, and threw the Slasher with a rolling hiplock. The Slasher went down with a thud.

Still groggy, he came to scratch again, but as they came together, he feinted suddenly. As the Slasher swung, Shaw threw his right, high and hard. It caught the Slasher coming in and knocked him to the ropes. As he rebounded Shaw hit him with a one-two, so fast the the two blows landed with almost the same sound.

The Slasher hit the ground all in one piece and rolled over. After ten minutes he was still unable to stand.

As he shoved, to his feet and held there, Harrington suddenly shouted. As one man, his thugs charged the ring and began tearing down the posts.

But even as they charged, the four cattlemen leaped into the ring, as did the man with the blue anchors on his hands. In a breath there was a cordon of men with guns drawn around Barney, around the two stakeholders, and around the shouting Turkey Tom.

Harrington's thugs broke against the flying wedge formed by the cattlemen and Shaw's friends, and the wedge moved on to the hotel.

Tess met them at the door, her eyes wild with anxiety.

"You're all right? Oh, I was so afraid! I was sure you'd be hurt!"

"You should see the Slasher, ma'am," Turkey Tom said, grinning to show his five gold teeth. "He don't look so good!"

"We've got the money to pay off now," Barney told her, smiling. His lips were puffed and there was a blue welt alongside his ear. "We can pay off and start over."

"Yes, and that ain't all!" One of the cattlemen, a big man wearing a black hat, stepped in. "When yuh wired about the water, I was in Zeb's office. We went to the governor and we got it all fixed up. So I decided it might be a right good idea for me to come up here and get yuh to feed about five hundred whiteface cows for me—on shares!"

"She can't," snarled a voice behind them.

As one man they turned. George Clyde stood in the doorway, his lips thinned and his face white.

"She can't, because there's mineral on that place, and I've filed a mining claim that takes in the spring and water source!"

His eyes were hard and malicious. Harrington, his face still bloody, loomed behind him. The big man with the anchors on his hands stepped forward and stared hard at Clyde.

"That's him, Sheriff," he said. "The man who killed Rex Tilden!"

George Clyde's face stiffened and went white.

"What do you mean?" he shouted. "I was here that night!"

"You were in Santos that night. You met Rex Tilden on the road outside of town and shot him. I was up on the hill when it happened and I saw you. You shot him with that Krag Jorgenson rifle! I found one of the shells!"

"He's got one of them Krags," the sheriff said abruptly. "I seen it! He won it from some Danish feller last year in a game of faro. I never seen another like it!"

Barney Shaw had pulled on his trousers over his fighting trunks and slipped on his shirt. He felt the sag of the heavy pistol in his coat pocket and put on the coat. Half turning, he slid the pistol into his waistband.

"That means," he said coolly, "that his mineral claim won't be any use to him. I know he hasn't done any assessment work, and without that he can't hold the claim!"

Clyde's eyes narrowed.

"You!" he snarled. "If you'd stayed out of this I'd have made it work. You'll never see me die! And you will never see me arrested!"

Suddenly his hand dropped for his gun, but even as his hand swept down, Barney Shaw stepped through the crowd, drew, and fired!

Clyde staggered half turned, and pitched over on his face. Harrington had started to reach, but suddenly he jerked his hand away from his gun as though it were afire.

"I had nothin' to do with no killin'," he said, whining. "I never done nothin'!"

When the sheriff had taken Harrington away, Barney Shaw took Tess by the arm.

"Tess," he asked hesitantly, "does the fifty-fifty deal still go?"

She looked up, her eyes misty and suddenly tender.

"Yes, Barney, for as long as you want it!"

"Then," he said quietly, "it will be for always!"

AUTHOR'S NOTE
MAN RIDING WEST

Frank Collinson, writing of buffalo hunter Jim White, whom he knew: "White was a fine shot, the best I ever knew . . . I once knew him to kill 46 buffalo on Duck Creek with 47 shots."

At another point he quotes White as saying: "I can hit a half-dollar at fifty yards."

Frank Collinson, from Yorkshire, England, began his western experiences in 1872, as a cowboy, buffalo hunter and rancher. He died in Texas in 1943.

Man Riding West

Three men were hunkered down by the fire when Jim Gary walked his buckskin up to their camp in the lee of the cliff. The big man across the fire had a shotgun lying beside him. It was the shotgun that made Gary uneasy, for cowhands do not carry shotguns, especially when on a trail drive, as these men obviously were.

Early as it was, the cattle were already bedded down for the night in the meadow alongside the stream, and from their looks they had come far and fast. It was still light, but the clouds were low and swollen with rain.

"How's for some coffee?" Jim asked as he drew up. "I'm ridin' through, an' I'm sure hungry an' tuckered."

Somewhere off in the mountains, thunder rolled and grumbled. The fire crackled, and the leaves on the willows hung still in the lifeless air. There were three saddled horses nearby, and among the gear was an old Mother Hubbard style saddle with a wide skirt.

"Light an' set up." The man who spoke was lean jawed and sandy haired. "Never liked to ride on an empty stomach, m'self."

More than ever, Gary felt uneasy. Neither of the others spoke. All were tough-looking men, unshaven and dirty, but it was their hard-eyed suspicion that made Jim wonder. However, he swung down and loosened his saddle girth and then slipped the saddle off and laid it well back under the overhang of the cliff. As he did so he glanced again at the old saddle that lay there.

The overhang of the cliff was deep where the fire was built for shelter from the impending rain. Jim dropped to an ancient log, gray and stripped of bark, and handed his tin plate over to the man who reached for it. The cook slapped two thick slabs of beef on the plate and some frying-pan bread liberally touched with the beef fryings. Gary was hungry and he dove in without comment, and the small man filled his cup.

"Headed west?" The sandy-haired man asked, after a few minutes.

"Yeah, headed down below the rim. Pleasant Valley way."

The men all turned their heads toward him but none spoke. Jim could feel their eyes on his tied-down guns. There was a sheep and cattle war in the valley.

"They call me Red Slagle. These hombres are Tobe Langer and Jeeter Dirksen. We're drivin' to Salt Creek."

Langer would be the big one. "My name's Gary," Jim replied. "Jim Gary. I'm from points yonder. Mostly Dodge an' Santa Fe."

"Hear they are hirin' warriors in Pleasant Valley."

"Reckon." Jim refused to be drawn, although he had the feeling they had warmed to him since he mentioned heading for the valley.

"Ridin' thataway ourselves," Red suggested. "Want to make a few dollars drivin' cattle? We're shorthanded."

"Might," Gary admitted. "The grub's good."

"Give you forty to drive to Salt Creek. We'll need he'p. From hereabouts the country is plumb rough, an' she's fixin' to storm."

"You've hired a hand. When do I start?"

"Catch a couple of hours sleep. Tobe has the first ride. Then you take over. If you need he'p, just you call out."

Gary shook out his blankets and crawled into them. In the moment before his eyes closed he remembered the cattle had all worn a Double A brand, and the brands were fresh. That could easily be with a trail herd. But the Double A had been the spread that Mart Ray had mentioned.

It was raining when he rode out to the herd. "They ain't fussin'," Langer advised, "an' the rain's quiet enough. It should pass mighty easy. See you."

He drifted toward the camp, and Gary turned up his slicker collar and studied the herd as well as he could in the darkness. They were lying quiet. He was riding a gray roped from the small remuda, and he let the horse amble placidly toward the far side of the meadow. A hundred yards beyond the meadow the bulk of the sloping hill that formed the opposite side of the valley showed blacker in the gloom. Occasionally there was a flash of heat lightening, but no thunder.

Slagle had taken him on because he needed hands, but none of them accepted him. He decided to sit tight in his saddle and see what developed. It could be plenty, for unless he was mistaken, this was a stolen herd, and Slagle was a thief, as were the others.

If this herd had come far and fast, he had come farther and faster, and with just as great a need. Now there was nothing behind him but trouble, and nothing before him but bleak years of drifting ahead of a reputation.

Up ahead was Mart Ray, and Ray was as much a friend as he had. Gunfighters are admired by many, respected by some, feared by all, and welcomed by none. His father had warned him of what to expect, warned him long ago before he himself had died in a gun battle. "You're right handy, son," he had warned, "one of the fastest I ever seen, so don't let it be known. Don't never draw a gun on a man in anger, an' you'll live happy. Once you get the name of a gunfighter, you're on a lonesome trail, an' there's only one ending."

So he had listened, and he had avoided trouble. Mart Ray knew that. Ray was himself a gunman. He had killed six men of whom Jim Gary knew, and no doubt there had been others. He and Mart had been riding together in Texas and then in a couple of trail drives, one all the way to Montana. He never really got close to Mart, but they had been partners after a fashion.

Ray had always been amused at his eagerness to avoid trouble, although he had no idea of the cause of it. "Well," he had said, "they sure cain't say like father, like son. From all I hear your pappy was an uncurried wolf, an' you fight shy of trouble. You run from it. If I didn't know you so well, I'd say you was yaller."

But Mart Ray had known him well, for it had been Jim who rode his horse down in front of a stampede to pick Ray off the ground, saving his life. They got free, but no more, and a thousand head of cattle stampeded over the ground where Ray had stood.

Then, a month before, down in the Big Bend country, trouble had come, and it was trouble he could not avoid. It braced him in a little Mexican cantina just over the river, and in the person of a dark, catlike Mexican with small feet and dainty hands, but his guns were big enough and there was an unleashed devil in his eyes.

Jim Gary had been dancing with a Mexican girl, and the Mexican had jerked her from his arms and struck her across the face. Jim knocked him down, and the Mexican got up, his eyes fiendish. Without a word, the Mexican went for his gun, and for a frozen, awful instant, Jim saw his future facing him, and then his own hand went down and he palmed his gun in a flashing, lightning draw that rapped out two shots. The Mexican, who had reached first, barely got his gun clear before he was dead. He died on his feet and then fell.

In a haze of powder smoke and anquish, Jim Gary had wheeled and strode from the door, and behind him lay a dead and awful silence. It was not until two days later that he knew who and what he had killed.

The lithe-bodied Mexican had been Miguel Sonoma, and he had been a legend along the border. A tough, dangerous man with a reputation as a killer.

Two nights later, a band of outlaws from over the border rode down upon Gary's little spread to avenge their former leader, and two of them died in the first blast of gunfire, a matter of handguns at point-blank range.

From the shelter of his cabin, Gary fought them off for three days before the smoke from his burning barn attracted help. When the help arrived, Jim Gary was a man with a name. Five dead men lay on the ground around the ranch yard and in the desert nearby. The wounded had been carried away. And the following morning, Jim turned his ranch over to the bank to sell and lit a shuck—away from Texas.

Of this, Mart Ray knew nothing. Half of Texas and all of New Mexico, or most of it, would lie behind him when Jim reached the banks of Salt Creek. Mart Ray was ramrodding the Double A, and he would have a job for him.

Jim Gary turned the horse and rode slowly back along the side of the herd. The cattle had taken their midnight stretch and after standing around a bit, were lying down once more. The rain was falling, but softly, and Gary let the gray take his own time in skirting the herd.

The night was pitch dark. Only the horns of the cattle glistened with rain, and their bodies were darker blobs in the blackness of the night. Once, drawing up near the willows along the stream, Jim thought he detected a vague sound. He waited a moment, listening. On such a night nobody would be abroad who could help it, and it was unlikely that a mountain lion would be on the prowl, although possible.

He started on again, yet now his senses were alert, and his hand slid under his slicker and touched the butt of a .44. He was almost at the far end of the small herd when a sudden flash of lightning revealed the hillside across the narrow valley.

Stark and clear, glistening with rain, sat a horseman! He was standing in his stirrups, and seemed amazingly tall, and in the glare of the flash, his face was stark white, like the face of a fleshless skull!

Startled, Gary grunted and slid his gun into his hand, but all was darkness again, and listen as he could, he heard no further sound. When the lightning flashed again, the hillside was empty and still. Uneasily, he caught himself staring back over his shoulder into the darkness, and he watched his horse. The gray was standing, head up and ears erect, staring off toward the darkness near the hill. Riding warily, Gary started in that direction, but when he got there, he found nothing.

It was almost daylight when he rode up to the fire which he had kept up throughout the night, and swinging down, he awakened Dirksen. The man sat up, startled. "Hey!" he exclaimed. "You forget to call me?"

Jim grinned at him. "Just figured I was already up an' a good cook needed his sleep."

Jeeter stared at him. "You mean you rode for me? Say, you're all right!"

"Forget it!" Gary stretched. "I had a quiet night, mostly."

Red Slagle was sitting up, awakened by their talk. "What do you mean—mostly?"

Jim hesitated, feeling puzzled. "Why, to tell you the truth, I'm not sure whether I saw anything or not, but I sure thought I did. Anyway, it had me scared."

"What was it?" Slagle was pulling on his pants, but his eyes were serious. "A lion?"

"No, it was a man on a horse. A tall man with a dead-white face, like a skull." Gary shrugged sheepishly. "Makes me sound like a fool, but I figured for a moment that I'd seen a ghost!"

Red Slagle was staring at him, and Jeeter's face was dead white and his eyes were bulging. "A ghost?" he asked, faintly. "Did you say, a *ghost?*"

"Shucks," Gary shrugged, "there ain't no such thing. Just some hombre on a big black horse, passin' through in the night, that was all! But believe me, seein' him in the lightnin' up on that hill like I did, it sure was scary!"

Tobe Langer was getting up, and he, too, looked bothered. Slagle came over to the fire and sat down, boots in hand. Reaching down he pulled his sock around to get a hole away from his big toe; then he put his foot into the wet boot and began to struggle with it.

"That horse, now," Langer asked carefully, "did it have a white star between the eyes?"

Gary was surprised. "Why, yes! Matter of fact, it did! You know him?"

Slagle let go of the boot and stomped his foot to settle

it in the boot. "Yeah, feller we seen down the road a ways. Big black horse."

Slagle and Langer walked away from camp a ways and stood talking together. Jeeter was worried. Jim could see that without half trying, and he studied the man thoughtfully. Jeeter Dirksen was a small man, quiet, but inclined to be nervous. He had neither the strength nor the toughness of Slagle and Langer. If Gary learned anything about the cattle it would be through his own investigation or from Jeeter. And he was growing more and more curious.

Yet if these were Double A cattle and had been stolen, why were they being driven toward the Double A ranch, rather than away from it? He realized suddenly that he knew nothing at all about Red Slagle or his outfit, and it was time he made some inquiries.

"This Double A," he asked suddenly, "you been riding' for them long?"

Dirksen glanced at him sharply and bent over his fire. "Not long," he said. "It's a Salt Creek outfit. Slagle's segundo."

"Believe I know your foreman," Gary suggested. "I think this was the outfit he said. Hombre name of Mart Ray. Ever hear of him?"

Jeeter turned sharply, slopping coffee over the rim of the cup. It hissed in the fire, and both the other men looked around at the camp. Jeeter handed the cup to Gary and studied him, searching his face. Then he admitted cautiously, "Yeah, Ray's the foreman. Ranch belongs to a syndicate out on the coast. You say you know him?"

"Uh-huh. Used to ride with him." Langer and Slagle had walked back to the fire, and Dirksen poured coffee for them.

"Who was that you rode with?" Slagle asked.

"Your boss, Mart Ray."

Both men looked up sharply; then slagle's face cleared and he smiled. "Say! that's why the name was familiar! You're *that* Jim Gary! Son of old Steve Gary. Yeah, Mart told us about you."

Langer chuckled suddenly. "You're the scary one,

huh? The one who likes to keep out of trouble. Yeah, we heard about you!"

The contempt in his tone stiffened Jim's back, and for an instant he was on the verge of a harsh retort. Then the memory of what lay behind him welled up within, and bitterly he kept his mouth shut. If he got on the prod and killed a man here, he would only have to drift farther. There was only one solution, and that was to avoid trouble. Yet irritating as it was to be considered lacking in courage, Langer's remark let him know that the story of his fights had not preceded him.

"There's no call, he said after a minute, "to go around the country killin' folks. If people would just get the idea they can get along without all that. Me, I don't believe in fightin'."

Langer chuckled, but Slagle said nothing, and Dirksen glanced at him sympathetically.

All day the herd moved steadily west, but now Gary noticed a change, for the others were growing more watchful as the day progressed. Their eyes continued to search the surrounding hills, and they rode more warily approaching any bit of cover.

Once, when Jeeter rode near him, the little man glanced across the herd at the other riders and then said quietly, "That was no ghost you saw. Red rode up there on the hill, an' there was tracks, tracks of a mighty big black horse."

"Wonder why he didn't ride down to camp?" Jim speculated. "He sure enough saw the fire!"

Dirksen grunted. "If that hombre was the one Red thinks it is, he sure didn't have no aim to ride down there!"

Before Gary could question him further, Jeeter rode off after a stray and cutting him back into the herd, rode on further ahead. Jim dropped back to the drag, puzzling over this new angle. Who could the strange rider be? What did he want? Was he afraid of Slagle?

A big brindle steer was cutting wide of the herd, and Jim swung out to get him, but dashing toward the stream, the steer floundered into the water and into quicksand.

Almost at once, it was down, struggling madly, its eyes rolling.

Jim swung a loop and dropped it over the steer's horns. If he could give the steer a little help now, there was a chance he could get it out before it bogged in too deep.

He started the buckskin back toward more solid ground and with the pull on the rope and the struggling of the steer, he soon had it out on the bank of the stream. The weary animal stumbled and went down, and shaking his loop loose, Gary swung his horse around to get the animal up. Something he saw on the flank made him swing down beside the steer. Curiously, he bent over the brand.

It had been worked over! The Double A had been burned on over a Slash Four!

"Somethin' wrong?"

The voice was cold and level, and Jim Gary started guiltily, turning. Then his eyes widened. "Mart! Well, for cryin' out in the nighttime! Am I glad to see *you!*"

Ray stared. "For the luvva Pete, if it ain't Gary! Say, how did you get here? Don't tell me you're drivin' that herd up ahead?"

"That's right! Your outfit, ain't it? I hired on back down the line. This steer just got hisself bogged down an' I had a heck of a time gettin' him out. You seen Red an' the boys?"

"Not yet, I swung wide. Get that steer on his feet an' we'll join 'em'."

Yet as they rode back, despite Ray's affability, Gary was disturbed. Something here was very wrong. This was a Slash Four steer with the brand worked over to a Double A, the brand for which Ray was foreman. If these cattle were rustled, then Mart Ray was party to it, and so were Slagle, Langer, and Dirksen! And if he was caught with these men and cattle, so was he!

He replied to Ray's questions as well as he could, and briefly, aware that his friend was preoccupied and thinking of something else. Yet at the same time he was pleased that Ray asked him no questions about his reasons for leaving home.

Mart Ray rode up ahead and joined Slagle, and he could see the two men riding on together, deep in conversation. When they bedded down for the night, there had been no further chance to talk to him, and Gary was just as well satisified, for there was much about this that he did not like. Nor was anything said about the midnight rider. When day broke, Mart Ray was gone. "Rode on to Salt Creek," Red said. "We'll see him there." He glanced at Jim, his eyes amused. "He said to keep you on, that you was a top hand."

Despite the compliment, Jim was nettled. What else had Ray told Slagle? His eyes narrowed. Whatever it was, he was not staying on. He was going to get shut of this outfit just as fast as he could. All he wanted was his time. Yet by midday he had not brought himself to ask for it.

Dirksen had grown increasingly silent, and he avoided Langer and Slagle. Watching him, Jim was puzzled by the man, but could find no reason for his behavior unless the man was frightened by something. Finally, Jim pulled up alongside Jeeter.

The man glanced at him and shook his head. "I don't like this. Not even a little. She's too quiet."

Gary hesitated, waiting for the cowhand to continue, but he held his peace. Finally, Gary said, speaking slowly, "It is mighty quiet, but I see nothin' wrong with that. I'm not hunting trouble."

"Trouble," Jeeter said dryly, "comes sometimes whether you hunt it or not. If anything breaks around this herd, take my advice an' don't ask no questions. Just scatter dust out of here!"

"Why are you warning me?" Gary asked.

Jeeter shrugged. "You seem like a right nice feller," he said quietly. "Shame for you to get rung in on somethin' as dirty as this when you had nothin' to do with it."

Despite his questions, Jeeter would say no more, and finally Gary dropped back to the drag. There was little dust because of the rains, but the drag was a rough deal, for the herd was tired and the cattle kept lagging back. Langer and Slagle, Jim observed, spent more time watching the hills than the cattle. Obviously, both men were as jumpy as Dirksen and were expecting something. Toward dusk Red left the herd and rode up a canyon into the hills.

Slagle was still gone, and Jim was squatting by the fire watching Jeeter throw grub together when there was a sudden shot from the hills to the north.

Langer stopped his nervous pacing and faced the direction of the shot, his hand on his gun. Jim Gary got slowly to his feet, and he saw that Jeeter's knuckles gripping the frying pan were white and hard.

Langer was first to relax. "Red must have got him a turkey," he said. "Few around here, and he was sayin' earlier he's sure like some."

Nevertheless, Gary noted that Langer kept back from the firelight and had his rifle near at hand. There was a sound of an approaching horse, and Langer slid his rifle across his knees, but it was Slagle. He swung down, glancing toward the big man. "Shot at a turkey an' missed." Then he added, looking right at Langer, "Nothin' to worry about now. This time for sure."

Dirksen got suddenly to his feet. "I'm quittin', Red. I don't like this a-tall, not none. I'm gettin' out."

Slagle's eyes were flat and ugly. "Sit down an' shut up, Jeeter," he said impatiently. "Tomorrow's our last day. We'll have a payday this side of Salt Creek, an' then if you want to blow, why you can blow out of here."

Gary looked up. "I reckon you can have my time then, too," he said quietly, "I'm ridin' west for Pleasant Valley."

"You?" Langer snorted. "Pleasant Valley? You better stay somewhere where you can be took care of. They don't sidestep trouble out there."

Gary felt something rise within him, but he controlled his anger with an effort. "I didn't ask you for any comment, Tobe," he said quietly. "I can take care of myself."

Langer sneered. "Why, you yaller skunk! I heard all about you! Just because your pappy was a fast man, you must think folks are skeered of you! You're yaller as saffron! You ain't duckin' trouble; you're just scared!"

Gary was on his feet, his face white. "All you've got to do, Tobe, if you want to lose some teeth, is to stand up!"

"*What?*" Langer leaped to his feet. "Why, you dirty—"

Jim Gary threw a roundhouse left. The punch was wide, but it came fast, and Langer was not expecting Jim to fight. Too late, he tried to duck, but the fist caught him on the nose, smashing it and showering the front of his shirt with gore.

The big man was tough, and he sprang in, swinging with both hands. Gary stood his ground, and began to fire punches with both fists. For a full minute the two big men stood toe to toe and slugged wickedly, and then Gary deliberately gave ground. Overeager, Langer leaped after him, and Gary brought up a wicked right that stood Tobe on his boot toes and then a looping left that knocked him into the fire.

With a cry, he leaped from the flames, his shirt smoking. Ruthlessly, Gary grabbed him by the shirtfront and jerked him into a right hand to the stomach and then a right to the head, and shoving him away he split his ear with another looping left, smashing it like an overripe tomato. Langer went down in a heap.

Red Slagle had made no move to interfere, but his eyes were hard and curious as he stared up at Gary. "Now where," he said, "did Ray get the idea that you wouldn't fight?"

Gary spilled water from a canteen over his bloody knuckles. "Maybe he just figured wrong. Some folks don't like trouble. That don't mean they won't fight when they have to."

Langer pulled himself drunkenly to his feet and staggered toward the creek.

Red measured Jim with careful eyes. "What would you do," he asked suddenly, "if Langer reached for a gun?"

Gary turned his level green eyes toward Slagle. "Why, I reckon I'd have to kill him," he said matter-of-factly. "I hope he ain't so foolish."

Dawn broke cold and gray, and Jim Gary walked his horse up into the hills where he heard the shot the night before. He knew that if Slagle saw him, he would be in trouble, but there was much he wanted to know.

Despite the light fall of rain the night before, there were still tracks. He followed those of Slagle's bay until he found where they joined those of a larger horse. Walking the buckskin warily, Jim followed the trail. It came to a sudden end.

A horse was sprawled in the clearing, shot through the head. A dozen feet away lay an old man, a tall old man, his sightless eyes staring toward the lowering skies, his arms flung wide. Jim bent over him and saw that he had been shot three times through the chest. Three times. And the wound lower down was an older wound, several days old, at least.

The horse wore a Slash Four brand. Things were beginning to make sense now. Going through the old man's pockets, Jim found a worn envelope containing some tallies of cattle, and the envelope was addressed to *Tom Blaze, Durango, Colo.*

Tom Blaze . . . the Slash Four!

Tom Blaze, the pioneer Kiowa-fighting cattleman who owned the Slash Four, one of the toughest outfits in the West! Why he had not connected the two Jim could not imagine, but the fact remained that the Slash Four had struck no responsive chord in his thoughts until now.

And Tom Blaze was dead.

Now it all fitted. The old Mother Hubbard saddle had been taken from Tom's horse, for this was the second time he had been shot. Earlier, perhaps when the cattle had been stolen, they had shot him and left him for dead, yet they had been unable to leave the saddle behind, for a saddle was two or three months' work for a cowhand and not to be lightly left behind.

They had been sure of themselves, too. Sure until Gary had seen Blaze, following them despite his wound. After that they had been worried, and Slagle must have sighted Blaze the afternoon before and then followed him and shot him down.

When the Slash Four found Tom Blaze dead all heck

would break loose. Dirksen knew that, and that was why he wanted out, but fast. And it was why Red Slagle and Tobe Langer had pushed so hard to get the cattle to Salt Creek, where they could be lost in larger herds or in the breaks of the hills around the Double A.

When he rode the buckskin down to the fire the others were all up and moving around. Langer's face was swollen and there were two deep cuts, one on his cheekbone, the other over an eye. He was sullen and refused to look toward Gary.

Slagle stared at the buckskin suspiciously, noticing the wetness on his legs from riding in the high grass and brush.

Whatever the segundo had in mind he never got a chance to say. Jim Gary poured a cup of coffee, but held it in his left hand. "Red, I want my money. I'm takin' out."

"Mind if I ask why?" Red's eyes were level and waiting.

Gary knew that Slagle was a gunhand, but the thought did not disturb him. While he avoided trouble, it was never in him to be afraid, nor did his own skill permit it. While he had matched gun speed with only one man, he had that sure confidence that comes from unerring marksmanship and speed developed from long practice.

"No, I don't mind. This morning I found Tom Blaze's body, right where you killed him yesterday afternoon. I know that Slash Four outfit, and I don't want to be any part of this bunch when they catch up to you."

His frankness left Slagle uncertain. He had been prepared for evasion. This was not only sincerity, but it left Slagle unsure as to Gary's actual stand. From his words Slagle assumed Gary was leaving from dislike of fight rather than dislike of rustling.

"You stick with us, Jim," he said. "You're a good man, like Mart said. That Slash Four outfit won't get wise, and there'll be a nice split on this cattle deal."

"I want no part of it," Jim replied shortly. "I'm out. Let me have my money."

"I ain't got it," Red said simply. "Ray pays us all off. I carry no money around. Come on, Jim, lend us a hand.

We've only today; then we'll be at the head of Salt Creek Wash and get paid off."

Gary hesitated. He did need the money, for he was broke and would need grub before he could go on west. Since he had come this far, another day would scarcely matter. "All right, I'll finish the drive."

Nothing more was said, and within the hour they moved out. Yet Gary was restless and worried. He could feel the tenseness in the others and knew they, too, were disturbed. There was no sign of Mart Ray, who should be meeting them soon.

To make matters worse, the cattle were growing restive. The short drives had given them time to recover some of their energy, and several of them, led by one big red steer, kept breaking for the brush. It was hot, miserable work. The clouds still hung low, threatening rain, but the air was sultry.

Jim Gary started the day with the lean gray horse he had ridden before, but by midafternoon he had exchanged the worn-out animal for his own buckskin. Sweat streamed down his body under his shirt, and he worked hard, harrying the irritable animals down the trail that now was lined with piñon and juniper, with a sprinkling of huge boulders. Ahead, a wide canyon opened, and not far beyond would be the spot where he expected to find Ray with the payoff money.

The big red steer suddenly made another bolt for the brush, and the buckskin unwound so fast that it almost unseated Gary. He swore softly and let the horse take him after the steer and cut it back to the herd. As it swung back, he glanced up to see Langer and Red Slagle vanishing into the brush. Where Dirksen was he could not guess until he heard a wild yell.

Swinging around, he saw a dozen hard-riding horsemen cutting down from the brush on both sides, and a glance told him that flight was useless. Nevertheless, Jeeter Dirkson tried it.

Slamming the spurs into his bronc, Dirksen lunged for the brush in the direction taken by Slagle and Langer, but he had made no more than a dozen yards when a rattle of gunfire smashed him from the saddle. His slender body hit the ground rolling, flopped over one last time, and lay sprawled and sightless under the low gray clouds.

Gary rested his hands on his saddle horn and stared gloomily at the strange little man, so badly miscast in this outlaw venture. Then horsemen closed in around him; his six-guns were jerked from their holsters and his rifle from its scabbard.

"What's the matter with you?" The voice was harsh. "Won't that horse of yours run?"

Jim looked up into a pair of cold gray eyes in a leatherlike face. A neat gray mustache showed above a firm-lipped mouth. Jim Gary smiled, although he had never felt less like it in his life. The horsemen surrounded him, and their guns were ready. "Never was much of a hand to run," Jim said, "an' I've done nothing to run for."

"You call murderin' my brother nothin'? You call stealin' cattle nothin'? Sorry, friend, we don't see things alike. I call it hangin'."

"So would I, on'y I haven't done those things. I hired onto this outfit back down the line. Forty bucks to the head of Salt Creek Wash . . . an' they ain't paid me."

"You'll get paid!" The speaker was a lean, hard-faced young man. "With a rope!"

Another rider, a girl, pushed a horse through the circle. "Who is this man, Uncle Dan? Why didn't he try to get away?"

"Says he's just a hired hand," Uncle Dan commented.

"That's probably what that dead man would have said, too!" the lean puncher said. "Let me an' the boys have him under that cottonwood we seen. It had nice strong limbs."

Gary had turned his head to look at the girl. Uncle Dan would be Dan Blaze, and this must be the daughter of the murdered man. She was tall and slim, but rounded of limb and undeniably attractive, with color in her cheeks and a few scattered freckles over her nose. Her eyes were hazel and now looked hard and stormy.

"Did you folks find Tom Blaze's body?" he asked. "They left him back yonder." Lifting a hand carefully to his shirt pocket he drew out the envelope and tally sheets. "These were his."

"What more do you need?" The lean puncher demanded. He pushed his horse against Jim's and grabbed at the buckskin's bridle. "Come on, boys!"

"Take it easy, Jerry!" Dan Blaze said sharply. "When I want him hung, I'll say so." His eyes shifted back to Jim. "You're a mighty cool customer," he said. "If your story's straight, what are you doing with these?"

As briefly as possible, Jim explained the whole situation and ended by saying, "What could I do? I still had forty bucks comin', an' I did my work, so I aim to collect."

"You say there were three men with the herd? And the two who got away were Tobe Langer and Red Slagle?"

"That's right," Jim hesitated over Mary Ray and then said no more.

Blaze was staring at the herd, and now he looked at Jim. "Why were these cattle branded Double A? That's a straight outfit. You know anything about that?"

Gary hesitated. Much as he had reason to believe Ray was not only one of these men but their leader, he hated to betray him. "Not much. I don't know any of these outfits. I'm a Texas man."

Blaze smiled wryly. "You sound it. What's your handle?"

"Jim Gary."

The puncher named Jerry started as if struck. "Jim Gary?" he gasped, his voice incredulous. "The one who killed Sonoma?"

"Yeah, I reckon."

Now they were all staring at him with new interest, for the two fights he had were ample to start his name growing a legend on the plains and desert. These punchers had heard of him, probably from some grub-line rider or drifting puncher.

"Jim Gary," Blaze mused. "We've heard about you. Old Steve's son, aren't you? I knew Steve."

Jim looked up, his eyes cold. "My father," he said grimly, "was a mighty good man!"

Dan Blaze's eyes warmed a little. "You're right. He was."

"What of it?" Jerry demanded sullenly. "The man's a killer. We know that. We found him with the cattle. We found him with some of Tom's stuff on him. What more do you want?"

The girl spoke suddenly. "There was another rider, one who joined you and then rode away. Who was he?"

There it was, and Jim suddenly knew he would not lie. "Mart Ray," he said quietly, "of the Double A."

"That's a lie!" The girl flashed back. "What are you saying?"

"You got any proof of that?" Jerry demanded hotly. "You're talkin' about a friend of our'n."

"He was a friend of mine, too." Gary explained about Mart Ray. "Why don't you turn me loose?" he suggested then. "I'll go get Ray and bring him to you. Chances are Slagle and Tobe will be with him."

"You'll get him?" Jerry snorted. "That's a good one, that is!"

"Tie him," Dan Blaze said suddenly. "We'll go into Salt Creek."

Riding behind Dan Blaze was his niece, whom he heard them call Kitty, Jim Gary was suddenly aware, almost for the first time, of the danger he was in. The fact that it had been averted for the moment was small consolation, for these were hard, desperate men, and one of them, perhaps more, had been slain.

Fear was something strange to him, and while he had known danger, it had passed over him leaving him almost untouched. This situation conveyed only a sense of unreality, and until now the idea that he might really be in danger scarcely seemed credible. Listening to these men, his mind changed about that. He realized belatedly that he was in the greatest danger of his life. If he had none of their talk to warn him, the mute evidence of Jeeter's body was enough. And Jeeter had died yelling to him, trying to give him a warning so he might escape.

Now fear rode with him, a cold, clammy fear that stiffened his fingers and left his mouth dry and his stomach empty. Even the sight of the scattered buildings of the town of Salt Creek did not help, and when they rode up the street, the red of embarrassment crept up his neck at the shame of being led into the town, his hands tied behind him, like a cheap rustler.

Mart Ray was sitting on the steps, and he shoved his hat back and got to his feet. Beside him was Red Slagle. There was no sign of Tobe Langer. "Howdy, Dan! What did you catch? A hoss thief?" Ray's voice was genial, his eyes bland. "Looks like a big party for such a small catch."

Blaze reined in his horse and stopped the little cavalcade. His eyes went from Mart to Slagle. "How long you been here, Red?" he demanded.

"Me?" Slagle was innocent. "No more'n about fifteen minutes, maybe twenty. Just rode in from the Double A. Somethin' wrong?"

Blaze turned his cold eyes on Jim Gary and then looked back to Ray. "We found a herd of Slash Four cattle east of here, Mart. They were wearin' a Double A brand worked over our Slash Four. How do you explain it?"

Ray shrugged. "I don't," he said simply. "How does that hombre you got with you explain it?"

Kitty Blaze spoke up quickly. "Mart, did you ever see this man before? Did you?"

Ray stared at Gary. "Not that I recall," he said seriously. "He sure don't look familiar to me!"

"Blaze," Gary said suddenly, "if you'll turn my hands loose and give me a gun, I can settle this in three minutes! I can prove he's a liar! I can prove that he does know me an' that I know him!"

"There's nothin' you can prove with a gun you can't prove without it!" Blaze said flatly. "Whatever you know, spill it! Else you're gettin' your neck stretched! I'm tired of this fussin' around!"

Jim Gary kneed his horse forward. His eyes were hot and angry. "Mart," he said, "I always suspected there was a streak of coyote in you, but I never knowed you'd be this low-down. I don't like to remind anybody of what I done for him, but I recall a stampede I hauled you out of. Are you goin' to talk?"

Ray shook his head, smiling. "This is a lot of trouble, Dan. Take him away and stretch his neck before I get sore and plug him."

"You'd be afraid to meet me with a gun, Mart. You always were afraid!" Jim taunted. "That's why you left Red and Tobe with the cattle. You wanted the profit but none of the trouble! Well, you've got trouble now! If I had a gun I'd see you eat dirt!"

Mart Ray's face was ugly. "Shut up, you fool! You call me yellow? Why, everybody knows you're yellow as—!" He caught himself abruptly, his face paling under the tan.

"What was that, Ray?" Dan Blaze's face had sharpened. "Ever'body knows what about him? If you've never seen him before, how could you say ever'body calls him yellow?"

Ray shrugged. "Just talkin' too fast, that's all!" He turned and stepped up on the sidewalk. "He's your man. You settle your own war." Ray turned to go, but Jim yelled at him, and Ray wheeled.

"Mart, if I don't know you, how do I know you've got a white scar down your right side, a scar made by a steer's hoof?"

Ray laughed, but it was a strained laugh. He looked trapped now, and he took an involuntary step backward. "That's silly!" he scoffed. "I've no such scar!"

"Why not take off your shirt?" Jerry said suddenly. "That will only take a minute." The lean-jawed cowhand's face was suddenly hard. "I think I remember you having such a scar, from one time I seen you swimmin' in the San Juan. Take off your shirt an' let's see!"

Mart Ray backed up another step, his face sharp and cold. "I'll be damned if I take off my shirt in the street for any low-down rustler!" he snapped. "This here nonsense has gone far enough!"

"Loose my hands!" Jim pleaded in a whisper. "I'll take his shirt off!"

Kitty stared at him. Her face was white and strained, but in her eyes he now saw a shadow of doubt. Yet it was

Jerry who acted suddenly, jerking him around before anyone realized what he had done and severing the bonds with a razor-sharp knife and jerking the ropes from his hands. With almost the same gesture, he slammed guns in Gary's holsters. "All right! Maybe I'm crazy!" he snapped. "But go to it!"

The whole action had taken less than a minute, and Mart Ray had turned his back and started away while Blaze waited in indecision. It was Red Slagle who saw Jim Gary hit the ground. "Boss!" he yelled. His voice was suddenly sharp with panic. "Look out!"

Ray wheeled, and when he saw Gary coming toward him, chafing his wrists, he stood still, momentarily dumbfounded. Then he laughed. "All right, yellow! You're askin' for it! This is one bunch of trouble you can't duck! You've ducked your last fight!"

Furious, he failed to realize the import of his words, and he dropped into a half crouch, his hands ready above his gun butts. It was Jerry who shook him, Jerry who made the casual remark that jerked Mart Ray to realization of what he was facing.

"Looks like whatever Ray knows about him, he sure ain't heard about Jim Gary killin' Miguel Sonoma!"

Mart Ray was staggered. "Sonoma?" he gasped. "You killed Sonoma?"

Jim Gary was facing him now. Some of the numbness was gone from his hands, and something cold and terrible was welling up within him. He had ridden beside this man, shared food with him, worked with him, and now the man had tricked and betrayed him.

"Yes, Mart, I killed Sonoma. I ain't afraid. I never was. I just don't like trouble!"

Ray's tongue touched his lips and his eyes narrowed to slits. He sank a little deeper into the crouch, and men drew away to the sides of the street. Scarcely twenty feet apart, the two faced each other. "Take off your shirt, Ray. Take if off and show them. Reach up slow an' unbutton it. You take it off yourself, or I'll take it off your body!"

"Go to blazes!" Ray's voice was hoarse and strange. Then, with incredible swiftness, his hands dropped for his guns.

In the hot, dusty stillness of the afternoon street, all was deathly still. Somewhere a baby cried, and a foot shifted on the boardwalk. For what seemed an age, all movement seemed frozen and still as the two men in the street faced each other.

Kitty Blaze, her eyes wide with horror, seemed caught in that same breathless time-frozen hush. The hands of the men were moving with flashing speed, but at that instant everything seemed to move hauntingly slow. She saw Mart Ray's gun swing up; she saw the killing eagerness in his face, his lips thinned and white, he eyes blazing.

And she saw the stranger, Jim Gary. Tall, lithe, and strong, his dark face passionless, yet somehow ruthless. And she saw his lean brown hand flash in a blur of movement, saw flame leap from the black muzzles of his guns, and saw Mart Ray smashed back, back, back! She saw his body flung sideways into the hitching rail, saw a horse rear, his lashing hoofs within inches of the man. She saw the gun blaze again from the ground, and a leap of dust from the stranger's shoulder, and she saw Gary move coolly aside to bring his guns better to bear upon the man who was now struggling up.

As in a kind of daze, she saw Jim Gary holding his fire, letting Ray get to his feet. In that stark, incredible instant, she saw him move his lips and she heard the words, as they all heard them in the silence of the street. "I'm sorry, Mart. You shouldn't have played it this way. I'd rather it had been the stampede."

And when Ray's guns swung up. His shirt was bloody, his face twisted in a sort of leer torn into his cheek by a bullet, but his eyes were fiendish. The guns came up, and even as they came level, red flame stabbed from the muzzles of Gary's guns and Ray's body jerked, dust sprang from his shirt's back, and he staggered back and sat down on the edge of the walk, and then as though taken with a severe pain in the groin, he rolled over into the street and sprawled out flat. Somewhere thunder rolled.

For a long moment, the street was motionless. Then somebody said, "We better get inside. She's rainin'."

Jerry swung from his horse and in a couple of strides was beside the fallen man. Ripping back the shirt, he exposed the side, scarred by a steer's hoof.

Dan Blaze jerked around. "Slagle!" he yelled. "Where's Red Slagle! Get him!"

"Here." Slagle was sitting against the building, gripping a bloody hand. "I caught a slug. I got behind Ray." He looked up at Blaze. "Gary's right. He's straight as a string. It was Ray's idea to ring him in and use him as the goat after he found him with us."

Dan Blaze knelt beside him. "Who killed my brother?" he demanded. "Was it you or Ray?"

"Ray shot him first. I finished it. I went huntin' him an' he busted out of the brush. He had a stick he'd carried for walkin' an' I mistook it for a gun."

"What about Langer?" Gary demanded. "Where's he?"

Red grinned, a hard, cold grin. "He lit a shuck. That whuppin' you gave him took somethin' out of him. Once he started to run he didn't stop, not even for his money."

He dug into his pocket. "That reminds me. Here's the forty bucks you earned."

Jim Gary took the money, surprised speechless. Slagle struggled erect. Gary's expression seemed to irritate him. "Well, you earned it, didn't you? An' I hired you, didn't I? Well, I never gypped no man out of honest wages yet!

"Anyway," he added wryly, "by the looks of that rope I don't reckon I'll need it. Luck to you, kid! An'," he grinned, "stay out of trouble."

Thunder rumbled again, and rain poured into the street, a driving, pounding rain that would start the washes running and bring the grass to life again, green and waving for the grazing cattle, moving west, moving north.

AUTHOR'S NOTES

FORK YOUR OWN BRONCS

Water was the most precious item in the West, and it still is. The ownership or control of land was nothing without water, and most cattlemen did not own the land on which their cattle grazed. They merely found the range and grazed their cattle until it became too crowded or they were impelled to move on. The West has ways of hiding its water. At Tinajas Altas, on the old California trail, dozens of men died of thirst with many thousands of gallons of water waiting in natural rock tanks above them.

To a man unfamiliar with the southwestern desert, those bare rocky ridges looked unpromising, and no one not knowing the country would dream there would be water in such unlikely places. Yet it was there, rainwater caught in natural basins, runoff from the bare rocks around.

Nobody ever claimed the way of the West was easy. It had rich rewards, but you had to earn them.

You still do.

Fork Your Own Broncs

Mac Marcy turned in the saddle and, resting his left hand on the cantle, glanced back up the arroyo. His lean, brown face was troubled. There were cattle here, all right, but too few.

At this time of day, late afternoon and very hot, there should have been a steady drift of cattle toward the waterhole.

Ahead of him he heard a steer bawl and then another. Now what? Above the bawling of the cattle he heard another sound, a sound that turned his face gray with worry. It was the sound of hammers.

He needed nothing more to tell him what was happening. Jingle Bob Kenyon was fencing the waterhole!

As he rounded the bend in the wash, the sound of hammers ceased for an instant, but only for an instant. Then they continued with their work.

Two strands of barbed wire had already been stretched tight and hard across the mouth of the wash. Several cowhands were stretching the third wire of what was obviously to be a four-wire fence.

Already Marcy's cattle were bunching near the fence, bawling for water.

As he rode nearer, two men dropped their hammers and lounged up to the fence. Marcy's eyes narrowed and his gaze shifted to the big man on the roan horse. Jingle Bob Kenyon was watching him with grim humor.

Marcy avoided the eyes of the two other men by the fence, Vin Ricker and John Soley, who could mean only one thing for him—trouble, bad trouble. Vin Ricker was a gunhand and a killer. John Soley was anything Vin told him to be.

"This is a rotten trick, Kenyon." Marcy declared angrily. "In this heat my herd will be wiped out."

Kenyon's eyes were unrelenting. "That's just tough," he stated flatly. "I warned yuh when yuh fust come in here to git out while the gittin' was good. Yuh stayed on. Yuh asked for it. Now yuh take it or git out."

Temper flaring within him like a burst of flame, Marcy glared. But deliberately he throttled his fury. He would have no chance here. Ricker and Soley were too much for him, let alone the other hands and Kenyon himself.

"If you don't like it," Ricker sneered, "why don't yuh stop us? I hear tell yuh're a plumb salty hombre."

"You'd like me to give you a chance to kill me, wouldn't you?" Marcy asked harshly. "Someday I'll get you without your guns, Ricker an' I'll tear down your meat house."

Ricker laughed. "I don't want to dirty my hands on yuh, or I'd come over an' make yuh eat those words. If yuh ever catch me without these guns, yuh'll wish to old Harry I still had 'em."

Marcy turned his eyes away from the gunman and looked at Kenyon.

"Kenyon, I didn't think this of you. Without water, my cows won't last three days, an' you know it. You'll bust me flat."

Kenyon was unrelenting. "This is a man's country, Marcy," he said drily. "Yuh fork your own broncs an' yuh git your own water. Don't come whinin' to me. Yuh moved in on me, an' if yuh git along, it'll be on your own."

Kenyon turned his horse and rode away. For an instant Marcy stared after him, seething with rage. Then, abruptly, he wheeled his grayish-black horse—a moros—and started back up the arroyo. Even as he turned, he became aware that only six lean steers faced the barbed wire.

He had ridden but a few yards beyond the bend when that thought struck him like a blow. Six head of all the hundreds he had herded in here! By rights they should all be at the waterhole or heading that way. Puzzled, he started back up the trail.

By rights, there should be a big herd here. Where could they be? As he rode back toward his claim shack, he stared about him. No cattle were in sight. His range was stripped.

Rustlers? He scowled. But there had been no rustling activity of which he had heard. Ricker and Soley were certainly the type to rustle cattle, but Marcy knew Kenyon had been keeping them busy on the home range.

He rode back toward the shack, his heart heavy.

He had saved for seven years, riding cattle trails to Dodge, Abilene, and Ellsworth to get the money to buy his herd. It was his big chance to have a spread of his own, a chance for some independence and a home.

A home! He stared bitterly at the looming rimrock behind his outfit. A home meant a wife, and there was only one girl in the world for him. There would never be another who could make him feel as Sally Kenyon did. But she *would* have to be old Jingle Bob's daughter!

Not that she had ever noticed him. But in those first months before the fight with Jingle Bob became a dog-eat-dog fight, Marcy had seen her around, watched her, been in love with her from a distance. He had always hoped that when his place had proved up and he was settled, he might know her better. He might even ask her to marry him.

It had been a foolish dream. Yet day by day it became even more absurd. He was not only in a fight with her father, but he was closer than ever to being broke.

Grimly, his mind fraught with worry, he cooked his meager supper, crouching before the fireplace. Again and again the thought kept recurring—where were his cattle? If they had been stolen, they would have to be taken down past the waterhole and across Jingle Bob's range. There was no other route from Marcy's corner of range against the rim. For a horseman, yes. But not for cattle.

The sound of a walking horse startled him. He straightened and then stepped away from the fire and put the bacon upon the plate, listening to the horse as it drew nearer. Then he put down his food, and loosening his gun, he stepped to the door.

The sun had set long since, but it was not yet dark. He watched a gray horse coming down from the trees leading up to the rim. Suddenly he gulped in surprise.

It was Sally Kenyon! He stepped outside and walked into the open. The girl saw him and waved a casual hand and then reined in.

"Have you a drink of water?" she asked, smiling. "It's hot, riding."

"Sure," he said, trying to smile. "Coffee, if you want. I was just fixin' to eat a mite. Want to join me? Of course," he said sheepishly, "I ain't no hand with grub."

"I might take some coffee."

Sally swung down, drawing off her gantlets. She had always seemed a tall girl, but on the ground she came just to his shoulder. Her hair was honey colored, her eyes gray.

He caught the quick glance of her eyes as she looked around. He saw them hesitate with surprise at the spectacle of flowers blooming near the door. She looked up, and their eyes met.

"Ain't much time to work around," he confessed. "I sort of been tryin' to make it look like a home."

"Did you plant the flowers?" she asked curiously.

"Yes, ma'am. My mother was always a great hand for flowers. I like 'em, too, so when I built this cabin, I set some out. The wild flowers, I transplanted."

He poured coffee into a cup and handed it to her. She sipped the hot liquid and looked at him.

"I've been hearing about you," she said.

"From Jingle Bob?"

She nodded. "And some others. Vin Ricker, for one. He hates you."

"Who else?"

"Chen Lee."

"Lee?" Marcy shook his head. "I don't place him."

"He's Chinese, our cook. He seems to know a great deal about you. He thinks you're a fine man. A great fighter, too. He's always talking about some Mullen gang you had trouble with."

"Mullen gang?" he stared. "Why, that was in—" He caught himself. "No, ma'am, I reckon he's mistook. I don't know any Chinese an' there ain't no Mullen gang around I know of."

That, he reflected, was no falsehood. The Mullen gang had all fitted very neatly into the boothill he had prepared for them back in Bentown. They definitely weren't around.

"Going to stay here?" she asked, looking at him over her coffee cup, her gray eyes level.

His eyes flashed. "I was fixin' to, but I reckon your old man has stopped me by fencin' that waterhole. He's a hard man, your father."

"It's a hard country." She did not smile. "He's got ideas about it. He drove the Mescaleros out. He wiped out the rustlers; he took this range. He doesn't like the idea of any soft-going, second-run cowhand coming in and taking over."

His head jerked up.

"Soft-going?" he flared. "Second-run? Why, that old billy goat!"

Sally turned toward her horse. "Don't tell me. Tell him. If you've nerve enough!"

He got up and took the bridle of her horse. His eyes were hard.

"Ma'am," he said, striving to make his voice gentle, "I think you're a mighty fine person, an' sure enough purty, but that father of yours is a rough-ridin' old buzzard. If it wasn't for that Ricker hombre—"

"Afraid?" she taunted, looking down at him.

"No, ma'am," he said quietly. "Only I ain't a killin' man. I was raised a Quaker. I don't aim to do no fightin'."

"You're in a fighting man's country,' she warned him. "And you are cutting in on a fighting man's range."

She turned her gray and started to ride away. Suddenly she reined in and looked back over her shoulder.

"By the way," she said, "there's water up on the rim."

* * *

Water up on the rim? What did she mean? He turned his head and stared up at the top of the great cliff, which loomed high overhead into the night. It was fully a mile away, but it seemed almost behind his house.

How could he get up to the rim? Sally had come from that direction. In the morning he would try. In the distance, carried by the still air of night, he heard a cow bawling. It was shut off from the waterhole. His six head, starving for water!

Marcy walked out to the corral and threw a saddle on the moros. He swung into the saddle and rode at a canter toward the waterhole.

They heard him coming, and he saw a movement in the shadows by the cottonwoods.

"Hold it!" a voice called. "What do you want?"

"Let that fence down an' put them cows through!" Marcy yelled.

There was a harsh laugh. "Sorry, amigo. No can do. Only Kenyon cows drink here."

"All right," Marcy snapped. "They are Kenyon cows. I'm givin' 'em to him. Let the fence down an let 'em drink. I ain't seein' no animal die just to please an old plughead. Let em through."

Then he heard Sally's voice. He saw her sitting her horse beside old Joe Linger, who was her bodyguard, teacher, and friend. An old man who had taught her to ride and to shoot and who had been a scout for the Army at some time in the past.

Sally was speaking, and he heard her say, "Let them through, Texas. If they are our cows, we don't want to have them die on us."

Marcy turned the moros and rode back toward his cabin, a sense of defeat heavy upon him. . . .

He rolled out of his blankets with the sun and after a quick breakfast, saddled the grayish-black horse and started back toward the rim. He kept remembering Sally's words, "There is water on the rim." Why had she told him that? What good would water do him if it was way up on the rim?

There must be a way up. By backtracking the girl, he could find it. He was worried about the cattle. The problem of their disappearance kept working into his thoughts. That was another reason for his ride, the major reason. If the cattle were still on his ranch, they were back in the breaks at the foot of the rim.

As he backtracked the girl's horse, he saw cow tracks, more and more of them. Obviously, some of his cattle had drifted this way. It puzzled him, yet he had to admit that he knew little of this country.

Scarcely a year before, he had come into this range, and when he arrived, the grass in the lower reaches of the valley was good, and there were mesquite beans. The cattle grew fat. With hotter and dryer weather, they had shown more and more of a tendency to keep to shady hillsides and to the canyons.

The cow tracks scattered out and disappeared. He continued on the girl's trail. He was growing more and more puzzled, for he was in the shadow of the great cliff now, and any trail that mounted it must be frightfully steep. Sally, of course, had grown up in this country on horseback. With her always had been Joe Linger. Old Joe had been one of the first white men to settle in the rim country.

Marcy skirted a clump of piñon and emerged on a little sandy level at the foot of the cliff. This, at one distant time, had been a stream bed, a steep stream that originated somewhere back up in the rimrock and flowed down here and deeper into his range.

Then he saw the trail. It was a narrow catwalk of rock that clung to the cliff's edge in a way that made him swallow as he looked at it. The catwalk led up the face of the cliff and back into a deep gash in the face of the rim, a gash invisible from below.

The moros snorted a few times, but true to its mountain blood, it took the trail on dainty feet. In an hour Marcy rode out on the rim itself. All was green here, green grass. The foliage on the trees was greener than below. There was every indication of water, but no sign of a cow. Not even a range-bred cow would go up such a trail as Marcy had just ridden.

* * *

Following the tracks of the gray, Marcy worked back through the cedar and piñon until he began to hear a muffled roar. Then he rode through the trees and reined in at the edge of a pool that was some twenty feet across. Water flowed into it from a fair-sized stream, bubbling over rocks and falling into the pool. There were a number of springs here, and undoubtedly the supply of water was limitless. But where did it go?

Dismounting, Marcy walked down to the edge of the water and knelt on a flat rock and leaned far out.

Brush hung far out over the water at the end of the pool, brush that grew on a rocky ledge no more than three feet above the surface of the water. But beneath that ledge was a black hole at least eight feet long. Water from the pool was pouring into that black hole.

Mac Marcy got up and walked around the pool to the ledge. The brush was very thick, and he had to force his way through. Clinging precariously to a clump of manzanita, he leaned out over the rim of the ledge and tried to peer into the hole. He could see nothing except a black slope of water and that the water fell steeply beyond that slope.

He leaned further out, felt the manzanita give way slowly, and made a wild clutch at the neighboring brush. Then he plunged into the icy waters of the pool.

He felt himself going down, down, down! He struck out, trying to swim, but the current caught him and swept him into the gaping mouth of the wide black hole under the ledge.

Darkness closed over his head. he felt himself shooting downward. He struck something and felt it give beneath him, and then something hit him a powerful blow on the head. Blackness and icy water closed over him.

Chattering teeth awakened him. He was chilled to the bone and soaking wet. For a moment he lay on hard, smooth rock in darkness, head throbbing, trying to realize what had happened. His feet felt cold. He pulled them up and turned over to a sitting position in a large cave. Only then did he realize his feet had been lying in a pool of water.

Far above he could see a faint glimmer of light, a

glimmer feebly reflecting from the black, glistening roar of a fall. He tilted his head back and stared upward through the gloom. That dim light, the hole through which he had come, was at least sixty feet above him!

In falling he had struck some obstruction in the narrow chimney of the water's course, some piece of driftwood or brush insecurely wedged across the hole. It had broken his descent and had saved him.

His matches would be useless. Feeling around the cave floor in the dark, he found some dry tinder that had been lying here for years. He still had his guns, since they had been tied in place with rawhide thongs. He drew one of them, extracted a cartridge, and went to work on it with his hunting knife.

When it was open, he placed it carefully on the rock beside him. Then he cut shavings and crushed dried bark in his hand. Atop this he placed the powder from the open cartridge.

Then he went to work to strike a spark from a rock with the steel back of his knife. There was not the slightest wind here. Despite that, he worked for the better part of an hour before a spark sprang into the powder.

There was a bright burst of flame and the shavings crackled. He added fuel and then straightened up and stepped back to look around.

He stood on a wide ledge in the gloomy, closed cavern at the foot of the fall's first drop, down which he had fallen. The water struck the rock not ten feet away from him. Then it took another steep drop off to the left. He could see by the driftwood that had fallen clear that it was the usual thing for the rushing water to cast all waterborne objects onto this ledge.

The ledge had at one time been deeply gouged and worn by running water. Picking up a torch, Marcy turned and glanced away into the darkness. There lay the old dry channel, deeply worn and polished by former running water.

At some time in the past, this had been the route of the stream underground. In an earthquake or some breakthrough of the rock, the water had taken the new course.

Thoughtfully, Marcy calculated his situation.

* * *

He was fearful of his predicament. From the first moment of consciousness in that utter darkness, he had been so. There is no fear more universal than the fear of entombment alive, the fear of choking, strangling in utter darkness beyond the reach of help.

Mac Marcy was no fool. He was, he knew, beyond the reach of help. The moros was ground hitched in a spot where there was plenty of grass and water. The grayish-black horse would stay right there.

No one, with the exception of Sally, ever went to the top of the rim. It was highly improbable that she would go again soon. In many cases, weeks would go by without anyone stopping by Marcy's lonely cabin. If he was going to get out of this hole, he would have to do it by his own efforts.

One glance up that fall showed him there was no chance of going back up the way he had come down. Working his way over to the next step downward of the fall, he held out his torch and peered below. All was utter blackness, with only the cold damp of falling water in the air.

Fear was mounting within him now, but he fought it back, forcing himself to be calm and to think carefully. The old dry channel remained a vague hope. But to all appearances it went deeper and deeper into the stygian blackness of the earth. He put more fuel on his fire and started exploring again. Fortunately, the wood he was burning was bone dry and made almost no smoke.

Torch in hand he started down the old dry channel. This had been a watercourse for many, many years. The rock was worn and polished. He had gone no more than sixty feet when the channel divided.

On the left was a black, forbidding hole, scarcely waist high. Down that route most of the water seemed to have gone, as it was worn the deepest.

On the right was an opening almost like a doorway. Marcy stepped over to it and held his torch out. It also was a black hole. He had a sensation of awful depth. Stepping back, he picked up a rock. Leaning out, he dropped it into the hole on the right.

For a long time he listened. Then, somewhere far

below, there was a splash. This hole was literally hundreds of feet deep. It would end far below the level of the land on which his cabin stood.

He drew back. Sweat stood out on his forehead, and when he put his hand to it, his brow felt cold and clammy. He looked at the black waist-high hole on the left and felt fear rise within him as he had never felt it before. He drew back and wet his lips.

His torch was almost burned out. Turning with the last of its light, he retraced his steps to the ledge by the fall.

How long he had been below ground, he didn't know. He looked up, and there was still a feeble light from above. But it seemed to have grown less. Had night almost come?

Slowly he built a new torch. This was his last chance of escape. It was a chance he had already begun to give up. Of them all, that black hole on the left was least promising, but he must explore it.

He pulled his hat down a little tighter and started back to where the tunnel divided into two holes. His jaw was set grimly. He got down on his hands and knees and edged into the black hole on the left.

Once inside, he found it fell away steeply in a mass of loose boulders. Scrambling over them, he came to a straight, steep fall of at least ten feet. Glancing at the sheer drop, he knew one thing—once down there, he would never get back up!

Holding his torch high, he looked beyond. Nothing but darkness. Behind him there was no hope. he hesitated and then got down on his hands and knees, lowered himself over the edge, and dropped ten feet.

This time he had to be right, for there was no going back. He walked down a slanting tunnel. It seemed to be growing darker. Glancing up at his torch, he saw it was burning out. In a matter of minutes he would be in total darkness.

He walked faster and faster. Then he broke into a stumbling run, fear rising within him. Something brought him up short, and for a moment he did not see what had caused him to halt in his blind rush. Then hope broke over him like a cold shower of rain.

There on the sand beneath his feet were tiny tracks! He bent over them. A packrat or some other tiny creature. Getting up, he hurried on, and seeing a faint glow ahead, he rushed around a bend. There before him was the feeble glow of the fading day. His torch guttered and went out.

He walked on to the cave mouth, trembling in every limb. Mac Marcy was standing in an old watercourse that came out from behind some boulders not two miles from his cabin.

He stumbled home and fell into his bunk, almost too tired to undress. . . .

Marcy awakened to a frantic pounding on his door. Staggering erect, he pulled on his boots, yelling out as he did so. Then he drew on his Levi's and shirt and opened the door, buttoning his shirt with one hand.

Sally, her face deathly pale, was standing outside. Beyond her gray mare stood Marcy's moros. At the sight of him the grayish-black horse lifted his head and pricked up his ears.

"Oh!" Sally gasped. "I thought you were dead—drowned!"

He stepped over beside her.

"No," he said, "I guess I'm still here. You're purty scared, ma'am. What's there for you to be scared about?"

"Why," she burst out impatiently, "if you—" She caught herself and stopped abruptly. "After all," she continued coolly, "no one wants to find a friend drowned."

"Ma'am," he said sincerely, "if you get that wrought up, I'll get myself almost drowned every day."

She stared at him and then smiled. "I think you're a fool," she said. She mounted and turned. "But a nice fool."

Marcy stared after her thoughtfully. Well now, maybe—

He glanced down at his boots. Where they had lain in the pool, there was water stain on them. Also, there was a small green leaf clinging to the rough leather. He stooped and picked it off, wadded it up, and started to throw it away when he was struck by an idea. He unfolded the leaf and studied the veins. Suddenly his face broke into a grin.

"Boy," he said to the moros, "we got us a job to do, even if you do need a rest." he swung into the saddle and rode back toward the watercourse, still grinning.

It was midafternoon when he returned to the cabin and ate a leisurely lunch, still chuckling. Then he mounted again and started for the old waterhole that had been fenced by Jingle Bob Kenyon.

When Marcy rounded the bend, he could see that something was wrong. A dozen men were gathered around the waterhole. Nearby and astride her gray was Sally.

The men were in serious conference, and they did not notice Marcy's approach. He rode up, leaning on the horn of the saddle, and watched them, smiling.

Suddenly Vin Ricker looked up. His face went hard.

Mac Marcy swung down and strolled up to the fence, leaning casually on a post.

"What's up?"

"The waterhole's gone dry!" Kenyon exploded. "Not a drop o' water in it."

Smothering a grin, Marcy rolled a smoke.

"Well," he said philosophically, "the Lord giveth an' He taketh away. No doubt it's the curse of the Lord for your greed, Jingle Bob."

Kenyon glared at him suspiciously. "Yuh know somethin' about this?" he demanded. "Man, in this hot weather my cattle will die by the hundreds. Somethin's got to be done."

"Seems to me," Marcy said drily, "I have heard them words before."

Sally was looking at him over her father's head, her face grave and questioning. But she said nothing, gave no sign of approval or disapproval.

"This here's a man's country," Marcy said seriously. "Yuh fork your own broncs an' you get your own water."

Kenyon flushed. "Marcy, if you know anythin' about this, for goodness sake spill it. My cows will die. Maybe I was too stiff about this, but there's somethin' mighty funny goin' on here. This waterhole ain't failed in twenty years."

"Let me handle him," Riker snarled. "I'm just achin' to git my hands on him."

"Don't ache too hard, or you'll git your wish." Marcy drawled, and he crawled through the fence. "All right, Kenyon, we'll talk business," Marcy said to the rancher. "You had me stuck yesterday with my tail in a crack. Now you got yours in one. I cut off your water to teach you a lesson. You're a blamed old highbinder, an' it's high time you had some teeth pulled.

"Nobody but me knows how that water's cut off and where. If I don't change it, nobody can. So listen to what I'm sayin.' I'm goin' to have all the water I need after this on my own place, but this here hole stays open. No fences.

"This mornin' when I went up to cut your water off, I saw some cow tracks. I'm missin' a powerful lot of cows. I follered the tracks into a hidden draw an' found three hundred of my cattle an' about a hundred head of yours, all nicely corraled an' ready to be herded across the border.

"While I was lookin' over the hideout, I spied Ricker there. John Soley then come ridin' up with about thirty head of your cattle, an' they run 'em in with the rest."

"You're a liar!" Ricker burst out, his face tense, and he dropped into a crouch, his fingers spread.

Marcy was unmoved. "No, I ain't bluffing. You try to prove where you were about nine this mornin'. An' don't go tryin' to git me into a gunfight. I ain't a-goin' to draw, an' you don't dare shoot me down in front of witnesses. But you take off those guns, an' I'll—"

Ricker's face was ugly. "Yuh bet I'll take 'em off! I allus did want a crack at that purty face o' yours."

He stripped off his guns and swung them to Soley in one movement. Then he rushed.

A wicked right swing caught Marcy before he dropped his gun belt and got his hands up, and it knocked him reeling into the dirt.

Ricker charged, his face livid, trying to kick Marcy with his boots, but Marcy rolled over and got on his feet. He lunged and swung a right that clipped Ricker on the temple. Then Marcy stabbed the rustler with a long left. They started to slug.

Neither had any knowledge of science. Both were raw and tough and hard-bitten. Toe to toe, bloody and bitter, they slugged it out. Ricker, confident and the larger of the two men, rushed in swinging. One of his swings cut Marcy's eye; another started blood gushing from Marcy's nose. Ricker set himself and threw a hard right for Marcy's chin, but the punch missed as Marcy swung one to the body that staggered Ricker.

They came in again, and Marcy's big fist pulped the rustler's lips, smashing him back on his heels. Then Marcy followed it in, swinging with both hands. His breath came in great gasps, but his eyes were blazing. He charged in, following Ricker relentlessly.

Suddenly Marcy's right caught the gunman and knocked him to his knees. Marcy stepped back and let him get up and then knocked him sliding on his face in the sand. Ricker tried to get up, but he fell back, bloody and beaten.

Swiftly, before the slow-thinking Soley realized what was happening, Marcy spun and grabbed one of his own guns and turned it on this rustler.

"Drop 'em!" he snapped. "Unbuckle your belt an step back!"

Jingle Bob Kenyon leaned on his saddle horn, chewing his pipestem thoughtfully.

"What," he drawled, "would yuh of done if he drawed his gun?"

Marcy looked up, surprised. "Why, I'd have killed him, of course." He glanced over at Sally, and then looked back at Kenyon. "Afore we git off the subject," he said, "we finish our deal. I'll turn your water back into this hole—I got it stopped up away back inside the mountain—but as I said, the hole stays open to anybody. Also—" Marcy's face colored a little "—I'm marryin' Sally."

"You're *what*?" Kenyon glared and then jerked around to look at his daughter.

Sally's eyes were bright. "You heard him, Father," she replied coolly. "I'm taking back with me those six steers he gave you so he could get them to water."

Marcy was looking at Kenyon when suddenly Marcy grinned.

"I reckon," he said, "you had your lesson. Sally an' me have got a lot of talkin' to do."

Marcy swung aboard the moros, and he and Sally started off together.

Jingle Bob Kenyon stared after them, grim humor in his eyes.

"I wonder," he said, "what he would have done if Ricker had drawed?"

Old Joe Linger grinned and looked over at Kenyon from under his bushy brows. "Jest what he said. He'd of kilt him. That's Quaker John McMarcy, the hombre that wiped out the Mullen gang single-handed. He jest don't like to fight, that's all."

"It sure does beat all," Kenyon said thoughtfully. "The trouble a man has to go to git him a good son-in-law these days!"

AUTHOR'S NOTE

HOME IN THE VALLEY

Many of my stories are based upon historical incidents, such as the ride from Knights Landing to Portland reported in this story. I liked the story very much and felt that the ride should be preserved for history, so I used it in my novel Sitka *as well. The ride was actually made by a man named Louis Remme, under much the same circumstances as repeated here.*

Western horses were no such pampered beasts as we have today. There are many splendid horses now, some of the finest stock a man could hope to see, but Western horses usually were mustangs or had a streak of the wild horse in them. They were accustomed to long runs across country under adverse conditions. To ride seventy miles on one horse in one day was not unusual, and more than one cowboy has ridden that far to a dance and then back the following morning.

In the endurance race in 1903 from Chadron, Nebraska, to Chicago, each rider was to ride one horse and lead another. To make the distance in time meant covering seventy-five miles a day for thirteen days. Nice work if you can do it and have the horses!

Home in the Valley

Steve Mehan placed the folded newspaper beside his plate and watched the waiter pour his coffee. He was filled with that warm, expansive glow that comes only from a job well done, and he felt he had just cause to feel it.

Jake Hitson, the moneylending rancher from down at the end of Pahute Valley, had sneered when he heard of the attempt, and the ranchers had shaken their heads doubtfully when Steve first told them of his plan. They had agreed only because there was no alternative. He had proposed to drive a herd of cattle from the Nevada range to California in the dead of winter!

To the north the passes were blocked with snow, and to the south lay miles of trackless and almost waterless desert. Yet they had been obligated to repay the money Hitson had loaned them by the first day of March or lose their ranches to him. It had been a pitifully small amount when all was considered, yet Hitson had held their notes, and he had intended to have their range.

Months before, returning to Nevada, Steve Mehan had scouted the route. The gold rush was in full swing, people were crowding into California, and there was a demand for beef. As a boy he had packed and freighted over most of the trails and knew them well, so finally the ranchers had given in.

The drive had been a success. With surprisingly few losses he had driven the herd into central California and had sold out, a few head here and a few there, and the prices had been good.

The five ranchers of Pahute Valley who had trusted their cattle to him were safe. Twenty thousand dollars in fifty-dollar gold slugs had been placed on deposit in Dake & Company's bank here in Sacramento City.

With a smile, he lifted his coffee cup. Then, as a shadow darkened his table, he glanced up to see Jake Hitson.

The man dropped into a chair opposite him, and there was a triumphant light in his eyes that made Steve suddenly wary. Yet with the gold in the bank there was nothing to make him apprehensive.

"Well, yuh think yuh've done it, don't yuh?" Hitson's voice was malicious. "Yuh think yuh've stopped me? Yuh've played the hero in front of Betty Bruce, and the ranchers will welcome yuh back with open arms. Yuh think when everything was lost you stepped in and saved the day?"

Mehan shrugged. "We've got the money to pay yuh, Jake. The five brands of the Pahute will go on. This year looks like a good one, and we can drive more cattle over the route I took this time, so they'll make it now. And that in spite of all the bad years and the rustlin' of yore friends."

Hitson chuckled. He was a big man with straw-colored brows and a flat red face. From one small spread down there at the end of the Pahute he had expanded to take in a fair portion of the valley. The methods he had used would not bear examination, and strange cattle had continued to flow into the valley, enlarging his herds. Many of the brands were open to question. The hard years and losses due to cold or drouth did not affect him, because he kept adding to his herds from other sources.

During the bad years he had loaned money, and his money had been the only help available. The fact that he was a man disliked for his arrogant manner and his crooked connections made the matter only the more serious.

Hitson grinned with malice. "Read yore paper yet, Mehan? If yuh want to spoil yore breakfast, turn to page three."

Steve Mehan's dark eyes held the small blue ones of Hitson, and he felt something sick and empty in his stomach. Only bad news for him could give Hitson the satisfaction he was so obviously feeling.

Yet even as Steve opened the paper, a man bent over the table next to him.

"Heard the news?" he asked excitedly. "Latch & Evans banking house has failed. That means that Dake & Company are gone, too. They'll close the doors. There's already a line out there a hundred yards long and still growin'!"

Steve opened his paper slowly. The news was there for all to read. Latch & Evans had failed. The managing director had flown the coop, and only one interpretation could be put upon that. Dake & Company, always closely associated with Latch & Evans, would be caught in the collapse. February of 1855 would see the end of the five brands of Pahute Valley. It would be the end of everything he had planned, everything he wanted for Betty.

"See?" Hitson sneered, heaving himself to his feet. "Try and play hero now! I've got you and them highfalutin' friends of yores where I want 'em now! I'll kick every cussed one of 'em into the trail on March first, and with pleasure! And that goes for you, Steve Mehan!"

Steve scarcely heard him. He was remembering that awful drive. The hard winds, the bitter cold, the bawling cattle. And then the desert, the Indians, the struggle to get through with the herd intact—and all to end in this. Collapse and failure. Yes, and the lives of two men had been sacrificed, the two who had been killed on the way over the trail.

Mehan remembered Chuck Farthing's words. He had gone down with a Mohave Indian's bullet in his chest.

"Get 'em through, boy. Save the old man's ranch for him. That's all I ask!"

It had been little enough for two lives. And now they were gone, for nothing.

The realization hit Steve Mehan like a blow and brought him to his feet fighting mad, his eyes blazing, his jaw set.

"I'll be eternally blasted if they have!" he exploded, though only he knew what he meant.

He started for the door, leaving his breakfast unfinished behind him, his mind working like lightning. The whole California picture lay open for him now. The news of the failure would have reached the Dake & Company branches in Marysville and Grass Valley. And in Placerville. There was no hope there.

Portland? He stopped short, his eyes narrowed with thought. Didn't they have a branch in Portland? Of course! He remembered it well, now that he thought of it. The steamer from San Francisco would leave the next morning, and it would be carrying the news. But what if he could beat that steamer to Portland?

Going by steamer himself would be futile, for he would arrive at the same time the news did, and there would be no chance for him to get his money. Hurrying down the street, his eyes scanning the crowds for Pink Egan and Jerry Smith, punchers who had made the drive with him, he searched out every possible chance, and all that remained was that seven hundred miles of trail between Sacramento and Portland, rough, and part of it harassed by warring Modocs.

He paused, glancing around. He was a tall young man with rusty brown hair and a narrow, rather scholarly face. To the casual observer he looked like a roughly dressed frontier doctor or lawyer. Actually, he was a man bred to the saddle and the wild country.

Over the roofs of the buildings he could see the smoke of a steamboat. It was the stern-wheeler *Belle*, just about to leave for Knights Landing, forty-two miles upstream.

He started for the gangway, walking fast, and just as he reached it a hand caught his sleeve. He wheeled to see Pink and Jerry at his elbow.

"Hey!" Smith demanded. "Where yuh goin' so fast? We run two blocks to catch up with yuh."

Quickly, Steve explained. The riverboat tooted its whistle, and the crew started for the gangway to haul it aboard. "It's our only chance!" Steve Mehan exclaimed. "I've got to beat that steamboat from Frisco to Portland and draw my money before they get the news! Don't tell anybody where I've gone, and keep yore eyes on Hitson!"

He lunged for the gangway and raced aboard. It was foolish, it was wild, it was impossible, but it was their only chance. Grimly, he recalled what he had told Betty Bruce when he left the Valley.

"I'll get them cattle over, honey, or I'll die tryin'!"

"You come back, Steve!" she had begged. "That's all I ask. We can always go somewhere and start over. We always have each other."

"I know, honey, but how about yore father? How about Pete Farthing? They're too old to start over, and the ranches are all they have. They worked like slaves, fought Indians, gave a lot in sweat and blood for their ranches. I'll not see 'em turned out now. Whatever comes, I'll make it."

As the riverboat pushed away from the dock, he glanced back. Jake Hitson was staring after him, his brow furrowed. Jake had seen him, and that was bad.

Mehan put such thoughts behind him. The boat would not take long to get to Knights Landing, and he could depend upon Knight to help him. The man had migrated from New Mexico fifteen years before, but he had known Steve's father, and they had come over the Santa Fe Trail together. From a mud-and-wattle hut on an Indian mound at the landing, he had built a land grant he got from his Mexican wife into a fine estate, and the town had been named for him.

Would Jake Hitson guess what he was attempting? If so, what could he do? The man had money, and with money one can do many things, Hitson would not stop at killing. Steve had more than a hunch that Hitson had urged the Mohaves into the attack on the cattle drive that had resulted in the death of Chuck Farthing. He had more than a hunch that the landslide that had killed Dixie Rollins had been due to more than purely natural causes. But he could prove nothing.

His only chance was to reach Portland before the news did. He was not worried about their willingness to pay him the money. The banks made a charge of one half of one per cent for all withdrawals over a thousand dollars, and it would look like easy profit to the agent at the banking and express house.

Nor was it all unfamiliar country, for Steve had spent two years punching cows on ranches, prospecting and hunting through the northern valleys, almost as far as the Oregon line.

When the *Belle* shouldered her comfortable bulk against the landing at Knights, Mehan did not wait for the gangway. He grabbed the bulwark and vaulted ashore, landing on his hands and knees.

He found Knight standing on the steps of his home, looking down toward the river.

"A hoss, Steve?" Knight repeated. "Shorest thing yuh know. What's up?"

While Steve threw a saddle on a tall chestnut, he explained briefly.

"Yuh'll never make it, boy!" Knight protested. "It's a hard drive, and the Modocs are raidin' again." He chewed on his mustache as Steve swung into the saddle. "Boy," he said, "when yuh get to the head of Grand Island, see the judge. He's an old friend of mine, and he'll let yuh have a hoss. Good luck!"

Steve wheeled the chestnut into the street and started north at a spanking trot. He kept the horse moving, and the long-legged chestnut had a liking for the trail. He moved out eagerly, seeming to catch some of the anxiety to get over the trail that filled his rider.

At the head of Grand Island, Steve swapped horses and started north again, holding grimly to the trail. There was going to be little time for rest and less time to eat. He would have to keep moving if he was going to make it. The trail over much of the country was bad, and the farther north he got toward the line, the worse it would be.

His friends on the ranches remembered him, and he repeatedly swapped horses and kept moving. The sun was setting in a rose of glory when he made his fourth change of mount near the Marysville Buttes. The purple haze of evening was gathering when he turned up the trail and lined out.

He had money with him, and he paid a bonus plus a blown horse when necessary. But the stockmen were natural allies, as were the freighters along the route, and they were always willing to help. After leaving Knights Landing he told no one his true mission, his only explanation being that he was after a thief. In a certain sense, that was exactly true.

At ten o'clock, ten hours out of Sacramento, he galloped into the dark streets of Red Bluffs. No more than five minutes later, clutching a sandwich in his hand and with a fresh horse under him, he was off again.

Darkness closed around him, and the air was cool. He had no rifle with him, only the pistol he habitually wore and plenty of ammunition.

The air was so cold that he drew his coat around him, tucking it under and around his legs. He spoke softly to the horse, and its ears twitched. It was funny about a horse—how much they would give for gentleness. There was no animal which responded so readily to good treatment, and no other animal would run itself to death for a man—except, occasionally, a dog.

The hoofs of the horse beat a pounding rhythm upon the trail, and Steve leaned forward in the saddle, hunching himself against the damp chill and to cut wind resistance. His eyes were alert, although weariness began to dull his muscles and take the drive and snap from them.

Twenty miles out of Red Bluffs he glimpsed a fire shining through the trees. He slowed the horse, putting a hand on its damp neck. It was a campfire. He could see the light reflecting from the front of a covered wagon, and he heard voices speaking. He rode nearer and saw the faces of the men come around toward him.

"Who's there?" A tall man stepped around the fire with a rifle in his hand.

"Mehan, a cattleman. I'm after a thief and need a fresh hoss."

"Well, 'light and talk. Yuh won't catch him on that hoss. Damn' fine animal," he added, "but yuh've shore put him over the road."

"He's got heart, that one!" Steve said, slapping the horse. "Plenty of it! Is that coffee I smell?"

The bearded man picked up the pot. "It shore is, pardner. Have some!" He poured a cupful, handed it to Steve, and then strolled over to the horse. "Shucks, with a rubdown and a blanket he'll be all right. Tell yuh what I'll do. I've got a buckskin here that'll run 'til he drops. Give me twenty to boot and he's yores."

Mehan looked up. "Done, but you throw in a couple of sandwiches."

The bearded man chuckled. "Shore will." He glanced at the saddle as Steve began stripping it from the horse. "Yuh've got no rifle?"

"No, only a pistol. I'll take my chances."

"Haven't got a rifle to spare, but I'll make yuh a deal on this." He handed Steve a four-barreled Braendlin repeating pistol. "Frankly, mister, I need money. Got my family down to Red Bluffs, and I don't want to come in broke."

"How much?"

"Another twenty?"

"Shore, if yuh've got ammunition for it."

"I've got a hundred rounds. And it goes with the gun." The man dug out the ammunition. "Joe, wrap up a couple of them sandwiches for the man. Got smokin'?"

"Shore thing." Steve swung into the saddle and pocketed the extra pistol. He put the ammunition in his saddlebags. "Good luck."

"Hope yuh catch him!" the man called.

Steve touched a spur lightly to the big buckskin and was gone in a clatter of hoofs. Behind him the fire twinkled lonesomely among the dark columns of the trees, and then as he went down beyond a rise, the light faded and he was alone in the darkness, hitting the road at a fast trot.

Later, he saw the white radiance that preceded the moon, and something else—the white, gleaming peak of Mount Shasta, one of the most beautiful mountains in the world. Lifting its fourteen-thousand-foot peak above the surrounding country, it was like a throne for the Great Spirit of the Indians.

In darkness and moving fast, Steve Mehan rode down the trail into Shasta and then on to Whiskeytown.

A drunken miner lurched from the side of a building and flagged him down. "No use hurryin'," he said. "It ain't true!"

"What ain't true?" Steve stared at him. "What yuh talkin' about?"

"That Whiskey Creek. Shucks, it's got water in it just like any creek!" He spat with disgust. "I come all the way down here from Yreka huntin' it!"

"You came from Yreka?" Steve grabbed his shoulder. "How's the trail? Any Indians out?"

"Trail?" The miner spat. "There ain't no trail! A loose-minded mule walked through the brush a couple of times, that's all! Indians? Modocs? Man, the woods is full of 'em! Behind ever' bush! Scalp-huntin' bucks, young and old. If yuh're headin' that way, you won't get through. Yore hair will be in a tepee 'fore two suns go down!"

He staggered off into the darkness, trying a song that dribbled away and lost itself in the noise of the creek.

Mehan walked the horse down to the creek and let him drink.

"No whiskey, but we'll settle for water, won't we, Buck?"

The creek had its name, he remembered, from an ornery mule who lost the barrel from its pack. It broke in Whiskey Creek, which promptly drew a name upon itself.

Steve Mehan started the horse again, heading for the stage station at Tower House, some ten miles up the road. The buckskin was weary but game. Ahead of him and on his right, still loomed the peak of Mount Shasta, seeming large in the occasional glimpses, even at the distance that still separated them.

He almost fell from his horse at Tower House, with dawn bright in the eastern sky beyond the ragged mountains. The stage tender blinked sleepy eyes at him and then at the horse.

"Yuh've been givin' her blazes," he said. "In a mite of hurry?"

"After a thief," mumbled Steve.

The man scratched his grizzled chin. "He must be a goin' son of a gun," he commented whimsically. "Want anything?"

"Breakfast and a fresh hoss."

"Easy done. Yuh ain't figurin' on ridin' north, are yuh? Better change yore plans if yuh are, because the

Modocs are out and they're in a killin' mood. No trail north of here, yuh know."

With a quick breakfast and what must have been a gallon of coffee under his belt, Steve Mehan swung into the saddle and started once more. The new horse was a gray and built for the trail. Steve was sodden with weariness, and at every moment his lids fluttered and started to close. But now, for a while at least, he dared not close them.

Across Clear Creek he rode into the uplands where no wagon road had ever been started. It was a rugged country, but one he remembered from the past, and he wove around among the trees, following the thread of what might have been a trail. Into a labyrinth of canyons he rode, following the vague trail up the bottom of a gorge, now in the water, then out of it. Then he climbed a steep trail out of the gorge and headed out across the long rolling swell of a grass-covered mountainside.

The air was much colder now, and there was an occasional flurry of snow. At times he clung to the saddle horn, letting the horse find his own trail, just so that trail was north. He rode into the heavily forested sides of the Trinity Mountains, losing the trail once in the dimness under the tall firs and tamaracks, but keeping on his northern route. Eventually he again hit what must have been the trail.

His body ached, and he fought to keep his eyelids open. Once he dismounted and walked for several miles to keep himself awake and to give the horse a slight rest. Then he was back in the saddle and riding once more.

Behind him somewhere was Jake Hitson. Jake, he knew well, would not give up easily. If he guessed what Mehan was attempting he would stop at nothing to prevent it. And yet there was no way of preventing it unless he came north with the boat and reached Portland before him. And that would do no good, for if the boat got to Portland before him, the news would be there, and nothing Hitson could do would be any worse than the arrival of that news.

Egan and Smith would have their eyes on Jake Hitson, but he might find some means of getting away. Certainly,

Steve thought grimly, nothing on horseback was going to catch him now.

The wind grew still colder and howled mournfully under the dark, needled trees. He shivered and hunched his shoulders against the wind. Once, half alseep, he almost fell from the horse when the gray shied at a fleeing rabbit.

As yet there were no Indians. He peered ahead across the bleak and forbidding countryside, but it was empty. And then, not long later, he turned down a well-marked trail to Trinity Creek.

He swung down in front of a log bunkhouse. A miner was at the door.

"A hoss?" The miner chuckled. "Stranger, yuh're shore out of luck! There ain't a hoss hereabouts yuh could get for love or money!"

Steve Mehan sagged against the building, "Mister," he mumbled, "I've just got to get a hoss. I've got to!"

"Sorry, son. There just ain't none. Nobody in town would give up his hoss right now, and they are mighty scarce at that! Yuh'd better come in and have some coffee."

Steve stripped his saddle and bridle from his horse and walked into the house. He almost fell into a chair. Several miners playing cards looked up. "Amigo," one of them said, "yuh'd better lay off that stuff."

Mehan's head came up heavily, and he peered at the speaker, a blond giant in a red-checked shirt.

"I haven't slept since I left Sacramento," he said. "Been in the saddle ever since."

"*Sacramento?*" The young man stared. "You must be crazy!"

"He's chasin 'a thief." said the miner Steve had first seen. He was bringing Steve a cup of coffee. "I'd want a man awful bad before I rode like that."

"I got to beat the steamer to Portland," Steve said. It was a lie in a way, but actually the truth. "If I don't the fellow will get away with fifteen thousand dollars!"

"Fifteen thou—" The young man laid down his hand. "Brother," he said emphatically, "I'd ride, too!"

Steve gulped the coffee and lurched to his feet.

"Got to find a hoss," he said and lunged outside.

It took him less than a half hour to prove to himself that it was an impossibility. Nobody would even consider selling a horse, and his own was in bad shape.

"Not a chance!" they told him. "A man without a hoss in this country is through! No way in or out but on a hoss, and not an extry in town!"

He walked back to the stable. One look at his own horse told him the animal was through. There was no chance to go farther with it. No matter what he might do, the poor creature could stagger no more than a few miles. It would be killing a good horse to no purpose. Disgusted and discouraged, numbed with weariness, he stood in the cold wind, rubbing his grizzled chin with a fumbling hand.

So this was the end. After all his effort, the drive over the mountains and desert, the long struggle to sell out, and then this ride, and all for nothing. Back there in the Pahute the people he had left behind would be trusting him, keeping their faith. For no matter how much they were sure he would fail, their hopes must go with him. And now he had failed.

Wearily he staggered into the bunkhouse and dropped into his chair. He fumbled with the coffeepot and succeeded in pouring out a cupful. His legs and feet felt numb, and he had never realized a man could be so utterly, completely tired.

The young man in the checkered shirt looked around from his poker game.

"No luck, eh? Yuh've come a long way to lose now."

Steve nodded bitterly. "That money belongs to my friends as well as me," he said. "That's the worst of it."

The blond young fellow laid down his hand and pulled in the chips. Then he picked up his pipe.

"My sorrel out there in the barn," he said, "is the best hoss on the Trinity. You take it and go, but man, yuh'd better get yoreself some rest at Scott Valley. Yuh'll die."

Mehan lunged to his feet, hope flooding the weariness from his body.

"How much?" he demanded, reaching for his pocket.

"Nothin'," the fellow said. "Only if yuh catch that

thief, bring him back on my hoss, and I'll help yuh hang him. I promise yuh."

Steve hesitated. "What about the hoss?"

"Bring him back when yuh come south," the fellow said, "and take care of him. He'll never let yuh down."

Steve Mehan rode out of Trinity Creek ten minutes later, and the sorrel took to the trail as if he knew all that was at stake, and pressed on eagerly for Scott Valley.

The cold was increasing as Steve Mehan rode further north, and the wind was raw, spitting with rain that seemed to be changing to snow. Head hunched behind the collar of his buffalo coat, Steve pushed on, talking low to the horse, whose ears twitched a response and who kept going, alternating between a fast walk and a swinging, space-eating trot.

Six hours out of Trinity Creek, Steve Mehan rode into Scott Valley.

The stage tender took one look at him and waved him to a bunk.

"Hit it, stranger," he said. "I'll care for yore hoss!"

Stumbling through a fog of exhaustion, Steve made the bunk and dropped into its softness. . . .

Steve Mehan opened his eyes suddenly, with the bright sunlight in his face. He glanced at his watch. It was noon.

Lunging to his feet, he pulled on his boots, which somebody had removed without awakening him, and reached for his coat. The heavyset red-haired stage tender walked in and glanced at him.

"See yuh've got Joe Chalmers' hoss," he remarked, his thumbs in his belt. "How come?"

Steve looked up. "Chasin' a thief. He let me have it."

"I know Chalmers. He wouldn't let Moses have this hoss to lead the Israelites out of Egypt. Not him. Yuh've got some explainin' to do, stranger."

"I said he loaned me the hoss," Steve said grimly. "I'm leavin' him with you and I want to buy another to go on with. What have yuh got?"

Red was dubious. "Don't reckon I should sell yuh

one. Looks mighty funny to me, you havin' Joe's hoss. Is Joe all right?"

"Well," Steve said wearily, "he was just collecting a pot levied by three treys when I talked to him, so I reckon he'll make out."

Red chuckled. "He's a poker-playin' man, that one! Good man, too." He hesitated and then shrugged. "All right. There's a blaze-faced black in the stable yuh can have for fifty dollars. Good horse, too. Better eat somethin'."

He put food on the table, and Steve ate too rapidly. He gulped some coffee, and then Red came out with a pint of whiskey.

"Stick this in yore pocket, stranger. Might come in handy."

"Thanks." Mehan wiped his mouth and got to his feet. He felt better, and he walked to the door.

"Yuh ain't got a rifle?" Red was frankly incredulous. "The Modocs will get yuh shore."

"Haven't seen hide nor hair of one yet!" Steve said, smiling. "I'm beginnin' to think they've all gone east for the winter."

"Don't you think it!" Red slipped a bridle on the black while Steve cinched up the saddle. "They are out, and things up Oregon way are bad off. They shore raised ructions up around Grave Creek, and all the country around the Kalamath and the Rogue is harassed by 'em."

Somewhere out at sea the steamer would be plowing over the gray sea toward Astoria and the mouth of the Columbia. The trip from there up to the Willamette and Portland would not take long.

The black left town at a fast lope and held it. The horse was good, no question about it. Beyond Callahan's, Steve hit the old Applegate wagon trail and found the going somewhat better and pushed on. Just seventy hours out from Knights Landing he rode into Yreka.

After a quick meal, a drink, and a fresh horse, he mounted and headed out of town for the Oregon line. He rode through Humbug City and Hawkinsville without a stop and followed a winding trail up the gorge of the Shasta.

Once, after climbing the long slope north of the

Klamath, he glimpsed a party of Indians some distance away. They sighted him, for they turned their horses his way, but he rode on, holding his pace, and crossed Hungry Creek and left behind him the cairn that marked the boundary line of Oregon. He turned away from the trail then and headed into the back country, trying a cutoff for Bear Creek and the village of Jacksonville. Somewhere, he lost the Indians.

He pushed on, and now the rain that had been falling intermittently turned to snow. It began to fall thick and fast. He was riding out of the trees when on the white-flecked earth before him he saw a moccasin track with earth just tumbling into it from the edge.

Instantly he whipped his horse around and touched spurs to its flanks. The startled animal gave a great bound, and at the same instant a shot whipped by where he had been only a moment before. Then he was charging through brush, and the horse was dodging among the trees.

An Indian sprang from behind a rock and lifted a rifle. Steve drew and fired. The Indian threw his rifle away and rolled over on the ground, moaning.

Wild yells chorused behind him, and a shot cut the branches overhead. He fired again and then again.

Stowing the Smith & Wesson away, he whipped out the four-barreled Braendlin. Holding it ready, he charged out of the brush and headed across the open country. Behind him the Modocs were coming fast. His horse was quick and alert, and he swung it around a grove of trees and down into a gully. Racing along the bottom, he hit a small stream and began walking the horse carefully upstream. After making a half mile, he rode out again and took to the timber, reloading his other pistol.

Swapping horses at every chance, he pushed on. One hundred and forty-three hours out of Knights Landing, he rode into Portland. He had covered six hundred and fifty-five miles. He swung down and turned to the stable hand.

"That steamer in from Frisco?"

"Heard her whistle," said the man. "She's comin' up the river now."

But Steve had turned and was running fast.

* * *

The agent for the banking express company looked up and blinked when Steve Mehan lurched through the door.

"I'm buying cattle," Steve told him, "and need some money. Can you honor a certificate of deposit for me?"

"Let's see her."

Steve handed him the order and shifted restlessly. The man eyed the order for a long time and then turned it over and studied the back. Finally, when Steve was almost beside himself with impatience, the agent looked up over his glasses at the bearded, hollow-eyed young man. "Reckon I can," he said. "Of course there's the deduction of one half of one percent for all amounts over a thousand dollars."

"Pay me," Steve said.

He leaned over the desk, and suddenly the deep-toned blast of the steamer's whistle rang through the room. The agent was putting stacks of gold on the table. He looked up.

"Well, what do you know? That's the steamer in from Portland. I reckon I better see about—"

Whatever he was going to see about, Steve never discovered, for as the agent turned away, Steve reached out and collared him. "Pay me!" he said sharply. "Pay me now!"

The agent shrugged. "Well, all right! No need to get all fussed about it. Plenty of time."

He put out stacks of gold. Mentally, Steve calculated the amount. When it was all there, he swept it into a sack—almost fifty pounds of gold. He slung the sack over his shoulder and turned toward the door.

A gun boomed, announcing the arrival of the steamer, as he stepped out into the street. Four men were racing up the street from the dock, and the man in the lead was Jake Hitson!

Hitson skidded to a halt when he saw Steve Mehan, and his face went dark with angry blood. The blue eyes frosted and he stood wide legged, staring at the man who had beaten him to Portland.

"So!" His voice was a roar that turned the startled townspeople around. "Beat me here, did yuh? Got yore money, have yuh?" He seemed unable to absorb the fact that he was beaten, that Mehan had made it through.

"Just so yuh won't kick anybody out of his home, Jake," Steve said quietly, "and I hope that don't hurt too much!"

The small man in the black suit had gone around them and into the express company office. The other men were Pink Egan and a swarthy-faced man who was obviously a friend of Hitson's.

Hitson lowered his head. The fury seemed to go out of him as he stood there in the street with a soft rain falling over them.

"Yuh won't get back there," he said in a dead, flat voice. "Yuh done it, all right, but yuh'll never play the hero in Pahute, because I'm goin' to kill yuh!"

"Like yuh killed Dixie and Chuck?" challenged Steve. "Yuh did, yuh know. Yuh started that landslide and the Mohaves."

Hitson made no reply. He merely stood there, a huge bull of a man, his frosty eyes bright and hard under the corn-silk eyebrows.

Suddenly his hand swept down.

When Steve had first sighted the man, he had lowered the sack of gold to the street. Now he swept his coat back and grabbed for his own gun. He was no gunfighter, and the glimpse of flashing speed from Hitson made something go sick within him, but his gun came up and he fired.

Hitson's gun was already flaming, and even as Steve pulled the trigger on his own gun, a bullet from Hitson's pistol knocked the Smith & Wesson spinning into the dust! Steve sprang back and heard the hard, dry laugh of triumph from Jake Hitson's throat.

"Now I'll kill yuh!" Hitson yelled.

The killer's eyes were cold as he lifted the pistol, but even as it came level, Steve hurled himself to his knees and jerked out the four-barreled Braendlin.

Hitson swung the gun down on him, but startled by Steve's movement, he swung too fast and shot too fast. The bullet ripped through the top of Mehan's shoulder, tugging hard at the heavy coat. Then Steve fired. He fired once, twice, three times, and then heaved himself erect and stepped to one side, holding his last shot ready, his eyes careful.

Hitson stood stock-still, his eyes puzzled. Blood was trickling from his throat, and there was a slowly spreading blot of blood on his white shirt. He tried to speak, but when he opened his mouth, blood frothed there and he started to back up, frowning.

He stumbled and fell. Slowly he rolled over on his face in the street. Blood turned the gravel crimson, and rain darkened the coat on his back.

Only then did Steve Mehan look up. Pink Egan, his face cold, had a gun leveled at Hitson's companion. "You beat it," Pink said. "You get goin'!"

"Shore!" The man backed away, staring at Hitson's body. "Shore, I'm gone! I don't want no trouble! I just come along, I—"

The small man in black came out of the express office.

"Got here just in time," he said. "I'm the purser from the steamer. Got nearly a thousand out of that bank, the last anybody will get." He smiled at Mehan. "Won another thousand on your ride. I bet on you and got two to one." He chuckled. "Of course, I knew we had soldiers to put ashore at two places coming north, and that helped. I'm a sporting man, myself."

He clinked the gold in his sack and smiled, twitching his mustache with a white finger.

"Up to a point," he added, smiling again. "Only up to a point!"

AUTHOR'S NOTE

WEST IS WHERE THE HEART IS

John Howard Payne, who wrote "Home, Sweet Home" in 1823 as part of an opera called Clari, The Maid of Milan, *planned to write a "History of the Cherokees." Although he collected many notes the work was never completed.*

Payne was both a playwright and an actor, born in New York in 1791 he attended college for three years and made his debut as an actor in 1809, becoming one of the most popular actors in America. Later, he lived and worked in England where he piled up huge debts and found his way into debtor's prison. He wrote Romulus, The Shepherd King, *collaborating with Washington Irving. Later he was American consul in Tunis, where he died in 1852.*

He was briefly imprisoned with John Ross, Chief of the Cherokees, when Ross was fighting the removal of the Cherokees to Indian Territory.

Aside from his interest in the Cherokees and his efforts to aid them, Payne was associated with the West only in so far as his song, "Home, Sweet Home" was for many years one of the most popular songs in the West.

It was one of the songs often sung in my own home.

West Is Where the Heart Is

Jim London lay face down in the dry prairie grass, his body pressed tightly against the ground. Heat, starvation, and exhaustion had taken a toll of his lean, powerful body, and although light-headed from their accumulative effects, he still grasped the fact that to survive he must not be seen.

Hot sun blazed upon his back, and in his nostrils was the stale, sour smell of clothes and body long unwashed. Behind him lay days of dodging Comanche war parties and sleeping on the bare ground behind rocks or under bushes. He was without weapons or food, and it had been nine hours since he had tasted water, and that was only dew he had licked from leaves.

The screams of the dying rang in his ears, amid the sounds of occasional shots and the shouts and war cries of the Indians. From a hill almost five miles away he had spotted the white canvas tops of the Conestoga wagons and had taken a course that would intercept them. And then, in the last few minutes before he could reach their help, the Comanches had hit the wagon train.

From the way the attack went, a number of the Indians must have been bedded down in the tall grass, keeping out of sight, and then when the train was passing, they sprang for the drivers of the teams. The strategy was perfect, for there was then no chance of the wagon train making its circle. The lead wagons did swing, but two other teamsters were dead and another was fighting for his life, and their wagons could not be turned. The two lead wagons found themselves isolated from the last four and were hit hard by at least twenty Indians. The wagon whose driver was fighting turned over in the tall grass at the edge of a ditch, and the driver was killed.

Within twenty minutes after the beginning of the attack, the fighting was over and the wagons looted, and the Indians were riding away, leaving behind them only dead and butchered oxen, the scalped and mutilated bodies of the drivers, and the women who were killed or who had killed themselves.

Yet Jim London did not move. This was not his first crossing of the plains or his first encounter with Indians. He had fought Comanches before, as well as Kiowas, Apaches, Sioux, and Cheyenne. Born on the Oregon Trail, he had later been a teamster on the Santa Fe. He knew better than to move now. He knew that an Indian or two might come back to look for more loot.

The smoke of the burning wagons bit at his nostrils, yet he waited. An hour had passed before he let himself move, and then it was only to inch to the top of the hill, where from behind a tuft of bunch grass he surveyed the scene before him.

No living thing stirred near the wagons. Slow tendrils of smoke lifted from blackened timbers and wheel spokes. Bodies lay scattered about, grotesque in attitudes of tortured death. For a long time he studied the scene below, and the surrounding hills. And then he crawled over the skyline and slithered downhill through the grass, making no more visible disturbance than a snake or a coyote.

This was not the first such wagon train he had come upon, and he knew there was every chance that he would find food among the ruins as well as water, perhaps even overlooked weapons. Indians looted hastily and took the more obvious things, usually scattering food and wasting what they could not easily carry away.

Home was still more than two hundred miles away, and the wife he had not seen in four years would be waiting for him. In his heart, he knew she would be waiting. During the war the others had scoffed at him.

"Why, Jim, you say yourself she don't even know

where you're at! She probably figures you're dead! No woman can be expected to wait that long! Not for a man she never hears of and when she's in a good country for men and a bad one for women!"

"She'll wait. I know Jane."

"No man knows a woman that well. No man could. You say yourself you come east with a wagon train in sixty-one. Now it's sixty-four. You been in the war, you been wounded, you ain't been home, nor heard from her, nor she from you. Worst of all, she was left on a piece of ground with only a cabin built, no ground broke, no close-up neighbors. I'll tell you, Jim, you're crazy! Come go to Mexico with us!"

"No," he said stubbornly. "I'll go home. I'll go back to Jane. I come east after some fixings for her, after some stock for the ranch, and I'll go home with what I set out after."

"You got any young'uns?" The big sergeant was skeptical.

"Nope. I sure ain't, but I wish I did. Only," he added, "maybe I have. Jane, she was expecting, but had a time to go when I left. I only figured to be gone four months."

"And you been gone four years?" The sergeant shook his head. "Forget her, Jim, and come with us. Nobody would deny she was a good woman. From what you tell of her, she sure was, but she's been alone and no doubt figures you're dead. She'll be married again, maybe with a family."

Jim London had shaken his head. "I never took up with no other woman, and Jane wouldn't take up with any other man. I'm going home."

He made a good start. He had saved nearly every dime of pay, and he did some shrewd buying and trading when the war was over. He started west with a small but good train, and he had two wagons with six head of mules to the wagon, knowing the mules would sell better in New Mexico than would oxen. He had six cows and a yearling bull, some pigs, chickens, and utensils. He was a proud man when he looked over his outfit, and he hired two boys with the train to help him with the extra wagon and the stock.

Comanches hit them before they were well started. They killed two men, and one woman and stampeded some stock. The wagon train continued, and at forks of Little Creek they struck again, in force this time, and only Jim London came out of it alive. All his outfit was gone, and he escaped without weapons, food, or water.

He lay flat in the grass at the edge of the burned spot. Again he studied the hills, and then he eased forward and got to his feet. The nearest wagon was upright, and smoke was still rising from it. The wheels were partly burned, the box badly charred, and the interior smoking. It was still too hot to touch.

He crouched near the front wheel and studied the situation, avoiding the bodies. No weapons were in sight, but he had scarcely expected any. There had been nine wagons. The lead wagons were thirty or forty yards off, and the three wagons whose drivers had been attacked were bunched in the middle with one overturned. The last four, near one of which he was crouched, had burned further than the others.

Suddenly he saw a dead horse lying at one side with a canteen tied to the saddle. He crossed to it at once, and tearing the canteen loose, he rinsed his mouth with water. Gripping himself tight against drinking, he rinsed his mouth again and moistened his cracked lips. Only then did he let a mere swallow trickle down his parched throat.

Resolutely he put the canteen down in the shade and went through the saddle pockets. It was a treasure trove. He found a good-sized chunk of almost iron-hard brown sugar, a half dozen biscuits, a chunk of jerky wrapped in paper, and a new plug of chewing tobacco. Putting these things with the canteen, he unfastened the slicker from behind the saddle and added that to the pile.

Wagon by wagon he searched, always alert to the surrounding country and at times leaving the wagons to observe the plain from a hilltop. It was quite dark before he was finished. Then he took his first good drink, for he had allowed himself only nips during the remainder of the day. He took his drink and then ate a biscuit, and chewed a piece of the jerky. With his hunting knife he shaved a little of the plug tobacco and made a cigarette by rolling it in paper, the way the Mexicans did.

Every instinct warned him to be away from the place by daylight, and as much as he disliked leaving the bodies as they were, he knew it would be folly to bury them. If the Indians passed that way again, they would find them buried and would immediately be on his trail.

Crawling along the edge of the taller grass near the depression where the wagon had tipped over, he stopped suddenly. Here in the ground near the edge of the grass was a boot print!

His fingers found it, and then felt carefully. It had been made by a running man, either large or heavily laden. Feeling his way along the tracks, London stopped again, for this time his hand had come in contact with a boot. He shook it, but there was no move or response. Crawling nearer he touched the man's hand. It was cold as marble in the damp night air.

Moving his hand again, he struck canvas. Feeling along it he found it was a long canvas sack. Evidently the dead man had grabbed this sack from the wagon and dashed for the shelter of the ditch or hollow. Apparently he had been struck by a bullet and killed, but feeling again of the body, London's hand came in contact with a belt gun. So the Comanches had not found him! Stripping the belt and gun from the dead man, London swung it around his own hips, and then checked the gun. It was fully loaded, and so were the cartridge loops in the belt.

Something stirred in the grass, and instantly he froze, sliding out his hunting knife. He waited for several minutes, and then he heard it again. Something alive lay here in the grass with him!

A Comanche? No Indian likes to fight at night, and he had seen no Indians anywhere near when darkness fell. No, if anything lived near him now it must be something, man or animal, from the wagon train. For a long time he lay still, thinking it over, and then he took a chance. Yet from his experience the chance was not a long one.

"If there is someone there, speak up."

There was no sound, and he waited, listening. Five minutes passed—ten—twenty. Carefully, then, he slid through the grass, changing his position, and then froze in place. Something was moving, quite near!

His hand shot out, and he was shocked to find himself grasping a small hand with a ruffle of cloth at the wrist! The child struggled violently, and he whispered hoarsely, "Be still! I'm a friend! If you run, the Indians might come!"

Instantly, the struggling stopped. "There!" he breathed. "That's better." He searched his mind for something reassuring to say, and finally said, "Damp here, isn't it? Don't you have a coat?"

There was a momentary silence, and then a small voice said, "It was in the wagon."

"We'll look for it pretty soon," London said. "My name's Jim. What's yours?"

"Betty Jane Jones. I'm five years old and my papa's name is Daniel Jones and he is forty-six. Are you forty-six?"

London grinned. "No, I'm just twenty-nine, Betty Jane." He hesitated a minute and then said, "Betty Jane, you strike me as a mighty brave little girl. There when I first heard you, you made no more noise than a rabbit. Now do you think you can keep that up?"

"Yes." It was a very small voice but it sounded sure.

"Good. Now listen, Betty Jane." Quietly, he told her where he had come from and where he was going. He did not mention her parents, and she did not ask about them. From that he decided she knew only too well what had happened to them and the others from the wagon train.

"There's a canvas sack here, and I've got to look into it. Maybe there's something we can use. We're going to need food, Betty Jane, and a rifle. Later, we're going to have to find horses and money."

The sound of his voice, low though it was, seemed to give her confidence. She crawled nearer to him, and when she felt the sack, she said, "That is Daddy's bag. He keeps his carbine in it and his best clothes."

"Carbine?" London fumbled open the sack.

"Is a carbine like a rifle?"

He told her it was, and then found the gun. It was carefully wrapped, and by the feel of it London could tell the weapon was new or almost new. There was ammunition, another pistol, and a small canvas sack that chinked softly with gold coins. He stuffed this in his pocket. A careful check of the remaining wagons netted him nothing more, but he was not disturbed. The guns he had were good ones, and he had a little food and the canteen. Gravely, he took Betty Jane's hand and they started.

They walked for an hour before her steps began to drag, and then he picked her up and carried her. By the time the sky had grown gray he figured they had come six or seven miles from the burned wagons. He found some solid ground among some reeds on the edge of a slough, and they settled down there for the day.

After making coffee with a handful found in one of the only partly burned wagons, London gave Betty Jane some of the jerky and a biscuit. Then for the first time he examined his carbine. His eyes brightened as he sized it up. It was a Ball & Lamson Repeating Carbine, a gun just on the market and of which this must have been one of the first sold. It was a seven-shot weapon carrying a .56-50 cartridge. It was almost thirty-eight inches in length and weighed a bit over seven pounds.

The pistols were also new, both Prescott Navy six-shooters, caliber .38 with rosewood grips. Betty Jane looked at them and tears welled into her eyes. He took her hand quickly.

"Don't cry, honey. Your dad would want me to use the guns to take care of his girl. You've been mighty brave. Now keep it up."

She looked up at him with woebegone eyes, but the tears stopped, and after a while she fell asleep.

There was little shade, and as the reeds were not tall, he did not dare stand up. They kept close to the edge of the reeds and lay perfectly still. Once he heard a horse walking not far away and heard low, guttural voices and a hacking cough. He caught only a fleeting glimpse of one rider and hoped the Indians would not find their tracks.

When night came, they started on once more. He took his direction by the stars and he walked steadily, carrying Betty Jane most of the distance. Sometimes when she walked beside him, she talked. She rambled on endlessly about her home, her dolls, and her parents. Then on the third day she mentioned Hurlburt.

"He was a bad man. My papa told Mama he was a bad man. Papa said he was after Mr. Ballard's money."

"Who was Hurlburt?" London asked, more to keep the child occupied than because he wanted to know.

"He tried to steal Daddy's new carbine, and Mr. Ballard said he was a thief. He told him so."

Hurlburt. The child might be mispronouncing the name, but it sounded like that. There had been a man in Independence by that name. He had not been liked—a big, bearded man, very quarrelsome.

"Did he have a beard, Betty Jane? A big, black beard?"

She nodded eagerly. "At first, he did. But he didn't have it when he came back with the Indians."

"What?" He turned so sharply toward her that her eyes widened. He put his hand on her shoulder. "Did you say this Hurlburt came back with the Indians?"

Seriously, she nodded. "I saw him. He was in back of them, but I saw him. He was the one who shot his gun at Mr. Ballard."

"You say he came back?" London asked. "You mean he went away from the wagons before the attack?"

She looked at him. "Oh, yes! He went away when we stopped by the big pool. Mr. Ballard and Daddy caught him taking things again. They put ropes on him, on his hands and his feet. But when morning came I went to see, and he was gone away. Daddy said he had left the wagons, and he hoped nothing would happen to him."

Hurlburt. He had gone away and then had come back with the Indians. A renegade, then. What had they said of him in Independence? He had been over the trail several times. Maybe he was working with the Indians.

Betty Jane went to sleep on the grass he had pulled for her to lie on, and Jim London made a careful reconnaissance of the area, and then returned and lay down himself. After a long time he dozed, dreaming of Jane. He awakened feeling discouraged, with the last of their food gone. He had not tried the rifle, although twice they had seen antelope. There was too much chance of being heard by Indians.

Betty Jane was noticeably thinner, and her face looked wan as she slept. Suddenly, he heard a sound and looked up, almost too late. Not a dozen feet away a Comanche looked over the reeds and aimed a rifle at him! Hurling himself to one side, he jerked out one of the Navy pistols. The Commanche's rifle bellowed, and then Jim fired. The Indian threw up his rifle and fell over backward and lay still.

Carefully, London looked around. The rim of the hills was unbroken, and there was no other Indian in sight. The Indian's spotted pony cropped grass not far away. Gun in hand, London walked to the Indian. The bullet from the pistol had struck him under the chin and, tearing out the back, had broken the man's neck. A scarcely dry scalp was affixed to his rawhide belt, and the rifle he carried was new.

He walked toward the horse. The animal shied back. "Take it easy, boy," London said softly. "You're all right." Surprisingly, the horse perked up both ears and stared at him.

"Understand English, do you?" he said softly. "Well, maybe you're a white man's horse. We'll see."

He caught the reins and held out a hand to the horse. It hesitated and then snuffed of his fingers. He moved up the reins to it and touched a palm to the animal's back. The bridle was a white man's, too. There was no saddle, however, only a blanket.

Betty Jane was crying softly when he reached her, obviously frightened by the guns. He picked her up and then the rifle and started back toward the horse. "Don't cry, honey. We've got a horse now."

She slept in his arms that night, and he did not stop riding. He rode all through the night until the little horse began to stumble, and then he dismounted and led the horse while Betty Jane rode. Just before daylight they rested.

Two days later, tired, unshaven, and bedraggled, Jim London rode down the dusty street of Cimarron toward the Maxwell House. It was bright in the afternoon sunlight, and the sun glistened on the flanks and shoulders of the saddled horses at the hitch rail. Drawing up before the house, London slid from the saddle. Maxwell was standing on the wide porch staring down at him, and beside him was Tom Boggs, who London remembered from Missouri as the grandson of Daniel Boone.

"You look plumb tuckered, stranger, and that looks like an Injun rig on the horse. Or part of it."

"It is. The Injun's dead." He looked at Maxwell. "Is there a woman aroud here? This kid's nigh dead for rest and comfort."

"Sure!" Maxwell exclaimed heartily, "Lots of women around! My wife's inside!" He took the sleeping child and called to his wife. As he did so the child's eyes opened and stared, and then the corners of her mouth drew down and she screamed. All three men turned to where she looked. Hurlburt was standing there gaping at the child as if the earth had opened before him.

"What is it?" Maxwell looked perplexed. "What's the matter?"

"That's the man who killed Mr. Ballard! I *saw* him!"

Hurlburt's face paled. "Aw, the kid's mistook me for somebody else!" he scoffed. "I never seen her before!" He turned to Jim London. "Where'd you find that youngster?" he demanded. "Who are you?"

Jim London did not immediately reply. He was facing Hurlburt and suddenly all his anger and irritation at the trail, the Indians, the awful butchery around the wagons, returned to him and boiled down to this man. A child without parents because of this man.

"I picked that child up on the ground near a burned-out, Injun-raided wagon train," he said. "The same train you left Missouri with!"

Hurlburt's face darkened with angry blood.

"You lie!" he declared viciously. "You lie!"

Jim did not draw. He stared at Hurlburt, his eyes unwavering. "How'd you get here, then? You were in Independence when I left there. No wagons passed us. You had to be with that Ballard train."

"I ain't been in Independence for two years!" Hurlburt blustered. "You're crazy and so's that blasted kid!"

"Seems kind of funny," Maxwell suggested, his eyes cold. "You sold two rifles after you got here, and you had gold money. There's a train due in, the boys tell me; maybe we better hold you until we ask them if you were in Independence."

"Like hell!" Hurlburt said furiously. "I ain't no renegade, and nobody holds me in no jail!"

Jim London took an easy step forward. "These guns I'm wearing, Hurlburt, belonged to Jones. I reckon he'd be glad to see this done. You led those Injuns against those wagons. They found out you was a thief and faced you with it. I got it from Betty Jane, and the kid wouldn't lie about a thing like that. She told me all about it before we got here. So you don't get to go to no jail. You don't get to wait. You get a chance to reach for a gun, and that's all."

Hurlburt's face was ugly. Desperately, he glanced right and left. A crowd had gathered, but nobody spoke for him. He was up against it and he knew it. Suddenly, he grabbed for his guns. Jim London's Prescott Navies leaped from their holsters, and the right one barked, a hard sharp report. Hurlburt backed up two steps, and then fell face down, a blue hole over his eye.

"Good work," Boggs said grimly. "I've had my doubts about that hombre. He never does nothing, but he always has money."

"Staying around?" Maxwell asked, looking at London.

"No," Jim said quietly. "My wife's waiting for me. I ain't seen her since sixty-one."

"*Since sixty-one?*" Boggs was incredulous. "You heard from her?"

"She didn't know where I was. Anyway, she never learned to write none." He flushed slightly. "I can't, neither. Only my name."

Lucian Maxwell looked away, clearing his throat.

Then he said very carefully, "Better not rush any, son. That's a long time. It'll soon be five years."

"She'll be waiting." He looked at them, one to the

other. "It was the war. They took me in the Army, and I fought all through."

"What about the kid?" Boggs asked.

"Come morning she'll be ready, I reckon. I'll take her with me. She'll need a home, and I sort of owe her something for this here rifle and the guns. Also," he looked at them calmly, "I got nine hundred dollars in gold and bills here in my pocket. It's hers. I found it in her daddy's duffle."

He cleared his throat. "I reckon that'll buy her a piece of any place we got and give her a home with us for life. We wanted a little girl, and while my wife, she was expectin', I don't know if anything come of it."

Both men were silent, and finally Maxwell said, "See here, London, your wife may be dead. She may have married again. Anyway, she couldn't have stayed on that ranch alone. Man, you'd better leave the child here with us. Take the money. You earned it packing her here, but let her stay until you find out."

London shoook his head patiently. "You don't understand," he said, "that's my Jane who's waiting. She told me she'd wait for me, and she don't say things light. Not her."

"Where is she?" Maxwell asked curiously.

"We got us a place up on North Fork. Good grass, water and timber. The wife likes trees. I built us a cabin there, and a lean-to. We aimed to put about forty acres to wheat and maybe set us up a mill."

He looked up at them, smiling a little. "Pa was a miller, and he always said to me that folks need bread wherever they are. Make a good loaf," he said, "and you'll always have a good living. He had him a mill up Oregon way."

"North Fork?" Boggs and Maxwell exchanged glances. "Man, that country was run over by Injuns two years ago. Some folks went back up there, but one o' them is Bill Ketchum. He's got a bunch running with him no bettern'n he is. Hoss thieves, folks reckon. Most anything to get the 'coon."

When he rounded the bend below the creek and saw the old bridge ahead of him his mouth got dry and his heart began to pound. He walked his horse, with the child sitting before him and the carbine in its scabbard. At the creek he drew up for just a moment, looking down at the bridge. He built it with his own hands. Then his eyes saw the hand rail on the right. It was cut from a young poplar. He had used cedar. Somebody had worked on that bridge recently.

The cabin he had built topped a low rise in a clearing backed by a rocky overhang. He rode through the pines, trying to quiet himself. It might be like they said.

Maybe she had sold out and gone away, or just gone. Maybe she had married somebody else, or maybe the Injuns. . . .

The voice he heard was coarse and amused. "Come off it!" the voice said. "From here on you're my woman. I ain't takin' no more of this guff!"

Jim London did not stop his horse when it entered the clearing. He let it walk right along, but he lifted the child from in front of him and said, "Betty Jane, that lady over yonder is your new ma. You run to her now, an' tell her your name is Jane. Hear me?"

He lowered the child to the ground and she scampered at once toward the slender woman with the wide gray eyes who stood on the step staring at the rider.

Bill Ketchum turned abruptly to see what her expression meant. The lean, raw-boned man on the horse had a narrow sun-browned face and a battered hat pulled low. The rider shoved it back now and rested his right hand on his thigh. Ketchum stared at him. Something in that steel-trap jaw and those hard eyes sent a chill through him.

"I take it," London said gravely, "that you are Bill Ketchum. I heard what you said just now. I also heard down the line that you was a horse thief, maybe worse. You get off this place now, and don't ever come back. You do and I'll shoot you on sight. Now get!"

"You talk mighty big." Ketchum stared at him, anger rising within him. Should he try this fellow? Who did he think he was, anyway?"

"I'm big as I talk." London said it flatly. "I done killed a man yesterday down to Maxwell's. Hombre name of Hurlburt. That's all I figure to kill this week unless you want to make it two. Start moving now."

Ketchum hesitated, then viciously reined his horse around and started down the trail. As he neared the edge of the woods, rage suddenly possessed him. He grabbed for his rifle and instantly a shot rang out and a heavy slug gouged the butt of his rifle and glanced off.

Behind him the words were plain. "I put that one right where I want it. This here's a seven-shot repeater, so if you want one through your heart, just try it again."

London waited until the man had disappeared in the trees, and a minute more. Only then did he turn to his wife. She was down on the step with her arm around Betty Jane, who was sobbing happily against her breast.

"Jim!" she whispered. "Oh, Jim!"

He got down heavily. He started toward her and then stopped. Around the corner came a boy of four or five, a husky youngster with a stick in his hand and his eyes blazing. When he saw Jim he stopped abruptly. This stranger looked just like the old picture on his mother's table. Only he had on a coat in the picture, a store-bought coat.

"Jim." Jane was on her feet now, color coming back into her face. "This is Little Jim. This is your son."

Jim London swallowed and his throat suddenly filled. He looked at his wife and started toward her. He felt awkward, clumsy. He took her by the elbows. "Been a long time, honey," he said hoarsely, "a mighty long time!"

She drew back a little, nervously. "Let's—I've coffee on. We'll—" She turned and hurried toward the door and he followed.

It would take some time. A little time for both of them to get over feeling strange, and maybe more time for her. She was a woman, and women needed time to get used to things.

He turned his head and almost automatically his eyes went to that south forty. The field was green with a young crop. Wheat! He smiled.

She had filled his cup; he dropped into a seat, and she sat down opposite him. Little Jim looked awkwardly at

Betty Jane, and she stared at him with round, curious eyes.

"There's a big frog down by the bridge," Little Jim said suddenly. "I bet I can make him hop!"

They ran outside into the sunlight, and across the table Jim London took his wife's hand. It was good to be home. Mighty good.

ABOUT LOUIS L'AMOUR

"I think of myself in the oral tradition—as a troubadour, a village taleteller, the man in the shadows of the campfire. That's the way I'd like to be remembered—as a storyteller. A good storyteller."

It is doubtful that any author could be as at home in the world re-created in his novels as Louis Dearborn L'Amour. Not only could he physically fill the boots of the rugged characters he writes about, but he has literally "walked the land my characters walk." His personal experiences as well as his lifelong devotion to historical research have combined to give Mr. L'Amour the unique knowledge and understanding of the people, events, and challenge of the American frontier that have become the hallmarks of his popularity.

Of French-Irish descent, Mr. L'Amour can trace his own family in North America back to the early 1600s and follow their steady progression westward, "always on the frontier." As a boy growing up in Jamestown, North Dakota, he absorbed all he could about his family's frontier heritage, including the story of his great-grandfather who was scalped by Sioux warriors.

Spurred by an eager curiosity and desire to broaden his horizons, Mr. L'Amour left home at the age of fifteen and enjoyed a wide variety of jobs including seaman, lumberjack, elephant handler, skinner of dead cattle, assessment miner, and officer on tank destroyers during World War II. During his "yondering" days he also circled the world on a freighter, sailed a dhow on the Red Sea, was shipwrecked in the West Indies and stranded in the Mojave Desert. He has won fifty-one of fifty-nine fights as a professional boxer and worked as a journalist and lecturer. A voracious reader and collector of rare books, Mr. L'Amour's personal library of some 10,000 volumes covers a broad range of scholarly disciplines including many personal papers, maps, and diaries of the pioneers.

Mr. L'Amour "wanted to write almost from the time I could walk." After developing a widespread following for his many adventure stories written for the fiction magazines, Mr. L'Amour published his first full-length novel, *Hondo*, in 1953. Mr. L'Amour is now one of the four bestselling living novelists in the world. Every one of his more than 85 novels is constantly in print and every one has sold more than one million copies, giving him more million-copy bestsellers than any other living author. His books have been translated into more than a dozen languages, and more than thirty of his novels and stories have been made into feature films and television movies.

Among Mr. L'Amour's most popular books are *The Lonesome Gods, Comstock Lode, The Cherokee Trail, Flint, Son of a Wanted Man, The Shadow Riders, Silver Canyon, Bowdrie, The Walking Drum*, his historical novel of the 12th century, and his series of novels which tells the continuing saga of the Sackett family, the latest of which is the bestseller *Jubal Sackett*.

The recipient of many great honors and awards, in 1983 Mr. L'Amour became the first novelist ever to be awarded a Special National Gold Medal by the United States Congress in honor of his life's work. In 1984 he was also awarded the Medal of Freedom by President Ronald Reagan.

Mr. L'Amour lives in Los Angeles with his wife, Kathy, and their two children, Beau and Angelique.